OPERATION
BLOWPIPE

JP CROSS

monsoon

monsoonbooks

First published in 2022
by Monsoon Books Ltd
www.monsoonbooks.co.uk

No.1 The Lodge, Burrough Court,
Burrough on the Hill, Melton Mowbray LE14 2QS, UK

ISBN (paperback): 9781915310064
ISBN (ebook): 9781915310071

Cover design by Cover Kitchen.

A Cataloguing-in-Publication data record is available from the British
Library.

MIX
Paper from
responsible sources
FSC
www.fsc.org   FSC® C018072

Printed and bound in Great Britain by Clays Ltd, Elcograf S.p.A.
24 23 22   1 2 3

monsoonbooks

OPERATION BLOWPIPE

Lt. Col. JP Cross is a retired British officer who served with Gurkha units for nearly forty years. He has been an Indian frontier soldier, jungle fighter, policeman, military attaché, Gurkha recruitment officer and a linguist researcher, and he is the author of twenty books. He has fought in Burma, Indo-China, Malaya and Borneo and served in India, Pakistan, Hong Kong, Laos and Nepal where he now lives. Well into his nineties, he still walks four hours daily.

Operation Blowpipe is the seventh in a series of historical military novels set in Southeast Asia including *Operation Black Rose*, *Operation Janus*, *Operation Red Tidings*, *Operation Blind Spot*, *Operation Stealth* and *Operation Four Rings*. The first four books may be read in any order; the final two are sequential. The series features Gurkha military units, and the author draws on real events he witnessed and real people he fought alongside in various theatres of war in Southeast Asia and India.

'Nobody in the world is better qualified to tell the story of the Gurkhas' deadly jungle battles against Communist insurgency in Malaya in the 1950s. Cross spins his tale with the eye of incomparable experience.'

John le Carré

'... a gripping adventure story ...
learn the ins and outs of jungle warfare from a true expert'

The Oldie (on *Operation Janus*)

Also by JP Cross

FICTION
The Throne of Stone
The Restless Quest
The Crown of Renown
The Fame of the Name
The Age of Rage
Operation Black Rose
Operation Janus
Operation Blind Spot
Operation Stealth
Operation Four Rings
Operation Red Tidings

NONFICTION
English For Gurkha Soldiers
Gurkha – The Legendary Soldier
Gurkhas
Gurkha Tales: From Peace and War
In Gurkha Company
It Happens with Gurkhas
Jungle Warfare: Experiences And Encounters
Whatabouts And Whereabouts In Asia

MEMOIRS
First In, Last Out:
An Unconventional British Officer In Indo-China

The Call Of Nepal:
A Personal Nepalese Odyssey In A Different Dimension

'A Face Like A Chicken's Backside':
An Unconventional Soldier In South-East Asia, 1948-1971

ORAL HISTORY
Gurkhas at War

List of Characters

Met with and spoken to by the author personally:

Imbi, Sumatran guide

Ismail Mubarak, ('Moby'), Head of Special Branch, Seremban

Kantan, Temiar headman

Kerinching, Temiar headman

Mandeh, Sumatran guide

Senagit, Temiar hunter

Templer, General Sir Gerald, High Commissioner-cum-Director
    of Operations, Malaya

Theopulos, John, manager Bhutan Estate

Those searched for on operations by the author:

Ah Soo Chye, guerrilla leader in north Malaya

'Blood Sucker', nickname of guerrilla

†Chien Tiang, chief confidant of Chin Peng (q.v.) and propaganda
    expert

†Chin Peng, alias of Ong Boon Hwa, Secretary General of the
    Malayan Communist Party

'Collector', nickname of guerrilla, sometimes known as 'Wang'

'Killer', nickname of guerrilla

†Lee An Tung, Head of the Central Propaganda Department,
    Malayan Communist Party

Lee Song, Communist politician and guerrilla

Lo See, guerrilla leader in north Malaya

*Tan Fook Loong, Commander 2 Regiment, Malayan Races
  Liberation Army, ('Ten Foot Long',
  British nickname)

Tek Miu, guerrilla leader in north Malaya

Yeong Kwoh, senior military member of the Malayan Communist
  Party

(† Operation Allenby)

(* Operation Jekyll)

Historical characters:

Akbar Khan, Pathan lawyer, Indian Association and Indian
  Independence League

Lai Tek, triple agent

Mao Tse-tung, Chairman, Chinese Communist Party

Sharkey, Lawrence Louis ('Lance'). Chairman, Australian
  Communist Party

Sun Tzu, author of *The Art of War*

Too Chee Chew ('C C Too') brilliant propagandist, Special
  Branch, Malayan Police

**Names either born in the author's imagination or changed to
avoid family embarrassment:**

Abdul Hamid Khan} nephews of Akbar Khan (q.v.)

Abdul Rahim Khan} parachutists for the Indian National Army

Ah Fat, police 'mole' and non-voting Central Committee member,
  Malayan Communist Party

Ah Wong, police detective at Sepang Police Station

'Bear', Hung Lo, nickname of Wang Ming, (q.v.)

Chakrabahadur Rai, Rifleman, 1/12 Gurkha Rifles

Chan Man Yee, Malayan Communist Party 'mole' in Police HQ, Kuala Lumpur

Chen Yok Lan, wife of Tan Fook Loong (q.v.)

Chow Hoong Biu, fresh ration contractor for 1/12 Gurkha Rifles

Deng Bing Yi, fitter in Seremban

'Emissary', nickname of Meng Ru (q.v.)

Fong Chui Wan, taxi girl at Yam Yam night club, Seremban

Goh Ah Wah, surrendered guerrilla, 2 Regiment, Malayan Races Liberation Army

Hemlal Rai, chief clerk Bhutan Estate

Heron, James, Lieutenant Colonel, Commanding Officer, 1/12 Gurkha Rifles

Hinlea, Alan, Captain, turncoat officer in 1/12 Gurkha Rifles

Hutton, Reggie, Special Branch officer, Singapore

Kamal Rai, worker on Bhutan Estate with wartime experience

Kent, Major, 1/12 Gurkha Rifles

K. Ramamathan Chettiyar, Malayan Indian Congress

Kulbahadur Limbu, Rifleman, batman and expert tracker, 1/12 Gurkha Rifles

Kwek Leng Joo, guerrilla courier and barman in Yam Yam night club, Seremban

Kwek Leng Ming, surrendered guerrilla, 2 Regiment, Malayan Races Liberation Army

Lau Beng, one-time schoolmaster and Regional Commissar

Lee Kheng, 'sleeper' in Special Branch, Seremban

Leong Bik Fong, table maid for Head of Special Branch, Seremban

'Lustful Wolf', Sik Long, nickname of Hinlea, (q.v.)

Mandhoj Rai, second cousin to Kamal Rai, (q.v.)

Mason, James, Colonel, Director of Intelligence, HQ Malaya Command

Meng Ru, Communist Party of China emissary, a.k.a. 'Emissary'

Minbahadur Gurung, Lance Corporal, radio operator, 1/12 Gurkha Rifles

Ngai Hiu Ching, one-time schoolmaster

Padamsing Rai, member of All-India Gorkha League and Rifleman, 1/12 Gurkha Rifles

P'ing Yee, Flat Ears, nickname of Ah Fat (q.v.)

Rabilal Rai, Bhutan estate worker who tried to get to India by Japanese submarine

Rance, Jason Percival Vere, Captain, later Major, 1/12 Gurkha Rifles,

Rance, Mr, } Jason Rance's parents
Rance, Mrs,}

Ridings, Edward, Lieutenant Colonel, Commanding Officer, 1/12 Gurkha Rifles

Ruwaman Limbu, Sergeant, 1/12 Gurkha Rifles

Shandung P'aau, Shandong Cannon, nickname of Jason Rance, (q.v.)

Sim Ting Hok, surrendered guerrilla, 2 Regiment, Malayan Races Liberation Army

Siu Tae, working name of Fong Chui Wan (q.v.)

Subramaniam Mudaliar, helpful comprador to British Army officer during the war

Sugiyama Torashima, Japanese agent in pre-war Malaya

Tan Wing Bun, alias of son of Tang Fook Loong (q.v.)

Tan Wing Hoon, proper name of Tan Wing Bun (q.v.)

Tan Yee Faat, Communist room boy in GHQ Officers' Mess, Singapore

Tay Wang Teik, interpreter at Seremban Police Station

Tor Gul Khan, son of Akbar Khan, (q.v.)

Vaughan, Eustace, Lieutenant Colonel, Commanding Officer, 1/12 Gurkha Rifles

Wang Liang, son of Wang Ming, (q.v.)

Wang Ming, close friend of Ah Fat (q.v.)

Wang Tao, female table servant of the Officer Commanding the Police District, Seremban

Xi Zhan Yang. Communist courier

Yap Cheng Wu, manager of the Yam Yam night club, Seremban

Yap Kheng, surrendered guerrilla 'gardener', 2 Regiment, Malayan Races Liberation Army

Zhong Han San, leader of Killer Squad in south Thailand

Abbreviations

2 ic	Second-in-Command
ADO	Assistant District Officer
CO	Commanding Officer, commander of major unit
CPO	Chief Police Officer
CT	Communist Terrorist/s, official name for guerrillas
DWEC	District War Executive Committee
GHQ	General Headquarters
GR	Gurkha Rifles
HQ	headquarters
ID	identity
INA	Indian National Army
Int	intelligence
JCLO	Junior Civil Liaison Officer
KL	Kuala Lumpur
LMG	Light Machine Gun
IO	Intelligence Officer
LP	landing point
MA	Military Adviser
MCP	Malayan Communist Party
MIC	Malayan Indian Congress
MRLA	Malayan Races Liberation Army
MTO	Mechanical Transport Officer

NCO	non-commissioned officer
OC	Officer Commanding, commander of sub-unit
OCPD	Officer in Charge Police District
'O' Group	'Orders Group': sub-commanders for whom any orders are relevant
QM	Quartermaster
Raj	British India
recce	reconnaissance
RV	rendez-vous, the appointed place for assembly
sitrep	situation report
SWEC	State War Executive Committee

Glossary

Chinese

I sincerely thank Mr Bernard C C Chan, MBE, AMN, for his unstinting help in matters Chinese.

cheongsam	long, tight-fitting, slit-sided 'skirt'
Ghee Hin	a Secret Society
Goo K'a bing	Gurkha soldiers
gwai lo	foreigner, literally 'devil chap', 'old devil'
Hai San	a Secret Society
Loi Pai Yi	Nepali
Min Yuen	Masses Movement
Sinsaang	Mr, sir
Siu Gaau	Major
tong	brotherhood
t'o yan	'soil man', aborigine
wei	hello (chiefly telephone calls)

Malay

atap	palm thatch, Nipa fruticus
ipoh	poison tree, Antiaris toxica
ladang	orang asli (indigenous people's) settlement
nasi lemak	rice cooked in coconut milk, with fried crispy anchovies, peanuts and cucumber
orang asli	indigenous people of Malaysia

parang	chopper, knife
ringgit	Malayan dollar
sampitan	blowpipe
Tuan	official, 'sir'

Nepali (Gurkhali)

Belayat	England
Cheena	Chinese, normally a man
daku	'dacoit', used for Communist guerrillas
dushman	enemy
inding pinding	independence
ita aija	come here
keta	lad
gora	fair-skinned, word for British troops
hajur	term of respect, inert conversational response (literally 'presence')
hunchha	is, okay
sal	a tree, Shorea robusta
sarkar	government, officialdom
ustad	'teacher', word used in some Gurkha units to an NCO

Note: the '-bahadur' at the end of names is often shorted to '-é' when talking, so, instead of Kulbahadur, it is Kulé etc

Temiar

Blau	blowpipe
senoi bar halaaq	shaman

Maps

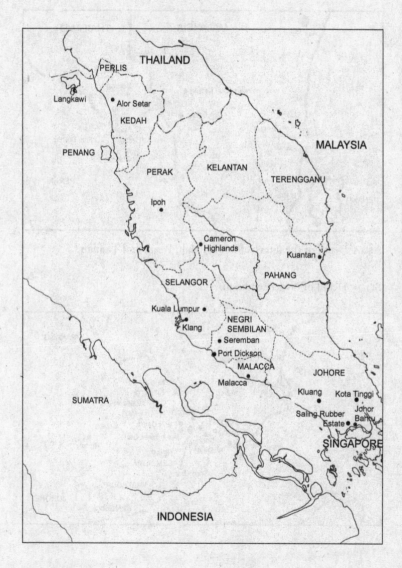

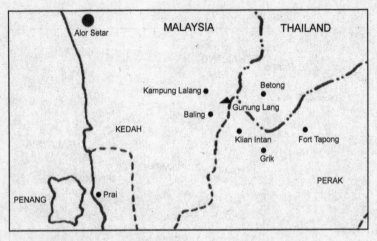

Above Detail of the intersecton of Kedah, Perak and Thailand.

Below Detail of Negri Sembilan.

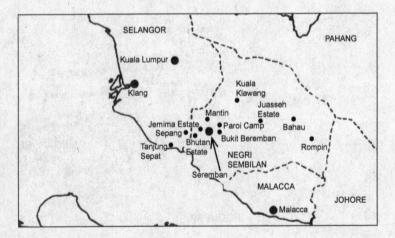

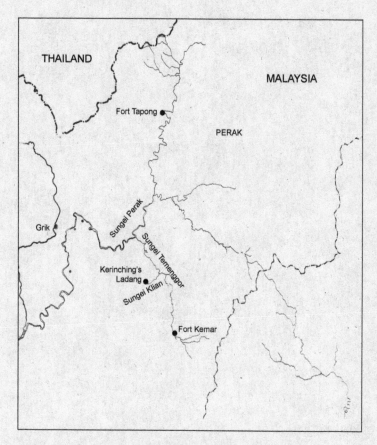

ABOVE Detail of Sungei Perak and its tributaries.

PROLOGUE

Late evening, sometime in 1943, in the Serting Forest Reserve, south of Seremban, Negri Sembilan, Malaya

As porters with a resupply of provisions reached the temporary camp of an anti-Japanese group of Communist Chinese guerrillas, they were shocked as muted but spine-chilling screams of unbearable pain throbbed around the thick jungle. A traitor, who had caused guerrilla casualties, had been identified and was suffering condign punishment: he had been tied to a wooden trestle, arms outstretched, legs apart, stomach stretched and gagged to lessen noise while the guerrilla, whose wife had been killed by the Japanese, had slit the traitor's belly crosswise with a kris, a pointed dagger with a curved blade. As the porters peered through the undergrowth, they saw the executioner slashing the belly downwards in a mockery of ritual hara-kiri. Noise from the tortured man shrank to a gurgle, then stopped as he died, blood flowing and guts slithering to the ground.

The leader of the porters was Kamal Rai: he and his men were Nepalis from Bhutan Estate, the nearest of the three estates that had a Nepalese labour force, some miles to the south. Kamal heard the voice of a guerrilla he recognised, Lee Soong, saying 'that is what we do to traitors. If there's another, his death will take longer, be slower and more painful. You all understand that, don't you?'

Kamal saw heads nod. He called out the password and it was answered. Into the camp area they went and dumped their loads. If Kamal had not made up his mind about the Communists before, the mangled and bloody remains of the tortured body turned him irrevocably against them.

It was unusual for any guerrilla group to be in such comparatively non-extensive jungle but it was considered safe. The previous year a group of Japanese had landed on the coast nearby and patrolled to Bhutan Estate. There the commander was overcome and sliced to death by Kamal who escaped unharmed. The rest of the Japanese were set on and killed by some returning hunters. After that, quite why no one could tell, the invaders regarded some buildings there to be haunted, so kept away.[1]

Kamal Rai was in his mid-twenties, immensely strong, had deep-set almond eyes that flashed dangerously, high cheek bones and a face that had a calm look, although there was an air of subtlety about it. He had been educated at King George V's School in Seremban where the medium of instruction was English and his teachers had regarded him as a scholar.

Among the guerrillas was a thin, austere, bespectacled and slightly balding Englishman, Reggie Hutton, a member of a stay-behind group who had joined forces with the Chinese fighting

---

1 The author's friend, Mr Denny, the proprietary owner of the nearby Sungei Pelek Estate, told him that the Japanese, believing his bungalow to be haunted, touched nothing the whole war when he was a prisoner. No local looted anything either.

the Japanese. Pre-war he had worked in the Singapore Police Special Branch. One of the guerrillas, Ah Fat, was secretly known to Hutton as a British 'mole'. Hutton had known Kamal since pre-war and the two men had joined the guerrilla group together. Hutton had persuaded them to go to the Serting Forest Reserve and once there Kamal had slipped away to Bhutan Estate to get some porters to bring new supplies back.

Before the porters left, Lee Soon warned them that any who told the Japanese where the camp was would also have similar condign punishment – or even more drastic. Reggie Hutton thanked the porters who, now unladen, were able to move faster and more easily avoid any Japanese who might just be lurking to nab them as they returned.

Calcutta, India, 19-30 March 1948

During that time an innocent-sounding Southeast Asia Youth Conference[2] – a youth being anyone up to thirty-five years old – composed of fanatical but untrained anti-colonialist revolutionaries from European Asian colonies, less Portugal, Timor being too small to matter, took place under the ægis of the Indian Communist Party. Its genesis lay in Soviet anti-imperialist policy and its aim was to teach the participants how best to prepare for the Communist-inspired risings against the imperialist colonialists. Knowing that fanaticism based solely

---

2 Its full name was The Conference of Youth and Students of Southeast Asia Fighting for Freedom and Independence. It lasted from the 19th to the 23rd of March. Its delegates were invited to attend the following 2nd Plenum of the Indian Communist Party.

on ignorance had to be rectified, the syllabus was designed to rectify this discrepancy. The Youth Conference was immediately followed by the second Plenum of the Indian Communist Party and its participants were invited to stay on and participate in it.

Billed as a 'star' was the Chairman of the Australian Communist Party, L L 'Lance' Sharkey, on a short-stay visa; the other attraction was a Communist from Singapore, Lee Soong, born there in 1927 and a fluent English speaker, who had already fought as a guerrilla against the Japanese.

Reggie Hutton, now Head of Singapore Special Branch, had come to hear about the Conference. He had learnt that a strong Soviet team had been in India for several months, preparing for it. The Russians could work more easily in India than anywhere else in Southeast Asia and now India was independent used their sources to help them. Whatever would transpire would be, he felt, of great significance so, even though Calcutta was not in his bailiwick, he intended to find out about it in as much detail as possible. He was extremely intrigued when his friend John Theopulos, the manager of Bhutan Estate, rang him to tell him that his chief clerk, Hemlal Rai, had received an invitation for one suitable person from the estate to attend, all expenses paid. 'Reggie, what is your advice and why do you think my estate has been chosen to send a representative to such a jamboree?'

Reggie considered his answer before saying 'John, why one of your men? I have heard rumours that several seriously anti-British Indian-domiciled hot-head Nepalis belonging to the Darjeeling branch of the All-India Gorkha League, have also been invited. Apart from the Indian Congress Party inspiring such political hatred of the British, even those in the Viceroy's Council had not fully realised the effect of Soviet and German liking for one of the more expensive brands of tea in the Darjeeling tea gardens, had, similarly, been a powerful albeit unobtrusive influence. The new British Gurkhas, announced just before the 15th of August, 1947, have made these hot heads think of joining up to try and influence, quite how they did not yet know, the Gurkha soldiers against their British officers with such bad discipline that they be disbanded. It could just be that the organisers of the conference see a Malaya-based Nepali estate worker as a useful conduit for dissatisfied Gurkha soldiers to desert and even join the guerrillas – a long shot and probably impossible to achieve but ...'

'Yes, that makes sense,' broke in John Theopulos. 'My Nepali labour force could be a link in their planning. But who to send?'

'I recommend Kamal Rai, whom I personally know, as he is the one and only man I trust to go and find out what it was all about. You know that he was my "eyes and ears" for much of the war. He could possibly find out if any such Nepalis attended the meetings, to recognise them and, were they to join the new British Gurkhas serving in Malaya, help to identify them.

'Another reason for recommending Kamal Rai to go is that a principal attendant is Lee Soong. They knew each other during the war. He was a member of the post-war British Military Administration's Singapore Advisory Council as well as now being on the Town Committee of the Communist Party of Malaya – they are not banned, you know – to say nothing of having been to Prague last year as a member of the World Federation of Democratic Youth. Tell Kamal to go to Singapore, contact me at a number I'll give you and I'll fully brief and finance him.'

John Theopulos was unhappy with all that but agreed to it, reluctantly: *after all, Reggie does know what he's talking about*

Lance Sharkey stayed over in Singapore and before embarking for Calcutta, Reggie Hutton had found out that had had a private meeting with Chin Peng, a member of the Malayan Communist Party (MCP), and Lai Tek, a double agent working for the British, both of whom were in Singapore. He also found out that nothing substantial was discussed and an invitation was given to the Australian to attend the MCP's 4th Plenary Session on his return from Calcutta.

There was a goodly gathering at the Youth Conference. When Kamal Rai set eyes on Lee Soong he felt sick at being so close to him. Lee Soong had originally thought Kamal had very little English but later he knew differently. Kamal and Reggie Hutton had wrongly presumed they had never conversed in English in his hearing.

The organisers of the programme were the same English-speaking Indians who later similarly organised the 2nd Plenum. The small group from French Indo-China who had been anti-Chinese longer than they had been anti-French, were keener to get rid of the latter than the former who had loomed over them for centuries, in this case being unable to change either history or geography. They did not speak English but an interpreter from the Air France office was found for them. Those from the Dutch East Indies were less lucky, speaking neither English nor French. One of them had learnt basic Arabic before going to Mecca and an Arabic speaker was found in one of the city banks. Despite not being altogether satisfactory, the all-powerful 'Cause' won the day.

It was Lee Soong who had asked about Mao Tse-tung and his guerrilla war. Luckily some homework had been done and copies of some of his dated writings were available for discussion. One was titled *A Single Spark Can Start A Prairie Fire*, published as far back as 3 January 1930. There were some extensive notes on guerrilla warfare, written in May 1938, but they were directed against Japan, not western imperialists and certainly not set in tropical rainforest terrain. But did it matter? It certainly brought forth more discussion than had the heavy-handed Soviet doctrine. It meant more to simple people. Eventually, much to Lance Sharkey's chagrin, it was the Chinese doctrines that caused the most interest. Such points as, for instance, *Six Specific Problems in Guerrilla War, Guerrilla Zones and Base Areas* and *The Basic Principle of War is to Preserve Oneself and Destroy the Enemy* brought a spark of interest where little or none had previously been observed. But, as ever, there was a negative side to it as much was made of ideology and political education, heady stuff if one was a zealot but pretty meaningless when many ethnic Southeast Asians had no political vocabulary – democracy? fascist? feudal? what are they? – and 'education' merely meant a village school and boring homework. As for 'ideology' ... ?

Sharkey's speech went on for too long as he had to make many pauses for the interpreters. It had seemed so easy in theory but, sadly, in practice, to him, the Conference had not come up to expectations. Not enough thought had been put into the programme to start with: strategy or tactics? politics or armed struggle? people or leaders? guerrilla warfare with weapons or trade unions stoppages? It was all very well to quote Soviet doctrine: *Surprise is the greatest factor in war. There are two kinds, tactical and strategic. Tactical surprise is an operational art. A skilled unit commander can generally achieve it. Strategic surprise is attained at the political level* but what meaning did that convey to most of the listeners who, till then, had probably only ever held a catapult in their hands? 'Look, what I've heard you talk about makes me realise that you have not got your act together. Here, in India, your communism stems from when the British tried to give you some of their educational ideas from way back in the nineteenth century. But since then you have split: some of you are Marxist, some are Marxist-Leninist and even some of you are trying to be Maoists. You will never achieve real communism until you all think alike. Can't you see what I am getting at?' he asked but no, his rhetoric was on too high a level and his Australian accent left the English speakers, including the interpreters, bewildered. 'Anyone got any questions for me?' he asked at the end.

'Yes, I have,' said a youth, holding up his arm.

'Who are you and what is it you want to ask?'

'I am a Darjeeling Nepali. My name is Padamsing Rai. My question is can you see any contradiction in the Chinese proposals and teaching compared with their Soviet counterparts?'

The Australian thought for a moment. *What is he getting at?* 'No, Marx and Lenin are the bedrock of them both. Why should there be any difference?'

'Because I have read that the Soviets try to impose their will on the countries of Europe, and even India, from the top downwards whereas the Chinese think that, once the masses know what is wanted and are converted, Communism will spread upwards. Would you agree with that? I want to know as I intend to work on the Gurkha soldiers in the British Army, in other words, start from the bottom. I can't start at the top.'

That caused some of the staff to look at each other, almost in dismay, that analysis being new to them. Sharkey, having no definite answer and not wanting to seem 'bested' by a mere lad, said that although tactically matters were always different, strategically the two parties would never be far apart.

'Thank you, sir,' said the man from Darjeeling and sat down, looking round as he did as though he were more than pleased with himself.

After it was all over, Lee Soong told Padamsing Rai to enlist in one of the eastern regiments he had heard that was now part of the British Army, 'Try to get a posting as a clerk, an intelligence man or an educational instructor, if possible in an army school, so as to spread the word among the Gurkha soldiers and to try and inveigle them to change sides or leave the army, in any case, so to disgrace the Gurkha name by indiscipline the War Office would disband them.'

Padamsing said he would try but, of course, there was no telling till he tried.

Lee Soong also spoke at length with Kamal Rai, telling him how he envisaged matters developing, with him to be a link with

Padamsing Rai. 'By the way, you remember when I had than man punished and killed for being a spy?' Kamal shivered as he remembered it. 'I'll let you into a secret,' continued the Chinese. 'He was the wrong man. I thought he was you with your friend Hutton.' He fixed the Gurkha with a gimlet-like stare. 'If you manage with Padamsing Rai my suspicions will be allayed.'

Lee Soong did not go straight back to Singapore as he had meetings in Bangkok, with whom he did not divulge. Kamal returned to Singapore on the same boat as did Sharkey and fully briefed Reggie Hutton on what had transpired. As for Sharkey, he had a long session with Chin Peng, Lai Tek not being present, and strongly urged him to change current MCP policy to military action to try and overcome the Security Forces ... thus setting the scene of much bloodshed and many brave deeds on both sides for the next decades.

It is, of course, a moot point indeed how much of what Calcutta tried to inculcate was responsible for the way in which events developed: what is not in doubt is that develop they did. What no one could have ever imagined was that one of very first, if not the first, British officer the Communists fired on to kill was, at the very last gasp of anti-British endeavour in 1968 after twenty years of Communist military activity, which would end not in the proverbial bang but the equally proverbial whimper, the very same British officer when three aborigine 'blowpipe marksmen' were ordered to aim their blowpipes at his head and shoot their poisoned darts to kill him ... never having yet missed their intended target.

PART I

1948-1954

1

When the troopship SS *Empire Pride* sailing from Burma– which had been given its independence five days earlier – carrying the 1st Battalion of the 12th Gurkha Rifles and two other British Army Gurkha battalions reached Prai, opposite the island of Penang, it was like coming back home after nearly ten years to only one of the passengers, Captain Jason Rance. With fair hair, penetrating, clear blue eyes, his features were almost hawk-like and stern. He showed his pleasure with a wonderful open smile. He was nearly six feet tall with a taut, lean body and the indefinable air of a natural commander. He was sixteen when he had left Malaya, hurriedly, for England and after a war in which he has seen action many times, here he was back again. Eyes fixed on Penang Hill, his mind drifted back all those years ...

He had been born in Kuala Lumpur where his father, unobtrusively working in a revenue office, had, in fact, been Britain's senior Intelligence officer in Malaya. Before her marriage, his mother had worked with her father's Punch and Judy show and had learnt how to be a ventriloquist, her son also mastering this rare skill. He had his own dummy and a model krait, this latter he had acquired after he had watched a Gurkha soldier

35

defang one of these lethal creatures with an elegant calmness.

Mr Rance's Chinese partner's son, Ah Fat, was the same age as Jason and the two boys became as close as brothers from when toddlers. They each had their Chinese nicknames, Ah Fat's was *P'ing Yee*, Flat Ears, as his ears were close to his head, and Jason's was *Shandung P'aau*, Shandong (Southern mountain) Cannon, as the people from that part of the world were strong and burly, as was Jason. By the time he was ten, Jason was a fluent Chinese speaker with a good knowledge of the writing. His Malay was almost as good as his Chinese. During their school holidays they used to go and camp in the jungle inland from the coastal village of Sepang and meet up with young Gurkhas from Bhutan Estate, becoming as 'at home' in the jungle as any seasoned Forest Ranger. He learnt to speak basic Gurkhali with one of his friends, Kamal Rai, his elder by a few years.

The crisis that had caused Jason to leave Malaya was instigated by Japanese intelligence operatives working with senior members of the banned Indian Independence League. It was thought that Rance senior had secret plans against any future Japanese militancy. The Japanese agent in Kuala Lumpur, Sugiyama Torashira, inveigled Akbar Khan, a Pathan lawyer for the overt Indian Association and, subversively, the Indian Independence League, to get his son, Tor Gul Khan, and his two nephews, Abdul Hamid Khan and Abdul Rahim Khan, to burgle Mr Rance's office, disguised as a humble tool shed at the back of the garden, to retrieve what they could of Japanese interest. There was a fourth man who went with them, a Gurkha, Rabilal Rai from Bhutan Estate, who happened to be in Kuala Lumpur with his father who had to go there on business. They were prevented by Rance junior who happened to look out of the lavatory window and see them in the moonlight. He skilfully ambushed them, laying low all four and capturing them. They were handed over to the police, all four of them vowing to kill him if ever they got the chance. For his son's safely, Rance senior sent him to England for the rest of his education – and then the war broke out.

Jason joined the army, was sent to India for officer training in the Indian Military Academy in Dehra Dun, where he outshone all the other cadets in his knowledge of jungle lore. He learnt to make a cuckoo call as well as the real bird which misled many a hearer on patrol exercises when a cuckoo answered his calls. On being commissioned he was posted to the 1st Gurkha Rifles. The three Indians and the Gurkha joined the Indian National Army, composed of Indian Army prisoners of war in Singapore. Intercepted by 'Magic', the highly guarded codeword given to the breaking of Japanese codes which the Indian National Army command in Singapore was allowed to use, the four men were captured; Rabilal Rai by Jason Rance and his men when he tried to get to India in a Japanese submarine; the two nephews, captured after parachuting into Burma and later hanged, and Tor Gul Khan, who was killed in Burma. Amazingly Jason Rance had been witness at the capture of the two Indians and the death of the one.

During the early stages of Japan's invasion of Malaya Jason's parents had escaped to India and his father had been commissioned in the Indian Intelligence Corps and worked in

General Headquarters in New Delhi. He had met his son when Jason went to GHQ for briefing for two special jobs; teaching units of the Chinese Army to use British Light Machine Guns; being loaned to the Nepalese Contingent's battalion in Burma to teach them the use of snipers' rifles. A third meeting was at the trial of the two captured parachutists.

At that time victory over the Japanese had yet to occur and the future of India was in doubt. The future of Gurkhas was, too, and no one expected either to be allowed to serve in the post-independent Indian Army or that there would be Gurkhas in the British Army. Having no civil job to go back to he had volunteered for a regular commission and been awarded one so when he heard that Gurkha regiments had been divided between the two armies he had volunteered for continued service with them and to his intense delight he had been commissioned into the 12th Gurkha Rifles, made up of men from the east of Nepal. After Indian independence, the British Army's Gurkhas were sent either to Hong Kong or Malaya. Jason's new battalion had been detailed to go the latter and that was why it was, in its way, a home-coming for him.

To date his soldering had been with Gurkhas from the west of Nepal, now he had to serve with easterners. He was to learn that both were as good as each other with one main difference: in the west, one could foster a friendship but in the east one had to wait until the other man took the initiative.

He heard orders for disembarkation over the Tannoy. He looked at his watch and saw it was half past three. He had yet to be given a job in charge of troops but his batman, Rifleman

Kulbahadur Limbu, was reputed to be the battalion's expert tracker. Jason wondered if that meant his future was to be the commander of the Recce Platoon.

'Saheb, time for us to leave the boat. I'll be happy to get off it and onto the firm ground again,' he heard a voice behind him and looking round there was Kulbahadur with Jason's and his own kit. 'I've been told we'll have our meal on the dockside before getting on the train', *rel* to Gurkhas, 'and moving all through the night. Do you know where we're going? It's all the same to me, new, green and fresh, so unlike it was in India.'

India, since the end of the war, had been a terrible place to serve in. Anti-British and anti-Gurkha tensions were constant: Hindu versus Moslem antipathy had resulted in a raging lust for religious superiority that caused myriad deaths, horrendous injuries, abject penury, widespread starvation and a collapse of all civil authority. Civil law and order were nowhere. The birth of the new country of Pakistan was something that generations of Britons who had loved and worked for India could never, in nightmares, have imagined or foretold. The final evacuation for Britons to leave in late December 1947 was Scheme QUIIM for Quit India Immediately, a name making those with a knowledge of one particular nickname of the most private part of a woman's body giggle.

So yes, the comparison between India and this new, green and fresh country, with no nose-to-tail, a-hundred-miles-long convoys of bullock carts of homeless refugees, no stench of death, no rotting corpses by the roadside and no hordes of hungry beggars.

'I agree with you, Kulé. It will a great change, too, no killings, proper peacetime, no war, training not operations, no casualties like there have been for so long.'

Jason was a born linguist and his Nepali, honed over the wartime years, was of a higher standard than many other British officers'. 'Saheb, your Nepali accent is as I have heard how the western Gurkhas speak, different from our eastern accent. Were you born in India and not in Belayat?' his batman asked.

'No, Kulé, I was born in this country.'

'So I suppose you speak Malay?'

'Yes' and fluently, but he did not let on that his Chinese was of a higher standard and, if his face were covered, he would be taken for a Chinese and not an Englishman, an *Angrej*, a *Belayati*. He somehow felt that he ought not to 'show off' his Chinese language ability, quite why he never really worked out, but at the back of his mind was the thought that it might be of the greatest use if he kept quiet about it.

Orders for entraining were given. Their destination was Seremban, a town south of Kuala Lumpur, in the state of Negri Sembilan. It had never had a regular army unit there before so there was no suitable accommodation ready for them. Going there pleased Jason as it meant he could go to Bhutan Estate where Rabilal Rai had lived, find out his parents and tell them that their son was dead, how they had become great friends, how Jason had managed to get him enlisted in the 1st Gurkha Rifles but how, sadly, he had been killed, by whom he never knew, as the Japanese were being driven south towards Rangoon.

The contrast between those last six months in India with the 1st Gurkha Rifles and the first three months in Malaya with 1/12 Gurkha Rifles took much getting used to. On the surface life was placid, humdrum, unexciting and boring. Initially the mass of paperwork required for the soldiers to change armies was time-consuming, mind-deadening but essential. Such matters as giving men their new army numbers, new pay books, a new currency, new accounting systems, new kit inventories and will forms in case a man died in service without a legal will had a high priority as did much else that was new. There were also a whole lot of new faces to recognise, new names and numbers to be learnt, a new accent and different words to get used to. There were many shortages: clerks, drivers, cooks, weapons specialists, signallers, pioneers and buglers, to say nothing of maps, compasses, wireless sets and even storage space, though there were several football grounds in the town. The weather was so different from what it had been in India, one could almost set one's watch by the daily afternoon showers at twenty past four so the footballers finished playing wet from rain and sweat.

Although life was, generally, boring, there were two surprises. The first, unpopular in the extreme, was, very early on, to be told that the battalion had become a gunner regiment, no longer were soldiers 'riflemen' and 'corporals' but 'gunners' and 'bombardiers', with 'companies' becoming 'batteries'. And indeed, the proposed 'new-look' Gurkha Division had the unit as 101 Field Regiment, Royal Artillery, (12 Gurkha Rifles) but they still called themselves 1/12 Gurkha Rifles. The soldiers were bemused but it only made a difference when 25-pounder artillery pieces arrived and with half a dozen new British officers, Gunners all, knowing nothing about Gurkhas or their language. Apart from a new weapon to be learnt, that meant a second lot of new sahebs to get used to: certain over-educated hot heads felt that they had made the wrong decision in becoming British Army Gurkhas. It also posed a dilemma for those British officers who had come across from the 1st Gurkha Rifles and who had no wish to be a 'nine-mile sniper' as the derogatory phrase had it: bug out to a British infantry regiment of the line, try to convert to be a Gunner or leave the army altogether? The majority decision was to stay for one three-year tour if only to help the Gurkhas by being a buffer between them and this new influx.

Apart for any administrative consideration, the main task of the battalion for the next four months was to learn what was known as 'gun drill' with the new 'pieces'. Peacetime routine also included drill, physical training, small arms weapon training and games, phantoms of memory in the past three and a half years. The regiment was badly under-strength as many men had opted to stay in the Indian Army, fed on anti-British propaganda by Congress Party sympathisers that there would be no rice in the rations which would only contain beef and bread. Likewise, it would be the first time ever that families were to live in a land beyond the Black Water, anathema to any Hindu.

But above all, people were thankful there was no war and peacetime conditions were now the norm ... but they were all wrong. What nobody knew was that, within six months, death and destruction, chaos and confusion would reign as the Communists launched a deadly offensive that would last a dozen years.

Mid-January 1948

Jason's parents had left India at the end of the war and settled in London. Jason's father became critically ill and Jason was allowed two weeks' compassionate leave, just in time to see him before he died. He was allowed to travel by air, an almost unknown privilege: it took two and a half days to get to England with night stops in Karachi and Rome. He almost had to wait for a ship to bring him back but was lucky to be given a flight instead. He decided to buy a Gurkha broach for his mother to wear. He went to Terrier's, a jeweller's shop in Regent's Street, and told the man there what he wanted, mentioning that he was returning to Malaya. 'I wonder you can do something for me?' he asked and Jason felt he was almost duty bound to say, 'I'll certainly try to.'

It transpired that before being taken a prisoner by the Japanese in 1942, a Tamil estate comprador, Subramanian Mudaliar, had helped him recover when wounded by hiding him till he was better, otherwise, as he said later, he would probably have died in captivity. 'I'd love to thank him and now is the chance of asking you to take a watch out for him as a present. Could you please manage that? Mind you, I don't know if he is dead or alive, but I'll risk it.'

'Of course. Where does he live?' and the address was Jemima Estate, not far from Seremban. Once back from leave Jason asked at the Police Station if they could help him find the man and the reason why. A week later Jason was asked to go to the Police Station where he found a frightened man who said yes, he had helped a British captain in 1942. When Jason told him what the captain had asked him to do, the man was overcome with surprise and delight. 'Tuan, as a thank you I can't do anything other than ask you to tell the captain how grateful I am and for you for having bothered to find me.' Here he hesitated then burst out with, 'if there is ever anything I can help you with, you must let me know.'

They parted and Jason put that out of his mind ... but Subramanian Mudaliar remembered.

In late February the Gunner CO, Lieutenant Colonel James Heron, a nice enough man but palpably out of his depth commanding Gurkhas, suggested holding a party for various local dignitaries and senior officers. Among the guests was one Reggie Hutton. When Jason Rance was introduced to him, he leant forwards and softly said, 'When there's a quiet moment come and talk to me.' It was only after Jason had drifted off that he realised that Hutton had not spoken English to him but Chinese.

When they did meet up Hutton, smiling, said, 'Congratulations, you have passed one most important test!'

Jason looked at him nonplussed so Hutton felt he had to explain himself. 'When I spoke to you in Chinese you didn't bat an eyelid in surprise. A great attribute.'

'How did you know I spoke Chinese, sir?'

'During the war I was in a stay-behind party in which was your boyhood friend Ah Fat and he told me all about you ...'

Rudely Jason interrupted. 'Is he still alive? I do hope so.'

'Yes, and you will learn what he's up to all in good time. Now, there's something I want to tell you about.' He came nearer and lowered his voice. 'I am in charge of Special Branch in Singapore and there is a Chinese, named Lee Soon, who worked with me in the same group during the war. He was one of the two Malayan Communist Party's representative at a so-called Youth Meeting in Calcutta in January when he was told that a Communist uprising was due to start here in Malaya sometime this year. At the meeting and then a Communist get-together there was a Gurkha from Bhutan Estate. He is Kamal Rai, who was my close companion in my hide-away years during the war. I spoke to him recently when I went to stay with the estate manager, Mr Theopulos. I took him to one side and told him about you and if ever it was suggested that he work with you, not to refuse.'

Jason gasped. 'Sir, I knew a Kamal Rai when I lived in Malaya pre-war. I wonder if he's the same.'

'Yes, he is the same as he knows you and your boyhood friend Ah Fat. Kamal has been my close agent ever since we met. That would be after you left Malaya, in 1936, wasn't it?' He took a sip from the glass in his hand.

'No, sir, 1938.'

'I arranged for him to go to Calcutta for the Youth meeting and to act dumb as I wanted to know what Lee Soong was up to and also what the two meetings, the Youth bit and a Communist Party Plenum, were about. On his return, apart from debriefing him, I was also keeping tabs on the Australian Communist leader, Sharkey, who had been at the Calcutta meeting and who stopped off in Singapore where he had a secret meeting with the MCP and urged them to become active.'

'If I do meet Kamal am I to know about that or will I just meet him as a one-time friend?'

A wine waiter offered them some drinks but both declined, too busy to break off their conversation.

'If you meet socially, keep it social,' Reggie continued as though he had not been interrupted. 'If any situation arises that involves his background, "yes". My name will be your passport for any skulduggery and when you do meet him, give him my regards. And, for your ears only, there are three Chinese Green Dragon men near Bhutan Estate in the Sepang area who are waiting for matters to turn active and have been warned that this Lee Soon will be visiting them. You don't know Lee Soong but Kamal does – and hates his guts.'

'Just one point, sir. A Rabilal Rai from Bhutan Estate tried to enter India by submarine during the war. I and my men captured him, prevented him from drowning. We became friends, he my gunman. He was killed at the end of the war by an Indian soldier who had volunteered for the *Azad Hind Fauj*, the Free Indian Army, in Burma and I need to go and tell his parents who will not have heard what's happened to him. When I am in Bhutan Estate looking for his folk, do I also look for Kamal?'

Reggie Hutton considered that then said, 'no. Let it happen of its own accord.'

Jason thanked him and, after a hand clasp, they drifted apart.

By early March Jason felt it was time for him to go and see Rabilal's parents and, if the occasion arose, 'bump into' Kamal. He asked the Adjutant for a weekend's leave. Many officers went the few miles to Port Dickson to swim and lounge and Bhutan Estate, under Mr Theopulos, whose uncle had brought the original workforce from Darjeeling in 1904, was not as far. Granted.

Jason rang the estate, using Malay.

'Bhutan Estate, chief clerk, Mr Hemlal Rai speaking.'

Jason answered in Nepali, hearing a gasp of surprise from the other end. He explained who he was and what he wanted. 'Yes, I remember Rabilal Rai. We all wondered what had become of him. So the poor man is dead.'

'Yes, Hemlal-jyu and I want to tell his parents about it.'

There was no immediate answer then 'although I would much like to meet you and talk face-to-face, if you can tell me without your coming here it will be more, how shall I say? it will be easier all round. Wartime captives under the Japanese still don't like talking to army officers if it can be avoided. You would have to meet the manager were you to come here. He was a prisoner of war.'

Jason had already found out that European planters who had been taken captive had such a low opinion of army officers for 'having let the side down' by being beaten by the Japanese that they would refuse to meet them if possible. He also knew that many officers from the ill-fated Malayan campaign looked on the planters as a 'whisky-swilling' lot and not wholly to be trusted. There was antipathy on both sides.

'In that case, chief clerk saheb, merely tell them that their son was my bodyguard and friend but was unfortunately killed at the end of the war. We made the correct obsequies for him.'

'Thank you, Rance saheb. I will tell them and please excuse my having to tell you it's better this way. I hope we can meet each other some time.'

Negri Sembilan-Selangor border, early April 1948

The village of Sepang, just inside the state of Negri Sembilan, was not much more than a group of Chinese shops huddled around a crossroads in one of the under-populated parts of the country. It had a small Police Station with a plain-clothed Chinese detective, and a minor Malay administrative functionary, the Assistant District Officer, known as the ADO. Chinese in government posts were unheard of other than when needed as linguists or in an Intelligence role.

To the east, a few miles off, was the sea, the Malacca Straits. Fishing villages, houses perched on stilts, bordered the shore and spread some short way inland. Those nearest the sea were inhabited by Sumatrans, more militantly inclined than Malays, who had sailed over from the Dutch East-Indies; those villages farther inland had Malays in them.

The other three sides were filled with rubber estates, all European-owned bar one, and, behind the westerly ones, the Serting 'forest reserve' jungle. Sandwiched between the two and peopled by Chinese – known as 'squatters' in that they were living on land without any title deed – was an untidy, overgrown area consisting of homesteads with vegetable plots, fruit, such as pomelo, papaya and jackfruit, pigs and poultry, out-lying tapioca patches and secondary jungle. This last was where the primary jungle had been cut down and a thick profusion of head-high growth, difficult to move through and always too hot for comfort during the day, proliferated. No Malay policeman would ever venture there except under extreme circumstances and then always led by a British gazetted officer, nor would any of the European rubber planting fraternity unless in a group with shotguns. As this area was just inside the Selangor boundary and a long way from the nearest Police Station it was seldom if ever visited by police.

Even before the war the area had a bad reputation. Received wisdom had it that many of the area's male inhabitants under forty years of age had been Communists fighting against the Japanese during the recent war. They had supposedly disarmed after the war so had no weapons or ammunition – or had they some hidden? Nowadays, on meeting any European, they avoided contact and a pernicious rumour was that they were preparing to re-start their armed struggle for Communism against the British imperialists now that they had got rid of the Japanese feudalists.

The immediate area around Sepang itself was quiet, not because there was no crime but because what crime there was went unreported as it was controlled by the Ghee Hin, or Green Dragons Secret Society, whose members lived in the squatter area and who made sure that whatever happened there was their business and nobody else's.

One evening in April, three middle-aged Chinese men were sitting round a small wooden table in the back room of a 'society' shop behind Boonoon Estate, the one estate not owned by a European concern but Chinese. It was thoroughly under the control of the Green Dragons, whose tattoo on one shoulder was a green dragon or, sometimes, 義興公司 or just 義興, the former including the full name, 'kongsi' whereas their enemies, originally based in Penang were a 'society'. They were still deadly enemies despite the truce, known as the Pangkor Treaty, signed in 1894 for reconciliation between the two factions.

The shop was owned and run by an elderly man whose eyes were described by the Chinese as 'fighting cock' eyes, so he was known as Dow Gai Ngaan Yeh Yeh', Boss-eyed Grandfather. He was famous for his breakfast char siu bao dumplings filled with barbecued pork and his speciality were dai bao, twice as big and filled with hardboiled egg, chicken meat and mushroom, to say nothing of his char siu, crispy roast pork belly. He was known to have tight lips, otherwise the three Chinese who had come to eat there would never have done so. The shop sold items the Chinese needed, amongst which were rice, dried fish, spices, vegetables such as brinjal, bean, bitter gourd and pumpkin, mostly brought in from the squatter area, as well as basic household articles, including cheap clothes, local medicines and condensed milk that Chinese mothers gave their babies.

The three Chinese, senior Ghee Hin men, all had nicknames, the Killer, who worked on assassinations, the Blood Sucker, because he was more insistent than any leech in getting under people's skin and got what he wanted, and the Collector, who raised money.[3] There were three others, similarly tattooed, bodyguard and understudy to each of the three senior men. All six were illegally armed with a pistol. Although the Green Dragons ruled supreme in this part of Malaya, they were always on their guard against another secret society, the Hai San, or Five Districts, whose sign was the numerals 108. They had regarded them as deadly enemies for more than a hundred years. Turf wars were endemic and the

---

3 These nicknames were told the author by Ismail Mubarak, Head of Special Branch, Seremban.

nearer a large town the more vicious they became.

'Before we start to talk seriously, let's have a drink,' said the Killer, a bullet-headed man with narrow-set eyes, a straggly beard and long arms. 'Shamsu or brandy?'

They decided on brandy, the grape making a better drink than did rice. 'Hey, you outside. Bring in two bottles of brandy and three glasses,' the Killer shouted out to the shop owner. This he quickly did, put them on the table and, 'Prepare a meal for us,' he was told as he left. He showed no interest or intimacy – neither would have been worth his while. The three bodyguards ate and drank by themselves in another room.

The Killer poured out four-fingers' worth into each glass and, with the obligatory toast of 'yam seng', 'drink to victory', they downed the contents in one. As custom dictated, hands were laid over each glass as if to say 'no more' but no resistance was made when their hands were removed so that more drink could be poured in. 'And again,' and again it was. Down it went in one and they wiped their lips with the back of their hand.

'Now listen, time to talk before our meal is ready,' said the Killer. 'You know how we thought that those arrogant British would not have the impudence to return here after the war in which their soldiers were so inferior, though better than those drunken Australians I will admit, and even though there were some of them who stayed in the jungle with us, none of them was anywhere as aggressive or skilled as we were.'

The other two fully agreed with him. 'However, they have yet to learn their lesson and they have come back. Early on today I received orders from our Politburo to prepare for active duty against them by defeating their army before taking over the government. We start by disrupting the economy by eliminating their European rubber planters and tin miners by threat and murder, so force the others to leave. We will then make the country into a Communist republic, without all those puppet Malay rulers.'

A gasp of surprise and appreciation burst from the other two. 'Not before time,' muttered the Blood Sucker.

'We have to wait for a couple or three months before we start. Between now and then we will open up that arms and ammunition dump so there will be no delay when we get executive orders. We must make sure that the 'cow-horn' type of machine guns, and the smaller ones, are in fully working order.'

The 'cow-horn' type referred to the Bren Light Machine Gun, the magazine of which curved as did a cow's horn.

They chatted about training, to include range work, tactics and jungle craft, until their meal was brought in. They kept quiet while they concentrated on scooping up the glutinous rice and fried pork with their chopsticks. No Chinese ever wanted to waste time talking at meals.

After belching their satisfaction, 'to continue: besides needing sufficient money and supplies, there is another matter we must not forget about. You,' and the Killer pointed at the Blood Sucker, 'are the best educated among us. You need to find out the latest situation about pamphlets, training ones and propaganda, while you,' and it was at the Collector that he looked now, 'get each of the huts in the whole of the squatter area to put some extra rations, not that there is a great deal, to one side. We may have to take them into the jungle at short notice.'

The other two nodded acceptance at these orders. It made sense and they were expecting them. It had happened during the war and now it was infinitely easier without any Japanese.

'My last point tonight is one that may make a difference to the way we have to operate. You know the estate of Tei Po Lo-Si' – the nearest he could get to Theopulos – 'don't you?'

Of course they did.

'His coolies are Goo K'a yan' – the nearest he could get to 'Gurkha men' – 'who did not fight with us against the Japanese. There were military Goo K'a bing who were beaten by the Japanese at the start of the war. There are now six battalions of Goo K'a bing in Malaya, the nearest being in Seremban. From what we know of them there will be little to fear from them. In any case, and this you will at all times keep to yourselves, I have learnt that there is a secret plan afoot that could make them into "paper tigers" just as the "running dogs", their masters, already are.' He was referring to the rumour of being gunners not infantrymen.

This the other two promised.

'Time to go back,' said the Killer, hawking and expertly spitting a gob of phlegm out of the opened wooden shutters and, heady from the drink and the excitement of what lay ahead of them, they called their bodyguards and quietly left for home, having given a right-handed, clenched-fisted salute, little realising that the Malay Communist Party now had a policy of not letting secret society men become members although they were extremely useful for strong-arm tactics.

Boss-eyed Grandfather pretended to hear nothing, likewise

his son who helped serve the food and drink, but both of them had heard everything.

'What have those soldiers based in Seremban been doing? What reports have you two had?'

It was a week after their last meal in the shop in the squatter area and the three Chinese Communist leaders had been busy. The Killer had visited Tanjong Sepat with a group of squatters and had taken out from a hidden dump sufficient arms and ammunition for their immediate needs and had also been deep into the jungle to inspect weapons and ammunition dumped there at the end of the war. Only about half seemed serviceable so a known armourer was put on the job of refurbishment where possible. Some he had brought back a couple of days later and suggested that a 'sample be tried out on the rifle range'. This was a tract of comparatively open land which was too far for firing to be heard from the Killer's own house and details of its use were left to a subordinate who lived nearer.

The Collector had visited a printing press in Seremban and picked up some Communist propaganda and receipt pads, while the Blood Sucker had made an extensive tour of the squatter area, detailing how many pigs and chickens had to be kept in reserve for emergencies as well as checking on rice stocks.

'And during your travels, what have your learnt about the *Goo K'a bing* and their "running dog" commander?' the Killer asked. 'What reports have you for me?'

Apparently they stayed in their camp in Seremban, doing nothing to disrupt the guerrillas' plans.

Saling Rubber Estate, 17½ Milestone, Johor Bahru-Kulai Road, Kulai, Johor, 10 May 1948

At the 5th Plenary Session of the Central Executive Committee, two months after the Australian Communist Leader who had 'had words' with Chin Peng now the Secretary General of the Malayan Communist Party, had gone back to Australia, a resolution was passed to take 'resolute action, concerted struggle and the use of violence when necessary,' but, in the minutes, there was no mention of any Soviet instruction for this. There was, after all, merit in starting what that uncouth and arrogant, 'white-skinned pig' barbarian, good communist though he was, and who, like all such people, smelled of bad meat, had said, even though Australian newspapers later denied that he had done any cajoling.

Malaya, 17 and 18 June, 1948

The High Commissioner declared an Emergency, first in one part of the country and the next day in the rest of it. This was because of increased Communist activity of murder, arson and sabotage. Orders for the use of firearms were also promulgated. At that time troops were not to fire unless first fired at.

Paroi Camp, Seremban, July 1948

The recruit intake at the small tented camp a few miles to the east of Seremban saw the arrival of the first batch of young men for the British Army's new 12th Gurkha Rifles, both battalions. Most were not of a high educational standard, many almost illiterate, strong men, even if unlettered being the criterion. One was a Darjeeling schoolboy, educated well enough for clerical duties, possibly an educational instructor or, maybe, with training, a member of the intelligence section. His name was Padamsing Rai.

Sepang and environs , August 1948

'Saheb, the Commanding saheb wants you in his office now.' The runner had found Captain Rance in the battery stores doing a routine check.

'Quartermaster ustad, you heard what the runner has said. I have to go away for a while. Let the fatigue party take a break until I come back.'

'*Hunchha, Hajur.*'

On his way to the CO's office, Rance started to question his conscience about any misgivings the CO might have ... but his thoughts snapped back to the present as a file of men marching past him gave him an 'eyes right', which he answered with a smart salute. He reported to the Adjutant. 'Straight in. You're wanted urgently.'

Jason entered the CO's office, saluted and waited, at attention, till the Colonel finished a telephone conversation. He noticed a wall map which had not been there before. The CO put the phone down. 'Rance, a surprise for you. One that you will enjoy, I feel sure. Come and look at the map. I have a man-sized task for you now that the Emergency has been declared.'

Jason thrilled. 'That sounds exciting, sir.'

'So far what trouble has occurred has chiefly been in the north and farther south but the CPO, the Chief Police Officer, of Negri Sembilan, is worried that a cell of wartime guerrillas, dormant till now, is dismantling an old arms and ammo dump left over from the war at …' and he peered at the map and made a stab with his right forefinger, 'here. At Tanjong Sepat, VU 4537, on the coast. All these new Malay names. I'm not used to them. From the shape of the area I guess it means promontory or something similar.'

Jason peered at the map. 'Got it, sir. Yes, "tanjong" means "promontory".'

'Farther inland is the small village of Sepang. Here we are. Grid reference VU 700417. No need to take that down yet. The CPO is worried that this suspected guerrilla gang that is believed to have its base in the squatter area between the jungle and the rubber estates is preparing to cause some sort of havoc. Special Branch has had information about an increase in donations, as a Chinese Blood Sucker politely calls them, as well as hearing what can only be range firing on several mornings and evenings a week and, curiously, bugle calls. It looks as if thorough and extensive preparations are being made for some major nastiness.'

Indeed, that is what it did look like.

'That's where you're going. Whether you actually come across the range in such a large area, always presuming the baddies fire their weapons in the same place and when you are in earshot, is highly questionable. It has not been pin-pointed and probably the clam-like civilians won't tell you, even if they do know. You don't have the time, the skill or the equipment to venture an approach to the area from the jungle so your entry into the area will be more difficult to keep secret.'

Obviously he's no idea how to use the jungle as we did in Burma. Why send a CO whose wartime experience was only in the desert and in Europe? Being a Gunner and not having served in India, he has a 'red-coat' mentality as we more irreverent junior officers say.

'The local police are not keen to go and investigate and the planting fraternity is worried. Your task, Rance, is to take a troop of Q Battery, a cook and two vehicles to the area and find out just what is happening. We are so short of kit you won't even have a wireless set. In case of an emergency you'll have to do the best you can until you get to a phone on a rubber estate or the Police Station in Sepang. Once there your initial task is to visit as many of the ten European estate managers in the area as you have time for. I have met some of them when they have come to the club in Seremban on a Saturday night. Many are anti-army, thinking that they were let down during the war. The last thing they want is more trouble now that the Japanese are no longer around. Make a note of the three estates with a Gurkha labour force, Bhutan, Bute and Lothian. You are to try and impress those three about how good Gurkhas are as I fear they do not have a particularly good opinion of them as fighters.'

Jason was stunned and his eyes burned. 'How come, sir? We wouldn't have won the war in Burma without them.'

'No, Rance. Those managers are like all the rubber planters I've met so far. Parochial in the extreme. I was not a Far East soldier but I have learnt that the three Gurkha battalions had no chance against the Japanese here in Malaya in 1942 – all stuffed full of too many raw soldiers with weak leadership at the top is one reason why they look down on us now and the other, believe it or not, is that apparently none joined the Chinese guerrillas or British stay-behind parties after the Japanese victory.' The CO wiped his sweaty forehead with a handkerchief.

'Jolly unfair and narrow-minded, if you ask me.' Rance automatically braced his back, an unconscious habit, in mute protest.

'I agree. Also you'll find, I think, that none of the three managers with Gurkhas speaks Nepali. Only Malay. We all know that our men only give of their best under certain conditions and weak leadership in a foreign language doesn't help. Talking about the club, what impressions have you come away with after your visits there? I mean as far as the European civilians are concerned, not types like the Garrison Engineer or the Claims and Hirings boffin.'

Jason pondered. 'The junior planters are mostly wartime servicemen, like myself. They seem a decent enough lot but as for their seniors, the managers, those of them who didn't get away to India or Australia in 1942, seem most reticent even to acknowledge our presence. They had a terrible time as prisoners of war and I suppose that took all the stuffing out of them.'

The CO listened intently. 'I fully agree. Also those who were in the bag tend to look down on those who did manage to get away. They see it as "unsportsmanlike". And, sadly, they look down on us British officers because "we" didn't put up a better show against those blasted Japs.'

'That means my job will have an extra dimension, sir,' commented Jason, with a quick intake of breath.

'Indeed so. And to add to what I've just said, they also have an inferiority complex as they think that we think of them as "whisky-swilling planters", not up to our standards as "pukka sahibs" or however they say that in their local language.'

Jason bit his lip. 'A two-fronted approach is needed and, probably, whichever way I play it will be wrong.'

'Now, back to your task after that digression,' said the CO, 'I've arranged for you to take over part of the ADO's place. It's empty – he's a Malay and has bugged out – and, apart from trying to help the morale of the managers, you are to do as much patrolling of the squatter areas and jungle fringes as you have time for. Even though the Emergency has been declared only shoot if they open fire first. You can't open fire at the tykes even if you see them in uniform and armed. Try and capture them, yes. You might also get the men to have a "flag march" in a vehicle when you're with the managers.' A thought struck him. 'By the way, how much Malay do you speak?'

Now is the time to tell him my background. 'Sir, you may not know it but I was born and bred in Malaya. I have a near perfect command of Chinese and am almost as equally fluent in Malay. The area you have pointed out to me is where my closest boyhood friend, a Chinese named Ah Fat, and I used to go camping during our school holidays. Once I'm in the area, which I presume will only be more overgrown and have more squatters than before, I'll almost be on home territory.'

'Thank you for telling me,' said the CO. 'You'll be of tremendous use for future operations' *and wonderful to be such a gifted linguist.*

'What are my orders if I find communist literature in a squatter's shack?'

'If you have the resources and the time, kick out the

inhabitants, bring them back to hand over to the police and, if there is not too much of it, bring the literature back with you.'

'And if we are fired on from inside a shack, retaliate and kill someone?'

The CO was, Jason saw, unsure of himself.

'Oh, tell the police about any corpses you left there and were probably burnt when you set fire to the shack.'

'Understood. Drastic and simple. When do you want me to leave, sir, and for how long?' *This has to be better than running round those 25-pounders on gun drill.*

'Today is, let me see – how quickly time flies with so much to do – Tuesday. Make it after your morning meal on Thursday for an initial ten days. Far too short a time with too few men for anything more than skimming the place but, who knows, you may have a lucky break. If you are on to something big you'll be extended and, probably, reinforced. Have a look at the map first and if there are any questions I'll try to answer them.'

Jason looked at the map. His practiced eye measured the area the CO had pointed out as the target. *Taking the western boundaries of the estates and the eastern boundary of the jungle the area is seventeen miles across and, from north to south, twenty-five miles long. You could lose a brigade there for a month and yet my few men only have ten days.* 'Before I mention anything operational, there is one tiny niggle, sir, the map shows Sepang inside Negri Sembilan and the outer reaches of my area in Selangor, yet the CPO of the former wants us there. Presumably he's cleared it with his opposite number so it's not my worry. It will be a change from just being in the lines and a great chance to see how these easterners compare to the westerners I was used to,' and he smiled in anticipation of assessing any differences.

'I know, I know. But whatever little you do find has to be more than nobody going there at all.' Jason nodded enthusiastically. 'Tell the Adjutant to alert OC Q Battery for the troop,' the CO continued, 'the Quartermaster for the rations to be drawn and the MTO for two vehicles to stay with you and spare fuel in jerry cans.'

'Wilco, sir,' called out Jason after his final salute, forgetting his customary decorum in his excitement. He glanced at his watch. *Twelve thirty. Just time to go back to the stores and let the Quartermaster Sergeant know that there'd be no more checking today or for quite some time.*

He reached the stores. The soldiers there stood up and saluted, a look of enquiry on each face. The answer was completely unexpected but then this new saheb was different from the others.

'*At the top of the* sal *trees how green the leaves are,*
We're on our way, we're on our way to the war.'

Jason's brown eyes a-twinkle and elastic face a-twitch, he sang an exact imitation of a Gurkha voice's timbre, patting his stomach as though it were a *madal*, the cylindrical Gurkha drum essential on all musical occasions.

The men burst out laughing and the song continued;
'*Even with gold and money proffered, all in vain,*
The happy days of carefree youth will ne'er be seen again.'

That resulted in more laughter as the men shared glances. 'Saheb,' one of the senior men ventured. 'Isn't that one of your western songs?'

'No longer. From now on it's as eastern as you are. And the reason I'm singing it is because the day after tomorrow we are going to the war, not all that far away and the leaves will not be of the *sal* trees but of the jungle and rubber trees. We are not chasing proper dushman but Cheena daku. I'm taking one troop from here. The others will come to support me if we run into trouble. We leave after our morning meal the day after tomorrow.'

'Saheb, I have a question,' the Battery Quartermaster Sergeant asked. 'After winning the war in Burma the British gave it away and after saving India from the Japanese they gave that away too. My question is, if there's a war in Malaya, will the British give that away after we've won?'

Jason's answer was noncommittal: 'In matters of god, government and games, only the referee can decide who wins and who loses.' Before dismissing them he had a thought. 'You may not know it but I was born in Malaya and had a Chinese childhood friend for many years. We used to go and camp in the area we're due to go to. I have not been there since I left Malaya when I was sixteen, about ten years ago but it may be of use if we meet anyone I knew before and I have to ask the way.'

'Saheb, if you had a Cheena as a friend, can you speak it?' one of his men asked.

Then, to his men's utter astonishment, Jason extended his arms and, with palms outwards, and as he opened and closed them, one hand spoke in Malay and the other answered in Chinese. He brought his arms down and smiled at the flabbergasted men. 'Yes, and write Chinese but I keep quiet about it so that if I hear any Cheena speak I can understand without them knowing about it so please try and keep it a secret.'

Heads nodded in assent and he dismissed them.

'Embuss!'

On Captain Rance's command, twenty-six men of 5 Troop, Q Battery, divided into three sections and a small headquarters, clambered aboard the three 15-cwt [hundred weight] trucks ready to drive off into the unknown, the first time a sub-unit of 1/12 Gurkha Rifles was going on operations in the British Army.

Earlier Jason had inspected them after Sergeant Ruwaman Limbu, the Troop Sergeant, handed them over to him; weapons, the Section Commanders' 9-mm Sten Guns and the soldiers' Number 4, Mark 1, Lee-Enfield rifles, bedding rolls, cooking equipment, ten days' rations and the spare fuel. So short of kit were they that there was only one map and one compass, no wireless set, no binoculars or medical pack although each man had his 'First Field Dressing'.

Satisfied that all was as it should be, he shouted out 'Start up and follow me!' got into the lead vehicle and away they went. The journey should take not much more than an hour. A straight line from Seremban to Sepang was no more than twelve miles but there was no direct route and the roads were winding and that more than doubled the distance they had to travel. Also the small convoy drove slowly as the drivers were only recently trained. As they drove past rubber estates with rows and rows of trees planted in straight lines at regular intervals, Jason let his mind wander. He was the only officer in the regiment with his linguistic background, he was going to an area where he had played around in the jungle when a youngster and Kamal Rai knew him from before as well as a lot else. It was an auspicious start.

He glanced at his watch. They had left the lines at half-past 11 and it was now a quarter to 1. Sepang, 2 miles' he saw on a mile stone. 'Nearly there,' he said to the driver. 'Once we're in the village keep your eyes open for a Police Station. The Commanding Saheb said he'd get a message sent down for them to be expecting us around now.'

They drove into the village and the Police Station was easy to spot. Also, a young Malay constable was waiting outside and waved them down. Jason got out of his vehicle and greeted him. '*Selamat tengah-hari, Enche.*'

The policeman grinned at this strange *orang puteh*, 'white man', getting both the greeting correct for 'midday' and knowing how to address a policeman. Many got it wrong, saying *Orang mata-mata* instead, '*Mata*', an eye: '*mata-mata*', eyes, the man with eyes, not the policeman but the detective. In fact the young Malay's eyes were not the only ones watching the Gurkhas' arrival. Furtive Chinese stares came from every shop that saw them and each shop keeper noted the trucks and saw that Gurkha soldiers were looking out of the back.

The Chinese detective, the only person in the Police Station who could speak English, came out and introduced himself. Jason did not let on that he was a Chinese speaker. 'Tuan, you are to drive to the ADO's compound which is your base. Here are the keys for it. The Tuan ADO is not there. It is completely empty, no telephone and no furniture but there is wood for cooking. You see that track leading up to that small hillock?' and Jason identified where he was pointing.

'Yes, I see where you mean. Is there anyone here I need to report to?'

'No, we know you're here. The Police Sergeant will make a note of it in the Station Diary.'

'May I know your name?'

'Call me Enche Ah Wong.'

'Have you a phone I can use, Enche Ah Wong?' and he was led inside. As Ah Wong leant forward to show Jason where it was his shirt was pulled open and Jason saw 海山 tattooed on his shoulder. He knew it was the sign for Hai San, the Five Districts secret society, based in Penang. More mischievously than anything else, he said to the detective in English, 'Inche, you come from a family based in Penang don't you?'

He was answered by a look of amazement. 'Yes, Tuan, how do you know that?'

'An inspired guess,' he answered lightly as he phoned the Adjutant, telling him that they had arrived safely and, once unloaded, would send back one of the trucks. 'I'll only contact you if there is anything important.'

The men in the shops saw them drive off to the ADO's house, realised that matters were to become more involved and that news of the troops' arrival needed passing on quickly. Eight to ten soldiers in each truck. Not Malays but those Goo K'a bing. A long-nosed devil in charge: why have they come and for how long? They bode no good.

'And who are you, then, driving up to my office in a military vehicle, armed to the teeth with a squad of soldiers, without any warning?' came an unseen angry voice.

Jason had got out of the vehicle, told the men with him to get down and stretch their legs and was looking around when the tirade came from behind him. He wheeled round and gave the angry man a butt salute, bringing his left arm over to the rifle he carried in his right hand, middle finger through the trigger guard and arm extended.

A tall man, with a lined, florid-face and angry eyes, greying at the temples and wearing a short-sleeved shirt with an open collar, thin slacks and black leather shoes, must have come out of the end room of a one-storied building, presumably his office. There was a small patch of grass in front of it and, on the others side, three larger buildings, an open-sided garage, a large, evil-smelling factory for processing the latex 'tapped' from the rubber trees and what looked like stores. One or two armed men in the uniform of Special Constables lounged unobtrusively in the shade.

'Good afternoon, sir. I presume you are Mr Theopulos, as this is Bhutan Estate. I am from the 1st/12th Gurkhas. I and my men are based in Sepang having come from Seremban,' he looked down at his watch, 'two hours ago.'

'Yet you have the impertinence not to forewarn me, the manager? I shall make a complaint to your CO.'

'Sir, I apologise on his behalf. I do not have your telephone number and had expected someone in Seremban, possibly the CPO, to have alerted you by now as we are here because he wants us here but he obviously hasn't.'

'Well, now you're here, what do you want?'

Jason had an aversion to being bullied yet he knew that he had to appease this angry and probably frightened man. He was

67

obviously in no mood to be asked about Reggie Hutton and Kamal Rai.

'I personally don't want anything more than to be of service to the planting fraternity who, I gather, are worried and upset by recent rumours of trouble caused by Chinese guerrillas in the vicinity.' That sounds high-falutin' and condescending. As that Indian babu once told me, 'Sir, lower your falutings.' He noticed an elderly Gurkha peering at him out of a window in the middle of the block.

The choleric manager stayed silent, gritting his teeth.

'As you seem to think I can be of no help, I'll leave and go now to see as many other managers as I can, who may think I can be of help to them, today and the next few days, to find out what information, if any, they can give me of the squatter area behind their estate. Then I will act on what information I have gleaned which may include pin-pointing a rifle range that has been reported and bugle calls that have been heard. Good day to you, sir.'

Without any more ado, Jason called out to his soldiers in crisp Nepali, 'Back into the vehicle. Driver start up.'

The order was obeyed instantly. Just as he himself was about to climb into his he saw the elderly Gurkha quickly come out and say something to Theopulos who had been taken aback by his uninvited guest's decisive way of taking the initiative from him. The Gurkha, who had to be a senior functionary in the office, Jason presumed, raised his hand almost as a protest at him, as though willing him not to move off, while the manager went back into his office.

The elderly Gurkha came up to Jason. 'Telephone, Saheb. The manager saheb has been called by your Commanding saheb. I am Hemlal Rai, the chief clerk here. How wonderful to hear an Englishman speak our language almost better than we do. We spoke on the phone and now you can understand why I felt it better you didn't come here in person. You'll be glad to learn I have told Rabilal's parents. They had thought that maybe he was dead as indeed an old shaman from Darjeeling had told them so but they are pleased to learn that you managed to carry out the correct obsequies.'

'Thank you, chief clerk saheb.'

'I have something else to ask that Rabilal's father asked me to enquire if you knew what had happened to the son, Tor Gul Khan, of Akbar Khan, a Pathan lawyer, Indian Association and Indian Independence League, and his two nephews so he can pass on any details you might have.'

Kindness rather than circumspection was Jason's uppermost reaction. 'All tried to kill me and, in turn, all were killed. Tor Gul was shot in a Burmese temple when I was there but it was not I who shot him and the other two had parachuted into Burma and were captured, both times trying to kill me. They were hanged in New Delhi on the Viceroy's order for wearing the uniform of the King-Emperor's enemies. There is no mercy in such cases. I had to give evidence against them and was there when the death sentences were delivered.'

'But they were not Indian Army soldiers,' said the chief clerk.

'No, but all of them had joined the *Azad Hind Fauj* even though none was an enlisted Indian soldier they were wearing uniform of an army fighting against the King-Emperor.'

'I understand, Saheb,' the chief clerk said, shaking his head and then Jason asked 'Doesn't the manager sahib speak Nepali?'

'No, Hajur. Only Malay.' He glanced round and saw his boss still on the phone. 'Got it! I remember you from when you and, what was his name? Mmmm. Yes, Ah Fat used to visit us before the war.' *Shall I? Yes.* 'Kamal Rai also seems to know you.'

'We met when I was a schoolboy. You see I was born in KL and used to come down this way with Ah Fat in our holidays, camping.'

'Captain saheb, yes, yes, it's coming back to me now. I tell you what, please arrange to visit us after work one day, with some of your soldiers and that will be a good time to meet up with him. We will really welcome you. You can tell us all that happened over in India during *inding-pinding*. We have heard so many stories that differ.'

'I am sure that can be arranged, Hemlal-ji. In due course I'll speak to the Tuan manager.'

'So will I. I know the men here will love it.'

'And you, chief clerk-ji. Where are your ancestors from?'

'My great-grandfather with his family moved to the Darjeeling area some years before the Tibetan War. That'll be about fifty years ago ...'

Before he could comment, Theopulos rejoined them. 'I understand you are Captain Rance. Please excuse my outburst earlier on. My nerves are not what they were or should be. That was a phone call from your CO asking for my cooperation and apologising for not having warned me before. Apparently the situation is worse than I thought. Your unexpected appearance rather threw me. What is your Christian name. Mine is John.'

Jason knew he had to be gracious after possibly being a bit too bombastic earlier. 'Not at all, John. Fully understandable. I am Jason,' and they shook hands.

'What do you plan to do now? Have you time to come up to my bungalow and have a cup of tea or a fresh lime with the Mem?'

'Thank you for the kind thought but I have to decline, this time anyway. I need to contact the other European managers as soon as I can and I don't have all that time to complete my task. However, what I really would like is to bring a group of my men here one evening, after your men have knocked off for the day and have a get-together. Mr Hemlal Rai has already sounded me out about it and will be mentioning it to you.'

'That sounds a good wheeze. *Kerani, apa pikaran-nya?*' Clerk, what do you think?

Hemlal had fully understood what was being said but Theopulos had 'lost points' so far and had, somehow, to make up for that. This he did by speaking Malay in front of Jason, wrongly assuming the army officer did not understand it.

'*Bagus-lah.*' Good.

'My chief clerk agrees that it is a good idea. Make a note of my phone number and we'll fix something.'

They bade farewell and Jason drove off to his next port of call.

Ah Wong came out of the tea shop, got on his bicycle that he had propped up outside and glanced up and down the road before mounting it. He rode off in the direction of the ADO's bungalow. Inside the shop a young Chinese girl, his niece, patted his $10 bill she had slipped into an inner pocket and went over to the older woman sitting at the counter. 'I'll buy a couple of tins of condensed milk now I'm here. A pity to waste a journey all this way and take nothing back for my sister's new baby. Just time to get back before dark.'

The elderly woman picked two tins off the small shelf behind her. 'We've at last got this new stock in. You're lucky. It's popular.'

The girl paid, took her change and put the two tins into her string bag. She went outside, got on her bike and rode off in the other direction, to the left, away from the village and towards the squatter area.

The elder woman in the shop took a small note book out of a drawer and wrote down the names of the two, with the time they had spent together and the $10 bill. *They'll come and ask me as they always do. I can't chance my luck not to as, although I can't swear to it, they're bound to have other sources they can check up with.*

Which was quite true: they had.

Akbar Khan, the Pathan lawyer who had worked for the overt Indian Association and, subversively, the Indian Liberation League, had reverted to what he considered his 'normal' duties now that India had got rid of the British and the *Azad Hind Fauj* sepoys had become heroes after the politically manoeuvred trials in the Red Fort in Delhi. He often wondered what had become of his son and nephews as no word of their fate had ever reached him and were they still alive surely by now he would have heard. He was totally unprepared for what he was about to hear when his telephone rang.

He answered in Malay, giving his name.

'I am the father of Rabilal Rai calling from Bhutan Estate. My son, your son Tor Gul and the two cousins all played together before the war, if you remember, whenever I went to Kuala Lumpur on business and brought him with me.'

Akbar caught his breath as he tried to answer too hastily. 'Yes, yes, of course I remember. What about them?' Good news, I hope. I've heard nothing. What have you for me?'

'Bad news, I fear. Your three are all dead, as is my son.'

'How did it happen? Do you know any details?'

He was told all that Captain Rance had told Hemlal Rai, the chief clerk.

'And who gave him that news?'

'A Captain Jason Rance from the 12th Gurkha Rifles now in Seremban.'

There was no answer. 'Are you still there?'

'Yes. Jason Rance you say?'

'Yes, that's the name.'

Akhbar Khan put the phone down after thanking his caller. *That little devil who ran away after I had told that Sugiyama Torashira and that other Japanese about the raid on Mr Rance's office? I'll get him one way or another however long it takes me* he thought gloatingly.

The three Green Dragon men were having another communal meal, their bodyguards in the next room. Military vehicles and soldiers had been seen, armed but not looking for any trouble, it seemed. 'No actual activity?' the Killer asked.

It appeared that nothing of obvious importance had occurred. One vehicle had been seen going to a number of estates, sometimes to the office and at other times to the bungalow, while the other vehicle had been travelling around the local area with soldiers in the back.

'Those men are nothing to be afraid of. I have heard that they went to *Tei Po Lo-Si* and sat around with the labour force singing songs. The long-nosed devil even sang and danced, yes, in their language and according to their culture. He also made his hands speak, so it was said. He should be in a circus, not the army. What sort of commander lowers himself to that extent, I ask you?' His smirk dripped irony. 'He's no threat to us,' he sneered, spitting his disgust.

The other two did not answer and the speaker continued. 'They are so lazy and ineffective it will be quite safe to see if the dumped weapons and ammo are good enough to use without fear of too many misfires. They won't hear anything.'

But he was wrong on both counts.

2

Sepang and environs, August 1948

The detective Ah Wong walked up to the Gurkha base, produced his identity card and showed it to the sentry on duty. '*Tuan ada*?' he asked and the sentry, knowing that Captain Rance was in, replied, '*Tuan ada*.' Simple Malay was indeed simple and by now every Gurkha had a working smattering.

'Take this Cheena to the Saheb,' the sentry told a bystander, who led him away. They found the British Army Captain sitting on the floor writing some notes.

'*Selamat petang*,' Rance greeted the detective, wishing him 'good afternoon'.

Ah Wong answered in like coin then, in English and in surprise, 'No chair, no table?'

'No, we sleep, sit and eat on the floor but at least the roof does not leak,' he replied with a smile, eyes a-twinkle. 'Join me and tell me what you have for me.'

He sat down. 'Tuan, you have been here about a week during which time you have visited all the European-owned estates.'

Rance nodded.

'You have, I know, put on plain clothes, taken a Gurkha wearing a Malay sarong and toured the estates up to the squatter area, driving and being driven in a car belonging to one of the managers.'

Rance tried not to show his surprise at Ah Wong's knowledge of his movements, especially about being in plain clothes. *If he knows, how many others do?*

'On your foot patrols into the secondary jungle you saw strips of meat hanging from branches. They were to be collected by men who don't want other people to see them.'

Yes, Jason had, wondered why the strips of meat were there and had reported it to the Police Station and to the regiment.

'Have you heard a bugle being blown followed by firing?'

'Yes, and I have reported it. So far it has been too remote to investigate. I must have more men before I do.'

'You have toured the villages, even going as far as Tanjong Sepat to look for that ammunition dump.'

'Yes, that's right. We did.'

His whole troop had gone there, left Sepang at 4 in the morning, picked up a Malay Police Inspector and reached the seaside village shortly before dawn broke. The houses, made of wood-plank walls, an *atap* roof and a mud floor, were spaced out just above the shore of golden sand and were backed by casuarina trees that 'sang' in the breeze coming off the water, coconut trees, banana plants and tapioca. Every villager had been collected in one place and, using local implements, the floors of ten houses had been dug up where the Inspector had said ammo was hidden. Nothing was found and no suspects were identified.

'We got back seven hours later.'

It had been hideously frustrating and it went against Rance's personal grain to dig up a person's house despite the Police Inspector telling him that is what should happen.

'You found nothing because there was nothing to find. The weapons and ammunition had never actually been in the houses. They had already been moved to a remote squatter area before you ever came to Sepang. Sadly you have made a lot of enemies in the village, especially in the ten houses where you dug up the mud floors.'

Rance, eyes burning, shook his head, partly in disgust and partly in despair. 'Is that what you have come to tell me? Just that and nothing else?'

'That and something else. The Sumatran villagers from Tanjong Sepat were made to move the weapons from the squatter area to near the jungle edge and two of them, Mandeh and Imbi, were kept there as prisoners. They managed to escape and have volunteered to lead you to where some of the weapons have been temporarily placed.'

'You trust them?'

'They are risking their life to take you.'

That's hardly answering my question. 'Why are they doing that?'

'Because at the new dump they were tightly bound so could not move and blindfolded. They were left like that for a day and a night while the Chinese guerrilla leaders were away somewhere else. They were to be untied after the Chinese returned but before that they managed to wriggle free and escape. They want revenge. Sumatrans are aggressive people.'

'Where is this place?'

'Behind Boonoon Estate. I expect you have been warned that it is a "bad" estate.'

'Yes, I have. All the European estate managers I have met have warned me against it. Why is it bad?'

'It is dominated by three powerful Chinese, nicknamed the Killer, the Blood Sucker and the Collector who live there. They rule the place and are preparing for some armed action. If you are willing to investigate the arms dump, it means a roundabout approach march to keep well away from the Boonoon squatter area. In the dark it will take a good five hours from the road. The guides only want to approach the area in the small hours, around 2 a.m. Any sentry there, they think, will be asleep or if not asleep, not alert. Working back, that means leaving the road leading into the far edge of the estate at 10 p.m. and that means we should leave here at 9 p.m. They would like to move off as soon as you are ready to take them in transport as far as … give me your map and I'll show you. Is tomorrow, Tuesday, too early?"

'Yes, give me a couple or so days, please. I'll let you know in good time when I'm ready.'

After a bit more talk and declining a mug of tea, Ah Wong left.

Captain Rance called his NCOs together. 'You'll be wanting to know why this Cheena came to see me. Bring a tot of rum each and I'll have a mug of tea.'

As they sat on the floor with their tot Rance briefed them on what the detective had told him and the NCOs listened carefully, sipping their rum from time to time. 'We must go and search for these weapons. It'll be pitch black as there's no moon. I have been promised two Sumatran guides. They were part of the group that shifted the arms and ammo from near the village we went to and took them way behind Boonoon Estate and once they had finished their last trip they were not allowed to leave but were bound and blindfolded for a whole day and a night. Uncomfortable.'

'Yes. They probably wet their pants,' said Sergeant Ruwaman.

'I didn't ask but none of us can hold it that long. Now, back to that shambles in Tanjong Sepat when we dug up those houses. I wasn't too keen on it myself and I did wonder if that Malay Police Inspector was trying to get his own back on the villagers, a sort of private quarrel.'

He looked at Sergeant Ruwaman and the three lance bombardiers. *I still think of them as havildar and lance naiks.*

'Saheb, we don't know enough about these people yet to say "yes" or "no" to that but you may well be correct.'

'Anyway, the arms and ammunition, I don't know types or totals, have been moved to the back of Boonoon Estate and I have been told that that estate is a bad one. Apart from being owned by a Cheena it is completely dominated by three daku. The Cheena who came here told me that the guides want to leave tomorrow after dark. I have told him that is too early and I'll let him know when we're ready.'

A flicker of interest showed on each Gurkha face. Rance moved his legs: sitting on the floor was not his favourite position. His next question changed tack. 'How did the Gurkha workforce on Bhutan Estate strike you when we went for that visit and had a sing-song? In any way as good as you from Nepal?'

'Hard to tell,' said the Sergeant. 'Anybody, even the lazy

and a coward can look happy at a party. Why are you asking us, Saheb?'

'Did any of you see me talking to a Kamal Rai?'

Jason and Kamal had had a heart-warming encounter, neither having ever expected to see the other again. After opening questions – health, family, circumstances generally – Jason had wandered around the labour force, introducing himself and cracking jokes. Later, after darkness fell and they'd had their meal, the estate workers put on a dance. While that was happening Kamal came and sat next to Jason and said, 'Saheb. It's wonderful meeting you again at that party after all those years. I have something I must tell you.'

Jason interrupted him. 'First I must tell you that Hutton saheb has told me all about you, your having met my friend Ah Fat and my ability to talk Malay and Chinese, which you knew already. That was not long ago. He asked me to give you his remembrances. He also has a message for you which I'll tell you in a minute.'

'Oh thank you. He is a good and brave man. I was with him during the war. It is a privilege to be with you, Saheb,' and he bowed his head with his hands joined together.

Jason, both pleased and embarrassed, did the same. 'Did Hutton saheb mention anything about a Chinese guerrilla named Lee Soong?'

'Yes, he did and how you disliked him and how and why you so bravely went to Calcutta that time and that there is a possibility that Lee Soong intends to meet up with the guerrillas in this district.'

'Quite right, Saheb, I have met him. Hutton saheb sent me to Calcutta when the Cheena went on some conference to find out what was said. That was about six months ago. I came back to Singapore but Lee Soong told me he was going first to Bangkok.'

Again there had been an interruption when Jason was hauled out to dance …

'… Yes, we saw you two talking together. He looked good enough to be a soldier,' answered Sergeant Ruwaman. 'Did you see our Mandhoj Rai and him talking together? No? It was when you were dancing. Apparently they found out their great-great grandfathers were one and the same. And they look like each other!'

'Now, that's really something, 'said Jason, then told his men about Kamal Rai. 'We were schoolboy friends and he secretly fought the Japanese. He has been offered to help us if we feel we need him. I think we do. I'll tell you why.' Rance had already informed them about the Killer, Blood Sucker and Collector. Now he told them of the possibility of Lee Soong and his escort being in the area and Kamal Rai recognising him. As he did an idea had started to grow in his mind and his gaze unfocussed as he pondered. His men waited in silence. At last Jason said, 'I have an idea. I want to go on a recce with Kamal Rai to where one of those three Cheena lives before we take these two Sumatrans to that dump. I'll talk as though I were Lee Soong's representative, find out where they will meet and try to ambush them. Any views?'

'Saheb, is this wise? What if you get lost?'

Jason smiled at them. 'As you know I was born in Kuala Lumpur, KL to us, and in my school holidays would come to this area and play in the jungle with a Chinese friend and Kamal Rai. Of course I don't know how much it has changed as it's ten years since I was last here but so far, looking around, there have not been many changes and a lot of memory of places has returned. What I'll do is ask for Kamal to come here, unseen, and we'll make a plan, taking two of you with us. You, Sergeant Ruwaman and Kulé.'

As a result of a phone call to the chief clerk, John Theopulos drove up to the ADO's bungalow in his estate jeep shortly after midday on the morrow, Tuesday. He had driven through Sepang and was duly noted: *Tei Po Lo-Si* and a uniformed and armed Malay special constable sitting beside him. Rance happened to be outside the house as he drove up. 'You can come out from under the tarpaulin now,' Theopulos said, turning his head round as he did.

The tarpaulin was pushed back and another armed and uniformed man sat up, blinked in the light, smiled at Rance and jumped out.

'I've enlisted Kamal Rai as a special constable. It makes a lot of sense for him and his family if anything were to happen to him,' explained Theopulos.

'Essential, John, I'd say,' countered Rance, not letting on that they knew each other. 'Are you staying long enough for me to brew you a cup of tea?'

The manager of Bhutan Estate looked around and decided he would have to sit on the floor as he could see no chairs. He had heard of the ADO's place being denuded of furniture and wondered how Rance could put up with it. *I know I couldn't.* 'No thanks. I'll get back right away. You'll arrange for Kamal's safe return whenever it suits you. As soon as possible, please.'

'Right ho! That's for sure. Kamal will be of great use to us and we'll look after him as one of ours.'

'Before you go anywhere I have had a message from Reggie Hutton, an old friend of mine who knows both you and Kamal. It was in veiled speech. "Kamal's 'best friend' is due to meet the local leaders near where they fire on their own range on Saturday," was the message and he asked that I try and get it to you,' he said with an automatic lowering of voice.

'Thank you, John. Reggie has told me it might happen.'

'Where are you making for?' asked Theopulos.

'The far end of the squatter area where I have been told the Chinese have cached some arms and ammunition taken from where they were hidden after the war somewhere near Tanjong Sepat. We are due to meet up with that Chinese detective and some guides well this side of Boonoon Estate. Then we move through the squatter area where we hope to find some, if not all, of the arms. I have already made a recce of the approach road, dressed as a civilian in a private car.'

'I know where you're talking about. A difficult place to reach at the best of times, even by day. None of us Europeans ever go there if possible. Good trip and good luck.'

Rance took him to his Jeep and saw him drive off. Again eyes followed him through Sepang. Only the dedicated few wondered why the tarpaulin in the back was not stretched as it had been on the way to the camp. *What has been left behind? What did that*

Rance and Kamal sat together, both with a drink of tea. 'I'll tell you why I asked for you, Kamal. It was as a result of our talk at that party. I have had a message from Hutton saheb telling me that Lee Soong is to visit the local Communist leaders near the range on Saturday. Do you know anyone I can ask where the local leaders actually live, somewhere in the squatter area? A shop where we can ask the shopkeeper?'

Kamal thought. 'Yes, there's a shop ...' and he explained where it was. 'We can ask there.'

Jason asked if it belonged to a Chinese who had a boss eye. '"Fighting-cock eyes" as I remember you teaching me. If so I know him from when I was a boy.'

'Yes, that's the one. We visited him, all three of us, you, me and that Ah Fat.'

'You and I with two of my men will go there and ask him. If possible we'll go to the house of the nearest of the three Cheena I've been told about and I'll talk to him.'

Kamal was initially nonplussed at such a daring and unusual move but, too reserved to counter what was, to him, a wild idea, merely said 'I'll stay as your shadow all the time we are together. I'm sure it will be worthwhile.' He cleared his throat. 'Have you any money on you?'

Jason felt in his pocket and took out $2 in small change and two $5 notes.

'I don't expect we will need any but one never knows. Bring yours along with you.'

Jason called his two men and told them of his newly thought-out plan. 'We will go by vehicle as though we were on an ordinary motor patrol and Kamal will tell us where to debuss. It will not be in the same place as where we will go as a troop later when we take those two Sumatrans.'

Jason was new to his men and none of them knew how skilled he was. For them the sahebs were clumsy and noisy in the jungle and they presumed Jason was similar. He saw them tense with doubt in their faces. 'I see you are worried about the standard of my fieldcraft,' he told them. 'Don't worry. I have complete faith in myself. If you are worried I'll give you a demonstration, day or night, any time you like.'

Yes, this saheb is different. The men relaxed and smiled. '*Hunchha, Hajur*,' they said.

'Who let those two men we left on guard get away?' asked the Killer, quietly furious, his narrow-set eyes flashing. 'If they turn traitor, Lee Soong's medicine will be their only cure.' The Collector was about to say that he thought they had probably worked themselves free and that no breach of security was to be worried about but one look at the Killer's angry face stopped him short.

The three guerrillas were sitting in a shack, just over a stream, some little way from the very last and remotest squatter hut at the back of Boonoon Estate, about fifty yards from the jungle edge. Patches of thick undergrowth and cultivated tapioca surrounded it. It was hard to see except from nearby even in daylight. That is where the carrying party had stashed the arms and ammunition.

'We dare not rule out the possibility of the Sumatrans

betraying us so we need to shift it all to near where we normally fire our weapons, keeping enough to fire with on the range. I'll alert the comrades to carry it. I'll get two comrades to remain in ambush there until Thursday morning, one dressed as a special constable.' The Killer was adamant. 'I have just received a highly secret message to say that a senior Politburo comrade, a man named Lee Soong, is bringing us our operational orders. He is expected this coming Saturday. He also wants to know how many of the weapons we have been able to collect are in operational use. Same for the ammunition. We dare not mess this up. Comrade Lee Soong and his escort will only come to the jungle edge below the hillock where we keep our sentry post. Once there I'll take him to the sentry post, just above the range, and, when ready, get the bugle blown to order our comrades to start the demonstration. Comrade Lee Soong will see the shooting and get an oral report before he returns.'

'It's most unlikely anything will happen after that extraordinarily ineffective "raid",' the Blood Sucker sneered, 'on Tanjong Sepat, those *Goo K'a bing* meddlers will never think of coming here. Who could have told them about going to Tanjong Sepat?'

'It was made to look as if the Malay Police Inspector was responsible,' observed the Collector. 'If it was that Ah Wong devil Hai San was responsible, that'll be him wiped out.'

'So will we be if we don't manage to please Lee Soong,' snarled the Killer.

The four of them carried water bottles and what was known as 'skeleton order', pouches in front and no pack. The two troop men were armed with sub-machine guns, Jason, armed with a pistol, had a green sweat rag round his neck that he would put over his face when he was talking so that, if a torch was shone, he would not be recognised as a non-Asian. Kamal had had his Special Constable's issue rifle. For footwear, their normal clumping leather studded boots would be too heavy so they decided on the canvas shoes they wore for basketball. In one of their pouches they had three chapattis, folded over on some potatoes. Jason had also put a civilian shirt in his pack.

At noon they moved off in their vehicle as though they were going to Tanjong Sepat but jinked down the first estate road they met with. After half a mile and before reaching the labour lines, Kamal, sitting next to the driver, said 'we'll get out here' and the vehicle halted. The four men got out. Kamal suggested to Jason that the vehicle pick them up where the estate round met the main road at 10 o'clock on the morrow. The driver was told. He turned the vehicle round at the first easy place and went back to base.

Kamal knew the best tracks to use, the ones that, even if they were spotted, no one would imagine they were interested in going to where the three guerrillas lived. They skirted the labour lines without alerting the dogs before Kamal found the track that ran through the squatters' area. By late afternoon they were near enough to their target, the shop, sat down and ate their rations. Jason put on his civilian shirt.

They waited till dusk and cautiously moved to the shop, approaching it from the back. It was empty. In cover but near enough to be seen, Jason called out, 'Oh *Dow Gai Ngaan Yeh*

Yeh' Boss-eyed grandfather. 'Come and meet a friend you have not seen for a long time. It's *Shandung P'aau* who ate your delicious *dai bo* dumplings with *P'ing Yee.*'

Nothing.

Louder still, Jason repeated what he had said. The shop owner was a bit deaf. 'Eh, what is that?' he asked his son.

'Someone named *Shandung P'aau* says he knows you and is calling you from behind. He remembers the *dai bao* dumplings you used to cook for him,'

'Go and ask him what he wants.'

As Jason saw a young men come out he, too, emerged and greeted him with the correct etiquette. 'I last came here about ten years ago and used to come here with my friend. I'd like to talk to you or your father but quietly,' and giving the boy 50 cents he spoke softly to him in Chinese: 'a bowl of rice and a piece of stewed bean curd only cost 15 cents. A plate of fried noodles costs 5 cents, a cup of coffee 2 cents. A packet of nasi lemak costs a few cents. A serving of Indian roti canai also costs a few cents. Think what a feast you'll have when your boss next sends to go Sepang on an errand.'

The boy's eyes gleamed.

'I'll mind the shop while father talks to you,' and back he went. Soon the father came out and he recognised Jason, who asked him to move into the bushes.

The shop owner smelt intrigue. 'So you remember my *dai bao* dumplings, *Shandung P'aau*? You were always hungry as a boy weren't you, and now you come back as a man. You must want something. What can I do for you?'

'*Dow Gai Ngaan Yeh Yeh*, please tell me about the bugle and the range. Why the bugle and where is the range?' A flash of provident inspiration. 'Are they for themselves or for someone else?'

'Promise not to mention my name or where you heard this from?'

Jason swore an oath of fidelity. 'Then I'll tell you. They are expecting a senior visitor on Saturday.'

Jason nodded. *Look quizzical but don't ask questions.*

He was rewarded. The shopkeeper's mouth came close to Jason's ear. 'I overheard them when they were drinking, talking about it. They thought I did not hear them, but I did.'

Jason would never know that the shopkeeper was angry because he was never paid and also asked for a 'contribution'.

He slid the two $5 notes into the elderly man's hand and, almost in a stage whisper, said 'I probably owe you more than that from when I was a child all those years ago.'

The shopkeeper's fighting-cock eyes twinkled. It wasn't so much the money but the courtesy and finesse he appreciated as he listened to Jason's question, 'Grandfather, if a ranking Communist would come, where do you think they'd meet?'

'They'll have a sentry, an outpost on the highest piece of land … yes, the range!' said with satisfaction and he described it. *Yes, got it! Where* P'ing Yee *and I stalked each other without being seen our last holiday together. Can't be anywhere else.* Jason thanked him warmly and asked for a pen and a piece of paper. Jason wrote out a message in Chinese – you are three stupid people who talk too much and do nothing. I will punish you like traitors were punished during the war if you fail me – signed it as from a messenger from Lee Soong, asked the shopkeeper which of the three top men's house was the nearest was told whose and where it was. 'I've told you more than I should so you tell me what it is you've written.'

Jason did and, to his surprise, the shopkeeper went back to the shop and returned with a couple of large bones. 'The dogs will bark. Throw these at them so they won't bite you.'

'Thank you, Grandfather,' Jason said and he drifted back to where the others were. He told them what he had done. He kept his white shirt on.

'Just one more job then we'll go back,' he said. 'Kamal, we must go to the shack this side of the next stream. It belongs to the Collector.'

'Yes, I know where you mean. It is about five hundred yards to our west.'

'In that case I think it wise to stay here until about 2 o'clock before moving in. By then the household will certainly be asleep. I want to talk to the Collector who won't know my voice so should not be scared in answering. I wonder if "Red Salaam" will be an appropriate introduction.'

'Yes, that is what I have heard the hotheads on the estate say and I am sure you are clever enough to know what will sound genuine. I'll try to keep out of sight.'

'You two also try and keep out of sight although I'd like you near me in case instant firing is needed,' Jason told Sergeant Hastabahadur and Kulbahadur. 'I can't give orders as this is something new to us. If we react to the unexpected in true Gurkha fashion, the gods will be on our side.'

At dusk they decided to doze, with one man awake one hour at a time till half past one.

There was enough moonlight to approach the house quietly but, on nearing it, two dogs started barking furiously and came running towards them. Jason had the bones ready and threw them away from the dogs which immediately smelled them, searched for them, found them and started gnawing them, one each. An agitated voice came from inside the house. 'Who's that outside? I am armed. I'll shoot if you come nearer.'

It was Jason's turn. 'I am a messenger from Comrade Lee Soong and have lost my way. I have a message for you. Keep your dogs off and I'll come up to the window. You can let me in to spend the rest of the night with you.'

'How do I know you are telling the truth?'

'*Bou mat*' Keep secret. '*Dei haa dau zang.*' Remember the underground struggle. 'My knowing that's proof enough, isn't it,' Jason answered harshly and arrogantly as only a ranked Communist would.

'Who are you?' the Collector again queried. 'May I know a name?'

'Keep quiet. *Zyut shuei bou mat.*' Absolutely Necessary to Keep Secret. 'I have a message for you from Comrade Lee Soong. It has to be obeyed. He has many methods of punishing people he doesn't like. He told me he thinks you three are nothing but dog shitters, idle boasters so you had better be good. I have his message with me. Come and get it.'

'Are you serious?'

'Would I waste my time on an idiot like you if I wasn't?'

The Collector tried not to show his burgeoning rage mixed with complete bewilderment.

'What is your name? You are not that arrogant Ah Wong from the Hai San are you? If you are you are as good as dead.'

Jason's Chinese gutter repartee came to his rescue after which he said, 'so do I sound like him? Would the comrade be so utterly stupid to do anything like that? You really are a dog-shitter.'

'No. Come into the house and we'll talk.'

'I'll give you the message when you come and get it.'

They heard the door open. A torch was flashed at Jason's group. The Collector saw Kamal Rai. *I'll recognise him if I see him again.*

'Turn that off or I'll shoot you,' Jason snarled. Off it went. Jason stuck the piece of paper on a twig and shoved it forward. 'Read it. Not Friday, Saturday is what we've been told.' Silence. 'Did you hear that?'

Jason flashed his torch at the voice just long enough to see a green dragon tattooed on one shoulder.

The four men almost slid away.

'Why don't you answer? Where are you?' came the querulous voice.

Lying low they saw the Collector come out of the house and move to where Jason had spoken from and take the note before going back inside the house.

The four men moved off. For the three Gurkhas there was nothing but amazement at the British officer's language skill.

Next morning the Collector took the message to the Killer to tell him what had happened. The Killer read it and said 'This is insulting. How can one so much younger than we are write like that? We must ask him, carefully mind you, as he can be savage and has more men than us few. Did the messenger have anything else to say?'

The Collector felt it better not to say anything.

A thought occurred to the Killer. 'Did you recognise the voice? It was not our enemy in the Police Station, surely?'

'No, I know his voice and he would not dare to come in the middle of the night. I don't think he knows where I live. No, it was someone else.'

'How could Comrade Lee Soong's messenger have known where you house is unless he was a local man? We'll check with him when he comes.'

Back in base Rance had another 'O' Group. 'First, the two Sumatrans and our visit to the arms dump. We must be back here, job done by Thursday as we must be ready to ambush some visiting guerrillas on Saturday.' He went into details about the arms' dump' and, at the end, asked Kamal if he had anything to add.

'It is beyond where we went to talk to the Collector. It is a difficult journey: a winding track, small streams to cross, shacks, where dogs bark, and in the dark. People don't move around at night in this area so if we are heard a warning will be somehow be given. Your men must move most quietly. I'll see if I recognise the guides. I'll stick near you unless you tell me otherwise.' *I like this man: so much easier than my boss.*

Rance said, 'I do have two other important points. First, if any of your section has anything wrong with his feet or a cough, do not take him. Second, how many of you have torches? The Troop Sergeant needs one as does each Section Commander.'

It transpired that two torches were needed and new batteries for the others. Rance called his batman, Gunner, no longer Rifleman, Kulbahadur Limbu who, he knew, was not far away. He told him to go down to the village, armed and with one other, and buy two torches and four batteries. 'Here is an old battery to show the shop keeper what kind you want and enough money to buy them. Off you go.'

Something unusual is happening, thought the shop keeper. *They'll have to know about that as well.*

Kulbahadur gave the new torches, the batteries and the loose change to Rance. 'Those Cheenas, Saheb, they're cold-blooded people. Wary, grudging, suspicious, unsmiling and silent.' The men listening in nodded in agreement.

On Wednesday evening, fed, watered, expectant and alert, it was time to fall in. Magazines loaded but no rounds up the spout. 'Embuss!' and they drove off in two vehicles, Kamal in the back of the leading one surrounded by soldiers. Their drive through Sepang was duly noted by 'eyes'.

Some time later Rance said to the driver 'We should be fairly near the RV by now.' Luckily the roads in Malaya were well provided with legible mile stones. 'Keep your eyes skinned for mile stone 14. Sing out if you see it and I'll do the same.'

They had driven slowly, the better for the rear vehicle to keep the front one's lights in sight.

'Saheb, there it is,' exclaimed the driver shortly afterwards.

'A few hundred yards beyond there should be a turning to the right.' And there was. At the same time a light flashed by the side of the road and Ah Wong stepped out and waved them down. Behind him were two men, dressed in black, only their outline visible.

'Halt!'

Rance jumped down from the vehicle, went round to the back and himself lowered the tailboard so it did not bang. In a low voice he said 'Here we are. Out as quietly as you can,' and went to the back of the second vehicle as it came to a standstill, opened its tailboard and gave the same orders.

Ah Wong came up to him. 'Spot on. We're in plenty of time. No one knows we are here.' But he was wrong: 'eyes' had watched and were watching, everything and everyone.

Rance told Kulbahadur to fetch the NCOs and the two drivers. 'Right! Five minutes for a pee and a last fag. No smoking from now on unless given permission. You can sling rifles, no need to carry them in front of you. And no shooting unless shot at or on my order.' Although there was no curfew there was little chance of their being spotted and even if they were, there was no telling their destination. Nor would any local be crazy enough to try and follow them when they moved off.

'Drivers?' Yes, both were there. 'We won't be back until, oh, hard to say. Certainly not before 0800 hours. Go back to Sepang and be back here by that time tomorrow, with two containers of hot tea. To stay here the rest of the night is to be eaten alive by mosquitoes.'

Indeed the voracious creatures were whining around everyone's head. Rain water in untapped parts of a rubber estate ran down the trunk into the little clay pots that normally collected latex and made perfect breeding grounds.

Rance turned back to his NCOs. He had given out their order of march beforehand. 'Keep closed up. If necessary catch hold of the equipment straps of the man in front. No torches unless I say so except in an emergency. Section Commanders, all your men present?'

Yes, they were.

'Every time we halt you must ensure that all your men are present. If not I must be told immediately. It is too easy to miss a man if anyone has to make a stop and can't catch up. Sergeant Ruwaman, at the back you must make sure no one gets left behind. If you want to pass a message to me at the front, do it as quietly as possible.'

Ah Wong introduced the two Sumatran guides, Imbi and Mandeh, to Rance and one of them told him they were happy to take the soldiers to the arms' dump and gave a brief description of its location.

'All ready now?' loud enough to be heard.

'Yes,' from Sergeant Ruwaman Limbu, after checking.

After a bit of shuffling, they moved off in single file. Imbi was in the lead, then the detective. Behind him came Rance, his batman, Kamal Rai and then the leading section. At the rear came the Troop Sergeant and Mandeh.

The drivers had turned round when a civilian approached the lead vehicle. A Chinese emerged and waved his arms. In halting Malay, which the driver barely understood, he asked for a lift to the next village. *Why not?* The man got in and, after a while asked, '*Bila balek?*'

Why does he want to know when we're coming back? '*Besok pagi, pukul lapan.*' Tomorrow morning at 8 o'clock. At the next village the Chinese asked the driver to let him get out, thanked him and disappeared in the night. The driver thought no more of it.

Moving slowly, Rance's men walked along more of an overgrown track than a normal laterite estate road. There was just enough residual starlight not to bump into the man in front. More than an hour later a blacker black loomed ahead, causing the front two men to stop. Rance bumped into Ah Wong. 'Tuan, this is the start of the squatter area. The guide reckons the weapons are at least another three hours' walk from here.'

Rance looked at the luminous dial of his watch. *A break here will do us good.* 'How far to the nearest dwelling?'

The detective and the guide conferred. 'Imbi here reckons at least half an hour's walk.'

Rance made his mind up. 'Kulé, fetch the NCOs.'

They soon came. 'Listen. We're in good time. We'll have a 15-minute break here. Yes, you can light up but keep all fags cupped. Use your water bottles if you want to. Sit down and take it easy. No need for sentries.'

The NCOs went away and Rance leant over to Kamal. 'Kamal, are you all right?'

'Yes, Saheb. It makes an exciting change. Shikar with two legs rather than with four,' said with a friendly giggle. 'You have done well to bring me. I can't say if the two Sumatrans are trustworthy but just suppose they get shot or run away scared or even captured and taken away, I'm the only one who can help you if you get lost.'

'Yes, we are lucky to have you with us. You were born in Malaya but have you never wanted to go to Nepal? Or Darjeeling?'

'It is not easy to travel when you're as poor as we are,' Kamal answered obliquely. 'Labourers don't get paid much. Nowhere else apart from that journey to Calcutta and back that I told you about.'

The quarter of an hour was soon up. Quiet orders were given to get ready, men were checked and the single file moved off. Weapons were only to be held in front of the body if visibility was more than ten yards. It was pitch dark for most of the time as clouds had formed and a few drops of rain fell. Sometimes they passed through an open patch of cultivation and once or twice a dog barked but mostly they moved along a narrow path through thick undergrowth. Occasionally a man strayed to the edge of the track and tripped on a tree root or stumbled on some protuberance.

Rance found himself walking like an automaton, his mind alert, almost floating through the darkness. *'Arms dump' sounds so grand but from what the Sumatrans and Ah Wong have said, 'small hovel', nothing else, is 'arms dump' the way to describe what we may find? And what do we do if we do find any, or many? We can't carry them out with us. After an all-night effort we'll be too tired. Make them unserviceable? But how? Throw away the bolts and magazines? Bend the barrels? But what with? Problem – but let's get there first.*

Plod, plod, plod, the small force, each man wrapped in his own thoughts, trudged on through the squatter area: *if the daku we meet are anything like the Pathans or the Japanese, we'll have quite a fight on our hands,* thought Sergeant Ruwaman. *They told us we'd be gunners but the Sarkar can't make its mind up as we are still infantry,* thought one of the Section Leaders. Other men had their own thoughts buzzing around as mosquitoes buzzed around their heads. Rance slapped one that was buzzing in his right ear and it set off a humming sound in it. *Mustn't do that or I won't hear anything suspicious.* His mind went back to his leave. He had had a letter from his Jenny just before leaving Seremban. *No good getting too worked up over her. Probably can't wait until I am entitled to a quarter in … another eight years!* He bumped into Ah Wong, who had slowed his pace, and inwardly cursed. *Pay attention, you fool. Keep your mind on the job!*

Plod, plod, plod. In the column at times it was so dark men held on to the straps of the man in front. A muffled curse came onto lips when the man behind trod on heels. After what seemed an age, the guide suddenly stopped and whispered something to the detective. All down the line men, not realising that the man in front had stopped, bumped to a standstill.

At the front, Ah Wong whispered to Rance, 'Imbi is frightened. He tells me that if a sentry shines a light and sees me, a Chinese, with him in the squatter area, fire will immediately be opened to kill me and the guide will also be killed as a traitor.'

Indeed the detective was a head taller than Imbi.

'Then you get three behind me,' Rance whispered back. 'I'll be right behind Imbi. Tell him not to worry. Also tell him that if he thinks that someone in front of him is about to open fire, to lie down on one side of the track. I'll return fire even if I can't see the target.' Prophylactic fire might make an untrained man with a weapon run away.

The leading NCO silently came up to Rance. 'Anything amiss, Hajur? Why have we stopped? I can't smell any human habitation and we are not in an open piece of ground.'

'Ustad, the guide's frightened and I must try and calm him before we move off. Pass a message down the line for the Troop Sergeant to come to me.'

Whispering, scuffling and the noise of water bottles being used, to say nothing of the ever-present night sounds; insects clicking or shrilling, frogs croaking, the 'chunk-chunk-chunk' of the larger kind of nightjars calling. Many of the men were sweating as there was not a breath of breeze and the undergrowth would have smothered it had there been any.

'Saheb. You sent for me. Here I am,' whispered Sergeant Ruwaman Limbu.

'Ustad. Imbi, the front guide, is frightened and will not go on with the detective behind him. Thinks that any Cheena shining a torch and aiming will immediately fire if they see another Cheena and that he, Imbi, will be killed. I will go behind him and help him along. I don't think I'll change him with Mandeh but I want you to be doubly sure that Mandeh stays with you and does not try to escape. This may be a trap to ambush us.'

100

'I've thought so all along, Hajur. There is something I don't like about him. Can't be too careful.'

Rance moved up to Imbi and softly said to him 'I will stay with you whatever happens.'

Imbi grunted in return.

'Right. We'll move off now. You, Sergeant ustad, stay here until the tail of the column reaches you and keep a close watch on Mandeh.'

Rance moved off. The others followed him. But when the end of the column reached Sergeant Ruwaman Mandeh was not with it. He had disappeared.

Mandeh knew exactly where he was. He and Imbi had been promised a large reward by the police and they had decided that their best bet was to be successful, claim the reward and, for safety's sake, return to Sumatra. Yet, the nearer he got to the place where he and Imbi had been tied up, the more nervous he had become and the more foolhardy did the present venture seem. There was no way he could safely let Imbi know of his decision and he now thought that the odds against Imbi's survival at the front were heavily against him. Mandeh turned round and went back the way he had come immediately the soldier at the end of the line moved forward.

Not long afterwards Rance heard a whispering coming towards him. *A message from Sergeant Ruwaman?* It was. 'The other Sumatran guide has run away. Do we stop and look for him?'

'Kulbahadur. Stay here until Sergeant Ruwaman reaches you

and tell him in no way will we stop to look for him, there is no change in orders but to be doubly alert against any ambush. Got that?'

'Saheb. I understand.'

'Kamal,' hissed Rance. 'Am I right in not mentioning this to Imbi?'

'Correct, Saheb. It will make him more afraid and he may also be tempted to run away. Also don't tell the Cheena detective. I sense that he, too, is frightened.'

Rance asked Imbi how longer until we reach the place where the arms are and was told anything from one hour to three hours,' Rance doubted it, thinking that he was too frightened to think properly. He probably hadn't learnt how to tell the time by looking at a watch.

It was then half past one.

Once on the move again, Imbi put his right arm back and searched for Rance's hand. Fumbled and found it. Grasped it. Rance involuntarily pulled his back but the grip was vice like. However hard he tugged he could not break lose.

'Imbi, as long as you clutch my hand I won't be able to fire my rifle.'

Imbi refused to let go and it was uncomfortable, inconvenient and sweaty but Rance bore it for, he later reckoned, about half an hour when, thankfully, the Sumatran let go, stopped and said 'Over there. We have arrived.'

Once more the column bumped to a halt. Rance, almost under his breath, sent for his NCOs. Waiting for them to come, he listened intently. He heard a trickle of water and, in a break in the clouds, saw a small stream in front of him. The NCOs reached him. 'Listen. We have arrived. I'll ask Imbi to describe the place.'

To their half right about thirty paces away, the weapons had been laid out under some waterproof covering on the ground and to their half left, not quite so distant, was the shack where the two guides had been held prisoner.

Rance gave out his orders. '1 Section, move silently to the shack and see what you can find. Do not go straight up to it. Move round to a flank, listen and, if after five minutes you have heard nothing, draw khukris, use your torch and see if there is anyone inside. You will take the detective with you and he will arrest anyone there. Fire if you have to but remember the others are off to a flank.

'2 Section. Take the guide with you to where he thinks the dump is. Once you have seen 1 Section's torch, use your own to examine the ground. Look for any tracks.

'Sergeant Ruwaman, go with 2 Section. If no one is there, wave your torch round and round. The other section will do the same if their area is empty of humans. I will stay here and use my voice to coordinate what follows. Any questions?'

There were none.

'On your way.' Ah Wong was standing next to him and was told in outline what was happening.

Both Section Commanders faded away, briefed their men and, apart from the odd rustle here and there, nothing was heard; an exemplary performance of professional fieldcraft. In the silence each man was conscious of his own pulse beat, the small crepitant rustle of clothing against his body and the thrill of the chase. Rance, Kulbahadur and Kamal stood quietly by the stream, straining their ears, waiting for an outbreak of shooting or the noise of a struggle as sleeping men were seized. They heard not a sound from either group.

In the hut Ruwaman's torch beam began to probe around, licking like a lizard's tongue into the corners. Tension broke when both sections waved their torch at about the same time. It was an absurd anti-climax. Rance broke the silence. 'Any weapons?'

'Nothing at all, only marks on the ground.'

'Everybody back here. Section Commanders check all your men are present.'

'Saheb, there are three tins in one corner of the shack. I haven't opened them. Do you want me to see what they contain?'

'Yes. Do that right away.'

The Section Commander and two men went back to the shack and brought back the three containers, opened them and looked inside. 'Only pamphlets written in Chinese. What do you want me to do with them?'

'Let's have a look at them,' said Rance and flashed his torch at the contents. He saw the outline of a hammer and sickle on a red background. *That trash. I suppose we ought to take it back with us but it's too much of a bore.* 'Ustad, distribute them equally to each man and tell them when we cross that small bridge to drop them in the water.'

After the pamphlets were distributed Rance said, loudly enough for all to hear, 'Listen to me, you have done well. Relax for a few minutes and light up if you want to but cup your hands. *To hell with the smell. The stream will carry it away.* I doubt the guerrillas know we're here but if they do I believe they will think we'll stay here, lie on the ground, go to sleep and, probably at first light, creep in and lob some grenades on us. As you have been told, on our way drop the daku propaganda into the stream. If we burn them it will take too long and might give our position away. They're not worth taking back with us.

'Kamal, fetch Imbi. I want to ask him where he thinks an ambush party might come from. And you, Enche Ah Wong,' he added, changing into English, he asked the same question. No response came from Kamal's questioning. There was no Imbi to answer. Neither he nor Mandeh were ever seen again.

'Everyone listen. This other guide has run away. Cigarettes out. Back for half an hour as quickly as we can. I smell trouble.'

Back they went. At a clearing but with no dwelling nearby, Rance ordered a halt. 'We'll spend the rest of the night here. I don't believe we're in danger of an ambush now. You can smoke and doss down anywhere you feel leeches, cockroaches, scorpions, snakes and centipedes won't molest you. Cover your face with the towel– if you have brought it – and try to sleep. At first light we'll move back to where the transport will be waiting for us.'

At dawn, three Chinese, one dressed as a Special Constable, made their way from the jungle edge, grenades ready, and moved towards the hovel. Seeing nobody, they presumed nobody had come earlier. Not being the brightest of people, the unusual amount of scuff marks they saw around where the weapons had been meant nothing to them. They crept towards the shack. Nothing. Had they ventured even as far as the stream, they would have been alerted. They didn't so they weren't.

On the Friday evening Rance took his troop to the rubber estate that adjoined the Serting Forest Reserve and, in the moonlight, moved along the edge of the jungle until the land started to rise. 'We'll stay the rest of the night here and move off at dawn. Put out sentries,' he told Sergeant Ruwaman and the others get as much sleep as they can.' Rather against his will he had allowed the Chinese detective to go with them.

The evening before, the Killer, as arranged, met Lee Soong. After fraternal greetings, 'Comrade, we got the message you sent to us. We found it insulting. We are not as big-mouthed or as useless as you think.'

Lee Soong looked at the Killer in amazement. 'Have you got it?'

The Killer took it out of his pocket and sullenly gave it over.

Lee Soong read it, anger seeping over his face. 'I never sent that. I only sent the one message for today's meeting and demonstration. When and who brought this?' and he gave it back. 'Keep it and if ever you find writing the same you'll know who wrote this. When did you get it?'

'Wang got it two nights ago.'

'I don't like it one bit,' said Lee Soong, wondering what or who was behind such an unexpected development. He looked sternly at his three hosts. 'Something is wrong. Did you recognise the man?'

'I saw the Gurkha who worked with you during the war,' said

the Collector.

'The traitor! I knew it all the time. When you see him, kill him. That does not stop you looking for the writer of the message as that man doesn't speak or write our language.' He turned and spat. 'I will depart as soon as your demonstration is over. As for the bogus messenger, he can't be anyone outside this area so I am ordering you to do your level best to find out who he is. Understand? If it turns out to be someone from here I will do to you what I do to all traitors.' And there was no doubt he meant every word of what he said.

Shortly after dawn Lee Soong sent some of his escort to clear the area. Standing orders. One, a local, had worked as a Forest Ranger, scoured the area and found nothing suspicious. They were now relaxed with no worry because peace and quiet had prevailed and sure that no soldiers had been anywhere near, the Killer put his plan into action. 'I am glad, Comrade Lee Soong, you are ready for us. We now go to our look-out point on a small hillock where no one can approach us unseen. The firing will start after my bugler, who will be at the look-out, blows the order to begin.'

'Comrade. That is most efficient. Well done. Red salute. Just don't forget my orders …'

Just after dawn Rance thought it time to move. As he was giving out orders everybody heard a bugle call. It came from not far away and a volley of fire was heard. There being no 'crack and thump' it had to be range firing. Vegetation was so thick there was no chance of seeing their target. So as not to miss it, Rance sent out patrols towards the noise but spaced out.

They moved off and twenty minutes later the bugle blew again, much nearer. The firing also ceased.

'Saheb, there is some high ground in front of us. It has good visibility all round. That'll be the place to make for now.'

Yes, it has to be the place the shopkeeper told me.

'Listen! 2 Section with Sergeant Ruwaman. Move off right with Kamal. I'll move off slightly left with 1 Section and with the Cheena detective. 3 Section in reserve behind me. I'll make cuckoo noises with my hands so we can keep in touch. If you shoot remember where we are.' Rance had only heard cuckoos when he was under training as a Gentleman Cadet in the Indian Military Academy in Dehra Dun, India, where he had learnt how to blow exactly like one.

'1 Section. With me. Inche Ah Wong come with me,' and he used hand signs for the advance to begin.

The ground rose steadily. Rance could not see where the other section was so made cuckoo noises from time to time, hoping his 'disguise' would fool any 'baddy'. *It fooled 'exercise enemy' when training in India, so why not here?*

The men, rifles at the ready and glad at a challenge, moved like the dedicated professionals they were.

Rance's group reached the top of the hill, unopposed, and saw a make-shift look-out point of rough *atap* palm thatch. It was unoccupied. They found an alarm warning that could be operated by being pulled by a piece of string from inside, a military belt, some .303 rounds of ammunition and a kettle on the hob with a fire burning underneath and some tea leaves in an open tin, ready to make a brew. Hanging on the wall by a plaited straw cord was a bugle[4] made from a buffalo horn. In one corner were two large tins. Inside one were a few more Chinese pamphlets with the hammer and sickle motif on the outside and in the other weapon training manuals and bill heads of receipts that the Collector, presumably, had given to those who had been forced to hand over money.

Damn and blast it. Just missed them. I really thought my trick would work. Rance was dismayed at their bad luck. Blue eyes burned. *I'll keep the bugle as a souvenir and have the hut burnt before we move off.*

As he was waiting for the other section to join him he heard the call of a bird that he had only ever heard at dawn and dusk come from the jungle below him. He recognised it as the *burong tetabu,* the great-eared nightjar. It was answered. Five minutes later he heard the call again, fainter, answered, also more faintly. Rance said 'Those are the escaping enemy who were here before we came. The guerrillas have split up so are using that call as a signal to keep contact with each other. We might have got them if we were a bit earlier.'

The other men joined them. Sergeant Ruwaman put out sentries. In broad daylight, the jungle below them lay black and foreboding.

'Sergeant ustad, what's that lying in a bush down there?' called out a soldier who had been put facing the jungle as sentry. 'It looks like a package of some sort.'

---

4 Many years later the bugle was presented to The Gurkha Museum in Winchester, England. Its accession number is 1994.05.15.

'Go and fetch it.'

The soldier brought the package up and gave it to the Sergeant who took it over to the British officer and, saluting first, handed it over. 'It was on a thorny bush at the jungle edge. It must have been torn out of the carrier's hand as he passed it and he was in such a hurry he failed to notice it.'

Inside were some papers, written in Chinese. Rance scanned them and saw they bore instructions from the Politburo of the MCP. *They'll mean a lot to Special Branch*. He showed them to Ah Wong.

As the detective was scanning them, Rance showed the Sergeant the contents of the tins. Before we leave, you will burn the hut and all the pamphlets with the hammer and sickle picture on the front. I have taken one which I will give in when I get back. As for the weapon training manuals and bill heads, distribute them for the men to carry back to the lines.'

'*Hunchha, Hajur*. That's the best thing to do with them. I'll get on with the burning.'

'Tuan Captain, this is a most important guerrilla operation order,' said Ah Wong. 'At the end there is a signature of one Lee Soong, a senior comrade who used to work in Singapore.'

'Thank you, Inche Ah Wong. That is most interesting. Quite a haul for one day. I'll take it back with me.' Then, in a louder voice, 'Sergeant Ruwaman. Now we'll move off. 1 Section in front and back to the RV. Once back in the lines the rest of the day is free after you've cleaned your weapon. We all need a sleep. You have shown the highest standards of discipline and night movement. I am proud of you. Well done.'

The tea Rance had told the drivers to bring with them was delicious. While they were drinking it, the detective asked Rance, 'Do you know why we did not catch those people?'

'I've no idea,' answered Rance, smothering a yawn. 'It had to be a sudden move otherwise they would have had their brew of tea first.'

Ah Wong smiled. 'You told them, Tuan. They knew we were coming,' said with gentle irony.

Rance gasped in disbelief. *Now's not the time to be funny with me.* 'How could they know? I told them? Impossible. I'm too tired for bad jokes,' unconsciously stiffening his back as he spoke.

'But you did, Tuan. You let them know we were coming. I'll tell you how. You made the noise of a bird that does not exist in Malaya. The people on the hilltop knew it had to be man-made, strangers, that is to say, soldiers, coming so, not wanting to be killed, wounded or captured, they made their escape, in two groups, before we got there – and only just in time. They probably thought that the maker of that strange bird noise would not have known that the *burong tetabu* was a dawn and dusk bird that never calls by day! They were likewise keeping track without a wireless.'

The Englishman put his head in his hands and groaned so loudly that Kulbahadur thought he had stomach ache. *Oh Lord. I'm the biggest cuckoo of them all,* he silently lamented. *With all my boyhood knowledge how could I have overlooked that?* 'It's time to back to the lines but I want to say one last thing. You were surprised when I asked you if you came from Penang. I'll tell you how I know. You have Hai San tattooed on your shoulder in

Chinese characters.'

The detective stared at Jason, so surprised he could find nothing to say before Jason continued, 'the people engaged in the firing are Green Dragons. I advise you to be more than extra careful. It is just possible they saw you after they escaped and so think you have got possession of the dropped package.'

Ah Wong did not know what to say, so said nothing.

'Embuss! Start up and back to Sepang just as quickly as we can,' Rance's order rang out.

At Sepang Rance rang Bhutan Estate for a vehicle and before Kamal got into it, the two of them shook hands. 'Saheb, I hope we meet again. I think I overheard one of the soldiers saying you were due back in Seremban soon.'

'Yes, Kamal. We don't have much longer here. It was good meeting you. Again my thanks and thank the manager Saheb for letting me have you.'

The vehicle drove off.

Rance sat on the floor to write his report. He fell asleep before he had written more than three lines. Kulbahadur only woke him the next morning with a mug of tea, still fully dressed.

Lee Soong[5] and his squad had been alerted by that strange bird call and, just in case it presaged a danger, they quickly made their way into the thick jungle of the forest reserve, spent the rest of that day hiding and, by a clever change of clothes and using taxis that worked for the Cause, reached their secret hideout, a cave

---

5 Lee Soong was killed by the Security Forces in Johor in 1954.

112

near the summit of Bukit Beremban, one of the tallest mountains to the east of Seremban, two days later, one of his old wartime hide-outs. He was confident his task had been a success. Before the alert he had complimented the Killer on his range planning, he had learnt that the *Goo K'a bing* were no match for him and his men and, to comfort any misgivings he had, he put that strange bird call down to a new, long-nosed devil rubber planter trying to make himself invisible as he explored the area at the back of his estate. It just so happened that the noise, a little too near for comfort, coincided with his giving the Killer his new operational orders.

The Killer, on the other hand, was in a quandary. *I must have dropped the package containing Lee Soong's orders shortly after that strange birdcall sounded, too near for safety.* He and his escort had returned to his house by a circuitous route. *I must go and look for that package in a couple of days*, he said to himself after he had had a wash.

Back in Seremban Rance reported to the CO, who debriefed him. At the end Jason said he had to go to Police HQ. 'I've an important policy document, some guerrilla training manuals and receipts of extorted money to give to Special Branch.'

'Yes, go and give them in, then have a couple of days to relax in. You have done a good job. Well done. I also have some news for you. It has been decided that 12 Gurkha Rifles will revert to infantry shortly so I will be leaving when it happens.'

'We'll be sorry to see you go, sir,' Rance said. 'We all know you have had a hard row to plough, often against the furrows. Please let me say how much all of us junior officers have recognised this.'

The CO was gracious enough to thank Rance who saluted, left the office and took a vehicle down to Police HQ to meet Head of Special Branch, one Ismail Mubarak – a charming Pakistani who bred crocodiles, was missing a finger, 'crocodile fodder', he said, and who liked his beer. His deputy was an ebullient Teochew, Tay Wang Teik, who was given the document to study. 'Once I have read this I must have a long talk with Captain Rance,' he told his boss, who spoke but did not read Chinese.

When Rance and Tay Wang Teik did meet up, the Chinese was delighted.

Rance told Tay Wang Teik about how he had heard firing and a bugle call so had gone to investigate. 'To keep in touch, I told my other section I'd make a noise like a cuckoo but apparently there are no cuckoos in Malaya so whoever was at the top of the hill in a hut, knowing that even though they did not recognise the "bird", ran away.'

A look of glee shone from Tay Wang Teik's face. 'I have a hunch. This document was due to go to the man we know as the Killer. You and I'll go back for three days and lay an ambush around the hut you burnt. I'll take the cover that the package that was dropped and you can pretend to hand it over to him. That way you'll be able to capture or kill the Killer or anyone who comes to look for it.'

'I can't just go back. It must be an order from the CO.'

Ismail Mubarak, listening in with intense interest, took up the phone. 'Get me the CO of 1/12 GR,' he ordered the operator.

'Rance, I can't not send you back,' the CO said, having explained the new plot. 'How will you tackle this? How can you get your targets to where you plan to go?'

Without putting it into so many words, somehow Jason inwardly realised that a turning point in the way he operated was at hand. For his foray to talk to the Collector, he was, in fact, back to his schoolboy days of adventure, almost on home ground, but augmented by real weapons and a real risk. No need for any new ideas of operating … but his task now was radically different from what he and his men had learnt in Burma: *new tactics but no time for new training! I'll ask for Kamal Rai who knows the ground better than I do.*

He came to a decision within seconds: 'With the fewest men compatible with success, sir. I only need a section with Sergeant Ruwaman Limbu.' *How to get the Chinese to where I want them? Yes, got it!* 'Let me take a bugler and the bugle. I'll teach him the call that was blown. I think I'll be able to remember the area from when I roamed around there as a boy but to make sure I'll ask for Kamal. We will approach the hill where we found the look-out point from the jungle edge, not the squatter area, and blow the bugle. That will, Ismail Mubarak said, so intrigue the Killer he'll come and investigate even if he does not come to search for the missing package.'

'That sounds sensible but we are only allowed to fire if fired on first. Try and capture the leader by challenging him. I'll also get the police to call Detective Ah Wong in and he can go with you,' said the CO. 'Take some cord to bind any prisoners.'

Why must we have a commander who knows nothing about

tactics?

'Sir, understood. Please ask the police to drive past the place where they drop us off four times a day from Day 1.'

'Sounds excessive. Why?'

'It will be the only way to communicate safely without going into the squatter area, sir. No wirelesses.'

And the plan worked. On Day 2, early in the morning the bugler blew his call at intervals of a quarter of an hour for an hour. The Killer heard it and presumed it was one of Lee Soong's men wanting to contact him although it did not occur to him that the bugler could be any other than one of Lee Soong's men. At half past eight he started again and just after a quarter to nine the Gurkha farthest down the slope in the ambush around the burnt-out lookout post, called out, 'There are three men coming up from the bottom of the hill, followed by another three men who must be their escorts. I see they are armed with pistols.' The bugler blew once more.

Rance was not to know that the men were the Killer, the Blood Sucker and the Collector and their special bodyguards. Tay Wang Teik recognised them and moved up to near Jason. Kamal stayed in the rear.

'Ready, all of you? Take up lying positions and try not to be seen. Open fire only if I am fired on. Try to wound, not to kill.' Rance remembered the strictures about not opening fire initially, *nobody had envisioned a situation quite like this, had they?*

To his men's surprise – *whoever saw a saheb like ours?* – Rance moved behind a tree and waited until the three leading

Chinese were passing and, throwing his voice to one side, softly called out, 'You have brains like pig dung, you eaters of dog meat. Forget your important package? Here it is' and he threw it to the other side from where his voice had come from.

The three turned round and saw nobody. The obvious leader turned to the man behind him and snarled, murderously 'curse me?' as he stooped to reach the package which he gratefully recognised but not comprehending how or why it had landed at his feet.

Simultaneously Jason showed his hat round the edge of the tree and, again with his voice at the feet of the leading man, sniggered. The leader whirled round, saw the hat and fired, the bullet just missing Jason's hand but hitting the hat.

Jason shouted 'Fire' and the forward man, Mandhoj Rai, opened fire first. Other itchy fingers ensured it was over in a trice. Two of the leading Chinese fell wounded, one in the arm and the other in the stomach. The third saw the firer and thought he was the man he had seen when he shone his torch on him a night or so ago before he and the three gunmen ran away.

'Cease fire,' shouted Rance. 'Come and help the casualties but disarm them first.'

The Gurkhas bound the wounds. They carried the man with the stomach injury, the Killer, down the hill while the Blood Sucker, wounded in the arm, bound by a rope to the detective, sullenly walked beside him. They left the seriously wounded Killer at the nearest squatter's house, Ah Wong telling them that they would return with medical help, but when it came it was too late. The Blood Sucker was handed over to the police and put in hospital under guard before being charged with the capital offence of carrying a firearm. That left the Collector, mouthing obscenities with two imperatives: one to find the man who had shot his friends – if I see him I'll recognise him – and the other to find out who had cursed – if I hear his voice again I'll recognise him – and thrown down the package … otherwise I'll find it hard to tell Comrade Lee Soong who it was who delivered that written message.

Two weeks after that, a Chinese from Boonoon Estate reported to the Sepang police that he had come across a mangled and tortured corpse. A squad of policemen went and there was a dead Ah Wong, butchered. A green dragon had been drawn on his left shoulder and a corresponding piece of skin had been cut off the right shoulder. That was where '海山' had been tattooed but, of course, none of the Malay policemen knew about that – nor would have been the slightest interested had they known.

3

Spring 1948

The Malayan Communist Party deliberated at length before deciding to move from what the military people then knew as Phase 1, the Passive Phase, of Communist Revolutionary Warfare[6], to Phase 2, the Active Phase[7] 'strong-arm' tactics. Some

---

6 In Malaya the Passive Phase started in 1928 by when Communist agents from China had established a South Seas Communist Party in Singapore, although the Malayan Communist Party (MCP) itself dates from 1930. It consisted of the penetration of such organisations as local government, trades unions, student unions, touring repertory groups, newspapers and broadcasting (especially the person who chose what items to broadcast and how to slant them), school masters and college professors, and even government security forces. Governments tried to foil this by use of their counter-intelligence agencies and police force, not by military means.

7 Guerrillas raided Police Stations for weapons, coerced, intimidated, burnt busses, destroyed or mutilated identity cards, slashed rubber trees and generally made life uncomfortable, if not dangerous, for those who did not submit to these pressures. Government forces could not give the public unlimited protection because the Communists had the initiative. Men attracted by a spirit of adventure joined them as did many criminals 'on the run' from the police, those whose womenfolk were threatened if their man did not join the cause and, lastly, the genuine zealot who, though few and far between, was the most deadly of them all. Such a

of the methods mooted in Calcutta were accepted, others not, but, in essence this meant a war waged by the Malayan People's Liberation Army, MRLA, from bases in the jungle.

In mid-June the government, shaken by the intensity of guerrilla action, declared an Emergency rather than war, even though a low-level war it was. That an 'Emergency' was declared rather than a war was purely on account of financial concerns for trade insurance. Severe restrictions on the movement of food and civil movement came into force, not all at once, but as the situation engendered them.

Despite the MRLA's tenacity of purpose, acceptance of dismal conditions and belief in its cause, it lacked any dependable system of communication other than a reliance on couriers and broadcasts on Radio Malaya. For arms and ammunition there were already what they had hidden after the war and what, certainly in the early stages of the campaign, they managed to capture. For information about the Security Forces, apart from any 'moles' there already were in the police or administration, and basic necessities, they relied heavily on their civil supporters, known as the *Min Yuen*, Masses Movement. These people lived, for the most part, in the waste land between the rubber estates the jungle fringes and were known as 'squatters'. There were, of course, other low level

---

situation provided the 'sea of people' for the Communist 'fish' to swim in. For the army that meant knowing how to live, move and operate in tropical rain forest terrain and become skilled in attacking Communist camps, tracking, ambushing, patrolling, river crossing and the other aspects of jungle movement that such work demanded – and always to be ready for that split-second contact – you or them.

sympathisers who could pick up useful snippets of knowledge for passing on, for instance shop keepers, barbers, and waiters in restaurants and hotels. One particular ready source was in night spots where Chinese 'taxi' girls, attractively dressed in their long, tight-fitting, slit-sided *cheongsams*, earned a pittance of a living. For a fee they would dance with sweaty, red-faced Europeans, chiefly British servicemen and at weekends junior planters who, once back at their tables, were inveigled to buy drinks at inflated prices while the girl they had danced with sipped lemonade and listened, nonchalantly, to the gossip of their temporary 'hosts'. The servicemen also stood at the bars and gossiped and the barmen, feigning a limited knowledge of English, picked up pieces of tactical information that could be used against the Security Forces, the drunken gossipers unaware they were passing on items of value to their military enemy. Brothels were also good sources for gaining such information.

If the 'taxi' girls did not report what they learnt from their garrulous partners to the barmen, they passed it on when they got back home locally or in the 'squatter' areas. It was of immense value to the Min Yuen who passed any worthwhile information upwards, either when they went into the jungle with edibles or when patrols from the jungle visited them. It was all local and low-level, each unit of the MRLA relying on its own Min Yuen supporters.

Similar uprisings against their colonial government were also taking place in French Indo-China and Dutch East Indies.

Over and above the MCP was a much larger and better organised system that embraced eastern India and most of colonial Southeast Asia. Many, if not most, operatives in various government Intelligence departments had no knowledge that it existed. Who organised it, where it was based, how it communicated was so secret, it is probably true to say it was never fully found out.

As examples of its octopus-like tentacles, in 1951 a three-week operation by A Company of 1/7 Gurkha Rifles, based in Seremban, took place in the top north-eastern corner of Malaya, the only time in ten years Gurkhas operated in that area. It was quickly reported to the Nepalese government in Kathmandu. Three weeks after the Gurkhas returned to base, over thirteen hundred Gurkhas, some with their families, sailed from Singapore to Calcutta going on leave to Nepal, called in at Rangoon. The Nepalese consulate there received a secret message saying that the Gurkhas were not going on leave but were a whole battalion, stationed in north-east Malaya, that had mutinied for the Communist cause so were being disbanded and sent back for discharge. Orders were that the Gurkhas should be left strictly alone and not visited by the consulate staff. In fact the vice-consul did visit the troops, taking his wife and the consul's wife with him. They were amazed not to find a load of disillusioned, bolshie people but happy soldiers, some with their family, going on leave.

Simultaneously Calcutta jute-mill coolies were paid 8 annas for half an hour's anti-British shouting outside the Transit Camp in Barrackpore, Calcutta, when leave men arrived there for documentation for their journey home. They were urged not to return to their units in Malaya. Around the same time, when matters were going against the Communists in Malaya, spurious calls for action by Gurkhas to quell riots in Sarawak were made, even though no such riots ever took place. Few people knew about such background machinations: fewer still ever found out how, whence or where they originated.[8] There was one unexpected and unseemly outcome from the Sepang incident. However successful the troops of 1/12 Gurkha Rifles had been there was an unseemly police quarrel between the Chief Police Officer of Selangor and his opposite number in Negri Sembilan. In the latter's keenness to get to grips in the Sepang area he had forgotten that the area he had allotted for the troops stretched into another state's and he either forgot to tell the CPO Selangor or didn't think of so doing. When the Selangor CPO learnt about the killing, so angry was he that he made a formal decision to charge Captain Rance with murder, sending the charge sheet to his opposite number in Negri Sembilan. Chan Man Yee, a clerk in the KL Police HQ's Registry, an MCP's 'mole', read, copied and filed the report. Later she sent the copy off to the MCP HQ by courier. There it was handed to a clerk in Ah Fat's presence. Ah Fat asked the clerk to show it to him. On reading it he saw that his friend Jason Rance was in serious trouble. 'I'll give this to the Secretary General myself,' he told the clerk and, once in his own quarter, burnt it and blew the ashes out of the window. *Jason, I hope that prolongs you life,* he whispered to himself.

The CPO Negri Sembilan sent the charge sheet letter to the OCPD Seremban who read it before filing it. There 'sleeper' Lee

---

8 Your author was the person who put the record straight in the Nepalese consulate in Rangoon and heard the coolies shouting.

Kheng got hold of it and that is how it came into the possession of an elderly, bespectacled, white wispy-bearded, one-time schoolmaster, named Ngai Hiu Ching, an original party member. He lived in 'plain sight' in Mantin, about ten miles north of Seremban, one of the villages that had always been a centre for people who wanted to hide from the Law, especially so during the Japanese occupation when it was almost a 'colony' of the wartime Chinese fighting against the invaders. He had helped many people evade enemy anger and had acted as a 'cell' for information. It was known by Special Branch as a recruiting centre for those who wanted to join the anti-British movement. He had been and was a coordinator for matters that needed retaliatory action by the MCP.

The Collector, whose only known name was Wang, was a harassed man. Without his two friends to consult he had, unusually for him, to work on his own. Comrade Lee Soong had asked him what sort of man the night-time messenger was. *I told him I had only a glimpse of him in the moonlight.* What was he wearing? Wang thought back. 'Not uniform. A white shirt.' 'That meant he was not a member of the MRLA,' had been Lee Soong's cutting reply – *why did I not think of that before?* Wang angrily asked himself, further recalling that he looked taller than most Chinese so … no that was too much of a puzzle. He was clever enough to keep the dogs off him by throwing them bones: did he think of that himself or was he put up to it? The idea of the man being a member of the army was too far-fetched and laughable to think about. He had not seen which way he had come or gone, he had just vanished. Were there only two of them, the unknown one and the 'traitor'? He knew Lee Soong wanted an answer and that his patience was not one of his strong points. He also knew he would have to go and report to Lee Soong but so secretly did he manage affairs one never really knew where he was. Nor did he ever take 'no' for an answer. He felt it prudent not to mention the bugle being blown at regular quarter-of-an-hour intervals nor about the package.

To try and find out he decided to work back along the line of squatters' huts till he came to Sepang, asking at each hovel and shop. He came to the shop they had always eaten at. 'Oh eh, *Dow Gai Ngaan Yeh Yeh,*' he called out as he went inside.

The man with fighting-cock eyes came out from the back, face bland as one of his dumpling skins. 'Can I help you?' he asked.

'Can you recall seeing any tall Chinese wearing a white shirt some time last month?'

'Tall Chinese wearing a white shirt?' he asked, screwing his eyes up as he thought of *Shandung P'aau.* 'No, no tall Chinese wearing a white shirt has ever come to my shop. Truly.' *He was a tall Englishman in a white shirt,* he giggled inwardly.

The Collector had no luck there or anywhere else and was at a loss. He also knew that if anyone had known anything, fear of reprisals would have kept them quiet. It was then that Wang, not one of nature's brightest, remembered something about who else in the area knew Lee Soong from the war years ... a man who worked on the estate of *Tei Po Lo-Si,* a *Loi Pok Yi* man, as the word Nepali formed in his mind. The name was ... was ... what was it? Yes, Kamal Lai. Wang decided to contact him. That was not easy but eventually a meeting was arranged.

Kamal denied all knowledge of any shooting incident and only when the Collector insisted he had seen him did Kamal say it was probably a look-alike second cousin serving in the 1/12 Gurkha Rifles.

'Weren't you the man who came to my house one night not so long ago?' Wang insisted.

Kamal played dumb. 'Sorry, I can't help you in any way.'

Then, a week later, the Collector's second cousin's third granddaughter, who worked as a 'taxi-girl' at the Yam Yam night club in Seremban, came home with a message from Kwek Leng Joo, the barman at the night club who was also a guerrilla courier. 'Comrade Lee Soong wants to talk to you and is sending two guides to take you to him. They know where to contact you at your house in the squatter area.' There was nothing to do but to wait.

They came. By this time the increase in Security Force activity decreed a circuitous approach to the RV. It had taken the guides two days, mostly downhill but it would take three to go back. Wang was no longer in the first flush of youth and by the end of that day he was finding the going harder than he had expected. Talking and planning were easy enough but it was a different matter entirely on the ground for real. Over-age for hard exercise and not as fit as he should have been because of his taste for liquor, he was an actor by inclination; dazzled by the footlights and indifferent to the audience behind them. Now he was learning. That first night he had spent the first six hours in a deep sleep but was awoken by a combination of mosquitoes, lice and the incessant rattling of mahjong pieces and voices in the next room. He was offered a glassful of tea and a plate of noodles while it was still dark. He was grateful for the food although he was not hungry. He was told that food that day would not be easy to come across.

The three of them moved off just before dawn, walked through a rubber estate that had a thick cover-crop between the trees which made steady walking difficult. His face brushed against vast spiders' webs, the spiders the size of small birds, their hairy legs and dangerously pointed claws trying to attack him or so, in his panic, he presumed as he tried to brush the stringy, sticky filaments from his face and clothes.

Their journey led them through patches of overgrown vegetation behind villages, often skulking if a civilian was seen or retracing their footsteps and making a detour. They had to cross some minor roads, always peering both ways to ensure no one could see them. By 10 o'clock it was uncomfortably hot and only when they were under tress were they a bit cooler. But rubber estates were the homes of myriads of mosquitoes: there were only different sorts of discomfort. In places they crossed swampy ground, home to large leeches that could suck a pint of blood if left unattached to the skin – four at once had been known to kill an old person as Wang knew as they took one off his leg that he had not noticed, already half full of blood. When there was a possibility of being tracked the three men walked in streams.

In his ignorance Wang had not bothered to take a water-bottle and was too proud to show he was thirsty. By the evening he was famished, parched and exhausted.

Before nightfall the same procedure as the night before was followed. One of the escorts went off to find shelter and a meal. Wang sat on a log and groaned. The escort with him got up and walked a short distance to an open area and looked up. There it was. Bukit Beremban. 'We should get there tomorrow midday,' Wang was told.

Halfway up the mountain were two traces, one made by pre-war surveyors and the other for a large water pipeline. Coming from farther north with a new policy directive, a three-man, well-trained, armed and uniformed courier group had spent the night at the junction of the two traces by a stream. They, too, had woken before dawn, brewed up and were about to set off. 'We're late,' said the senior. 'Wouldn't have been if I hadn't banged my knee and hurt my ankle on that slippery rock yesterday. This area has had no activity for quite some time. There's nothing fresh, no tracks, no cutting, none of those camps the soldiers make. You, Great King of the Air Flavour,' the leader turned to his Number 2, using a nickname that described his powers of sniffing and smelling. 'You have always been correct in telling me if any *gwai lo* foreigner is around – that is why we two are still alive – different tobacco, shit that smells of a meat diet, hair oil, toilet soap, anti-mosquito cream. Have you noticed anything like those around here?'

The Sniffer, grinning in appreciation, sniffed loudly and smiled. 'No, Comrade. Your morning farting has drowned any other stink that might have been sniffable even before you made yourself scarce for your morning rear,' and laughed, gently and not loudly, at his jibe. Luckily, the camaraderie between the two overcame normal discipline. The early morning mist over the trees as well as the down current of air the hill water brought with it, masked whatever olfactory clues that just might possibly have assailed his nostrils.

'So, on our way. I said we're late. Make haste slowly. They were probably expecting us to reach them yesterday. I expect we'll meet some of them looking for us fairly soon.'

Off they went.

The escort with Wang ordered a meal to be cooked before they left the rude dwelling at the back of the last village. 'No food until tonight in the camp where Comrade Lee Soong is waiting for you.'

What will he do to me when I have no news of the traitor? Wang wondered, dismally. *I'll have to have a really good excuse for him.* Thoroughly disheartened, dirty and downcast, his spirits fell further when the meal was slow in coming. It was no good being impatient. They eventually moved off, still a bit hungry, at about 8 o'clock and happened to meet the three-man courier group. Before they reached the camp they were met by a messenger telling them that comrade Lee Soong had just received a new directive so had already moved. In fact he would have lost face had he said that the new directive had laid down nothing of the sort but he was scared that his location could now be easily penetrated because his whereabouts were too well known.

Greatly relieved, back Wang's small group went and a famished, limp, bedraggled, exhausted but thoroughly relieved Collector eventually staggered back into his own house. Administration and common sense were two uncommon aspects of all Communist planning everywhere.

By the end of 1948, even if Big Brother had not heard details of some people in Malaya who were seeking revenge if not recompense for how a certain British officer had been present at the deaths of their family members, the people in the Seremban area concerned certainly did. The name was also known to them, a Captain Rance of a Gurkha regiment.

A large envelope had, earlier on in the day, been handed to Ngai Hiu Ching by someone he already knew, a Min Yuen courier who operated between Seremban and Mantin. In it were the names of six people who had a grievance against the government that would not be redressed except by help from 'other sources'. Ngai Hiu Ching was the coordinator for such matters. The more he read, the more it intrigued him. A couple of them were of a recent nature but the others concerned people missing from as far back as 1942 and 1943.

A British captain was accused of being responsible for the deaths of three Indians: Tor Gul Khan, Abdul Hamid Khan and Abdul Rahim Khan. The first named was the son of Akbar Khan, a pre-war Pathan lawyer for the Indian Association and, subversively, the Indian Independence League, in Malaya and the other two his nephews. Akbar Khan was not a Seremban man but the report had been initiated from, Ngai Hiu Ching squinted to the top of the page, yes, Bhutan Estate which was certainly in Negri Sembilan. *So that's why it's come to me.* He read it with growing interest and frustration.

Although the three were Malayan boys living in Kuala

Lumpur, they had gone to Singapore and joined the Indian National Army, the INA, that fought alongside the Japanese in Burma. The schoolmaster knew about it: it was composed of Indian Army soldiers made prisoners-of-war by the Japanese who then took sides with them against the British and Indian armies. The son had been killed at a village named Negya, near Mount Popa in Burma in 1945. The report came from a Captain Rance, at that time attached to a battalion of the Nepalese Contingent in Burma, who was there at the time of his death. Details were fully given. The same officer had reported that the other two, the nephews, had parachuted into different places in Burma, been captured when this officer had been there, and executed by order of the Viceroy of India. *Too much of a coincidence, surely?* Ngai Hiu Ching thought.

The next case was stranger. It concerned a Nepali lad from Bhutan Estate. His father had business with Akbar Khan in Kuala Lumpur and had taken his son, Rabilal Rai, with him and the boy had become friendly with the Indians. He too had joined the INA but had not gone to Burma but taken to India by Japanese submarine. His task was to go to the Gurkha recruiting depot in Darjeeling and to spread alarm among possible recruits to prevent them joining up, so weakening the Indian Army in Burma thereby making it easier for the Indian National Army. But, unbelievably, he had been picked up in the water by this same omnipresent Britisher and had even joined the captain's regiment, the 1st Gurkha Rifles, part of the army he had been sent against. He had even become the captain's gunman and killed near where Tor Gul Khan had met his death, probably by an Indian National

131

Army soldier who knew he had reneged. However, that was never proved. His father, too, wanted revenge.

Ngai Hiu Ching took his glasses off, polished them, rubbed his eyes that had grown tired and called for some tea. Waiting for it to come he thought deeply about how one man could have been at all four captures and all four deaths.

Sipping his tea he looked at the other list in the envelope. It had complaints from three families who lived in the squatter area near Sepang. The schoolmaster had been there and could visualise the place and the people, scraping a living, trying to feed their children, with life always precarious. Glancing down the pages he saw that even now this man Rance was causing trouble. Three men, he read their names which meant nothing to him, had apparently been climbing a hill in open country near the jungle edge, reason not given, and had met this man and some *Goo K'a bing*. They were fired upon and two of them were wounded. One died later and the other was hanged on a trumped-up charge of carrying a weapon. The third man, responsible for collecting money to help the Cause and was responsible for getting the wives and sons of the other two to make their report, had escaped. The third man's report was lucid enough to envisage the whole scene. If there was no party action he was willing to try by himself except that his one difficulty was that he would not recognise who was responsible for the killing if he ever saw him again.

As the elderly Chinese gentleman sat thinking about what to do, another envelope was delivered. *Unusually busy day today!* This was from the Sumatran villagers of Tanjong Sepat, bitterly complaining about how a British Army captain had had the gall,

132

the effrontery, to come into their peaceful village with some Gurkha soldiers and a Malay Police Inspector and, having evicted the inhabitants of ten houses, dug up their floors, 'looking for weapons' was the given reason. The elderly schoolmaster knew all about how weapons had been hidden after the war and how rumours of hidden weapons were now rampant.

Ngai Hiu Ching knew that such a man as this *gwai lo*, so monstrously evil, could not be allowed to remain unpunished, preferably personally. *What, I wonder, is the best way?* Get the armed comrades to deal with him? But how to find out where he was, either in a base camp or in the jungle? Or was it a case of increasing punishment on the Security Forces generally by more potent ambushes and attacks on their jungle camps? He was not enough of a military man to suggest tactical methods. Could he suggest any method of finding where this *gwai lo* was operating?

Ngai Hiu Ching sat long and thought hard. Yes, maybe there was an answer, maybe two answers how to pinpoint this captain for a 'one-off' operation: the troops had to have fresh rations. Therefore there would be a fresh ration contractor, unless they bought their own rations in the bazaar when their company was not in Seremban. The contractor was the more likely: he would know where to deliver his goods. And even if the company was in the jungle there would be a rear party in base. If the contractor could get hold of a transistor radio that could net in on the same wavelength as the companies passed their evening reports – what did they call them in English? Yes, 'sitreps', surely there could be a way of alerting the comrades in the jungle. And the second answer? It would take a lot to find out but ... yes, got it. He knew about Comrade Lee Soong's activities. He had read about his plans for a Gurkha 'mole'. Was there one in place yet, and how could he find out?

His answer came in another long and detailed report handed to him the following week. It contained a new name, a Captain Alan Hinlea, a British officer of the Gurkhas stationed in Seremban and had been written by the owner of the Yam Yam night club, Yap Cheng Wu, who had personally interviewed this Hinlea person.[9] It was of the greatest interest. In the report were details of what work this Hinlea did in the battalion. He was the Intelligence Officer who had on his staff a Gurkha from Darjeeling with similar ideas as his, a Padamsing Rai. Hinlea also had entry into the secret part of the Seremban police set-up and had met Lee Kheng, the MCP's 'sleeper'. *Sounds most promising!*

Ngai Hiu Ching wondered where all that was leading to and read on expectantly. Apparently Captain Hinlea frequented the Yam Yam, where he had illicit relations with so many of the 'taxi' girls he was known as *Sik Long*, the Lustful Wolf. After some time he had fallen for one of the girls, Siu Tae, and wanted to marry her, so he had confided with the barman, Kwek Lee Joo, who was a card-carrying member. He had also told the barman that he had no time for his brother officers and did not like any, except for a Captain Rance. Even that did not prevent his one great wish, namely to join the MCP and help the Politburo by advising its members how best to organise propaganda against the British as well as anything else similar that came his way.

---

9 See *Operation Janus*.

The name of Rance appearing in this context gave pause to the elderly schoolmaster's reading. He personally knew Yap Cheng Wu, a dedicated senior Communist cadre and who could be relied on for anything other than being a manager. Ngai Hiu Ching knew that such matters could not be hurried, seeds of any kind took time to mature, the bigger the plant or tree the longer it took.

There were other difficulties in taking revenge against anybody, especially a British officer. Few people had a weapon and hardly anyone knew how to kill bare-handed and a trained 'hit man' would be expensive even if one could be found. Also, apart from anything else, travel on the roads was dangerous and people tended not to go far unless they had to. Trains were being ambushed and civilian casualties occurred too often for people to risk travelling by rail. Ngai Hiu Ching considered his options: could a disguised member of the MRLA shoot a British officer in the town when, say, he was out shopping if ever a willing operative could be found to risk it? It had not happened so far. The best chance was on operations, getting the target to an area where comrades outnumbered the military patrol even if they did not dominate the area. And he knew that Gurkha soldiers, the *Goo K'a bing*, were tenaciously protective of their officers.

He sighed at his inability to do anything positive there and then. This Hinlea was promising but remote from him and, in any case, needed 'hands-on' treatment. Was there anyone else he could use for details that could lead to a successful outcome? Yes, there were three: one was Lee Kheng he had already noted in the report, one was the woman Wang Tao, a table servant of the Officer in Charge of the Police District, the OCPD; and one was the fresh-ration contractor he had already thought about. He was ... yes Chow Hoong Biu. *For now that's all the thinking and planning I can do.*

He put the reports in a safe place and, to stretch his legs, went for a short stroll – before the evening rain.

Just as it was difficult to take one's revenge and ensure success and a clean getaway, it was also difficult for Alan Hinlea to plan his clean getaway. He had to be convinced that there was a good chance of succeeding so *maskirovka* – 'a trick to fool "them" the MGB (Ministry of State Security) taught me taught me when I was in Russia, son,' his father had told him – had to be used. His trade craft had to be immaculate. Outwardly he remained loyal, making Jason Rance his friend; inwardly he plotted and planned ... and waited ... and the time did ripen, but so slowly it was not until June 1952 that matters came to a head.

Before then two things happened. The first was in 1950, when the Malayan Indian Congress, MIC, met in Kuala Lumpur to elect a new president. He was K. Ramanathan Chettiar who only lasted till 1951. At the meeting that elected him, despite travelling difficulties because of the Emergency, there was a goodly gathering. Many old friends who had not met for some time had a chance to renew contacts. After one long session, there was a chance meeting between Akbar Khan and Subramanian Mudaliar, the comprador of Jemima Estate. They were joined by other participants and, for ease, talk was in English as had been the meeting. English was better known than Malay. After their second cup of tea the conversation turned to the campaign against the guerrillas who, although they professed Communism which the MIC did not, did have their support as they were anti-British colonial rule in sentiment.

'I wonder if any of you had any relative who was lost during the war and have had no news about him?' Akbar Khan asked.

The others looked at him with curiosity. *A strange question to ask five years after the war has ended*, they thought.

'No? Three of mine were missing, a son and two nephews. It was in 1948 I heard how they had died, all killed fighting for our Indian freedom. Shall I tell you how?' and as the others did not gainsay him, out came the details.

'So how did you find out?' one of the listeners asked. 'Surely the Viceroy's wartime orders were not broadcast, were they?'

'I very much doubt it,' agreed Akbar Khan and, warming to his subject, went on to say 'I found out details of all three deaths from one Britisher, a captain, who was there at their capture and death.'

That produced a collective gasp of amazement. *Quite a coincidence!*

'Details have been given to,' he cleared his throat, 'certain authorities but I gather nothing has been done either to the officer or for compensation to my family. I am incensed.'

The others nodded agreement.

Akbar Khan continued, 'I want to get the guerrillas to make that captain a target so, even if there is no recompense, he will be punished. In case any of this comes your way, please take any action you can. He is a Captain Rance of the 1st/12th Gurkha Rifles, based in Seremban.'

'We will, we will,' the others chanted – all except one man, Subramanian Mudaliar, the comprador of Jemima Estate. *He's not that sort of man at all, otherwise I'd have heard about it. If I get the chance I'll warn him.* His firm features gave no clue as to his inner thoughts and after a bit more chit-chat the group broke up and they went their various ways.

Juasseh Estate, east of Seremban , mid-1952

This was an all-Tamil estate, with the owner living in Seremban. It was neither large nor all that profitable but the District War Executive Committee, DWEC, felt it provided a source of information to the guerrillas operating to the west of Bahau. DWECs, and their seniors, SWECs, State War Executive Committees, were the brainchild of General Templer, the High Commissioner-cum-Director of Operations. He wanted 'jointery' and the committees comprised the senior Malay government official, senior policeman and senior military man in the area it controlled, with some others, such as planters and railway men, being called in for advice if necessary. It was decided to station a company of Gurkhas there for a few months to see if relations could be so established that at best could bring those antis over to the government side or, at worst, to negate their power. The estate lay on the main road to Bahau so it was easy for sympathisers to count troops who passed and find out, if possible, their destination.

Captain Jason Rance, as a known linguist, was thought to be the man best able to do what was wanted so A Company, 1/12

Gurkha Rifles, was detailed to go there. There were two main buildings, in front and on the right as one entered and on the left was open ground. For accommodation a number of Nissen huts were erected. These were portable structures of ribbed aluminium over a frame of arched steel ribs. The floor was concrete. Ten men could be squeezed into one hut.

The main Seremban-Bahau road ran on the fourth side. Left and right of the entrance to the estate buildings on the road two parallel lines of barbed wire frames – 'knife rests' – were set eighty feet apart. No troops had ever been billeted there before and as it was a 'first' the news quickly spread. The local member of the MIC, who had been one of those who had listened to Akbar Khan in Kuala Lumpur, soon alerted those he thought could take advantage of what he wanted, so he contacted them and worked out a plan. Get a quarrel going among the locals, ask Captain Rance to be a neutral judge and, while he was adjudicating, let the quarrel spill over and kill him – quite accidently of course 'because he stepped into the way of a knife strike.'

It was purely by chance that Subramanian Mudaliar had to go to Seremban to organise some new machinery for his drying sheds and, on the off chance of a gossip, he went to the local MIC office to see what was what. Just as he was leaving, the 'plotter' came in. They knew each other and the 'plotter' said, 'I have something to tell you. Let's go and have something to eat and I'll tell you about it.' It was over a bowl of noodles that the plan was, voice suitably lowered, explained.

'Now, that is a good idea,' Subramanian Mudaliar chortled, sycophantically. 'Where exactly is that to take place, did you say?'

'Juasseh Estate.'

The comprador thanked his informer and wondered how best he could warn Captain Rance, *who had been so charming when he gave me the watch* he remembered, glancing at it in admiration. *It really is a beauty.*

Subramanian thought that he himself going to Juasseh was out of the question and, anyway, time was against him. *I'll ask the Telephone Office for the battalion's number.* He rang it.

'May I speak to Captain Rance, please?' he asked the battalion exchange.

He was told that Rance saheb was away in Juasseh Estate and could not be got hold of.

'Is there no telephone there?'

'No, we have to use the wireless or send mail.'

'Thank you,' said the Tamil and rang off. He went to a stationary shop and bought paper and an envelope, went to a cafe, sat down with a cup of tea and wrote Jason a letter, explaining what had been planned. He then took a taxi and told the driver to go to the Gurkha battalion lines and to wait for him. Once there he asked the way to the Adjutant's office and told that overworked man what he wanted. He told the Adjutant about his watch and showed it to him. 'In this envelope is a letter to the man who sent the watch. Captain Rance knows his address, I don't. I am asking him to send my letter to England.'

'Yes, that's reasonable. I'll send it to him by the next convoy.'

The comprador thanked him and went back to the town in the taxi. He returned to Jemima Estate in a bus.

When the letter reached Rance he read it with mixed feelings.

The main message ended, 'whatever rumpus happens, keep well away. Do not interfere even if you are asked to sort the quarrel out. You are the target because you were at the deaths of those three Pathan boys during the war. This I know to be true.'

Hardly possible, is it, after all this time? But as Subramanian Mudaliar has warned me I'll take his advice.

Rance was liked in the estate lines, the labourers were amused at how quickly he picked up Tamil and made the children laugh. He told his 2 ic, the Gurkha Captain, and his batman about his warning. And indeed, one morning the day after he had come back from a local operation, an unseemly row did break out. Jason was in his office, catching up with the mail and looked out of the window. A large crowd was gathering with much raucous shouting, feverish gesticulations and hand-to-hand scuffles. The main contestants seemed to be two men who were quarrelling about a young girl who was trying to hide behind her mother. Someone came and asked Rance to help sort out the row. 'You are neutral. We respect you.'

Rance, remembering his warning, said that he felt he could not become involved.

Another man ran into the office and asked the first man something, in Tamil, which Rance did not fully understand. The second man turned to him and said 'you are here to protect us, aren't you?'

'No, I am not,' he answered gruffly but as he looked out of the window he saw a man creep up behind the two men quarrelling, lift a stick and thwack one of them full in the face, drawing blood and knocking him to the ground. In no time at all a knife was drawn and Rance saw the man with the stick stabbed in the belly. He fell down bleeding. The man with the stick then went and struck the mother of the girl hiding behind her, reaching out and trying to grab her.

Instinctively Rance just felt he had to try and help the girl and to see if he could render any medical help. As he reached the crowd he saw that the stabber was out of control and very close to him. Glancing at the stabbed man he saw he was dead. Subramanian Mudaliar's message was temporarily forgotten in his urge to save the girl. His batman and another soldier charged up to him, Kulbahadur pulling him away and the soldier defending the two of them with a khukri. They ran back to his office and his company 2 ic said, 'Saheb, you were warned not to go. These hot blooded people are a danger.'

'Captain saheb, yes, thank you. I know I should not have gone but I went automatically to save the girl.' He put both hands on his ears and twisted them, a punishment used to recalcitrant riflemen. The 2 ic laughed, 'Saheb, you are forgiven but please do not do it again.'

Radio Malaya, suitably prompted, announced the death of 'a senior person at Juasseh Estate whose name cannot be made public.' This was taken by Akbar Khan as the authorities not wanting to mention a British officer's death. He exalted, feeling that justice had been done and, after a while, forgot about it.

In due course Jason thanked Subramanian Mudaliar for his timely warning and kept up a friendship for as long as he was in the country.

The second event was, in practice, so insignificant it hardly mentioned anything but temporary comment and an hour's frustration for all the listeners of all three channels of Radio Malaya, the red, green and blue for Chinese-, Malay- and English-language programmes. One afternoon none of the three channels broadcast anything and nobody knew why. The reason was that it had been decided, at the very top, that the final of the inter-battalion Nepal Cup, the annual football competition, should be broadcast on a wavelength that the 68 Radio sets used by soldiers in the jungle could receive the running commentary. The headset would be hung from a low-lying branch and, less the sentries, the men could gather round it and listen. Two broadcasters were detailed, a Gurkha from the British Forces Broadcasting Service and Captain Rance. They were to take turn and turn about. The Gurkha quickly became tongue-tied and Jason Rance spoke for most of the time.

The Collector, wanting to listen to his favourite programme, found nothing. Twirling the knob on his set he heard the Gurkhali voice coming over. There was something about it that was familiar. He understood not a word but, after resounding cheers had faded into the background, silence broke out. He decided to try the red channel for the Chinese programmes and switched on in time to hear the announcer explaining the disruption of normal programmes. 'It was the final of the Nepal Cup football competition being broadcast for the Gurkhas in the jungle and it was one of their officers, Captain Rance, speaking in their language making a running commentary. Radio Malaya makes no apologies as we approve of our fighting services getting the benefit of being able to listen into once a year and the only way for us to do that was to stop broadcasting on our normal channels and using a special one ...'

The Collector switched off. *So that's who that 'Chinese' voice belongs to.* He congratulated himself on recognising it. *One day ...* he vowed. Even his dreadful walk to and from near the top of Bukit Beremban seemed worth it. He decided to go and visit the one-time schoolmaster in Mantin, not only for old-times' sake.

June 1952

The guerrilla camp, base of the Negri Sembilan Regional Committee, part of the political wing of the MCP, was situated in a flat space surrounded by thick jungle not far from the summit of Bukit Beremban, 3293 feet high and easily seen from Seremban. It was guarded by elements of the MRLA, both at the base and around its edges. 1/12 GR's camp could be seen from there.

The Regional Commissar, Lau Beng, was a one-time schoolmaster from Seremban and a veteran activist from pre-war days, who knew Ngai Hiu Ching. The military commander was Wang Ming, a short, almost square, powerfully built man – he looked like a bear and his nickname was *Hung Lo,* Bear – who, at low level, was tactically astute. He was a veteran from the Second World War, fighting against the Japanese.

This particular day it so happened that the camp was on high alert, with sentries placed around the bottom of the camp entrance. A high-powered conference was taking place with members from the Politburo in the Cameron Highlands, who were on an unusually long visit to the south of the country. They were Yeong Kwoh, the MCP's military chief, Chien Tiang, chief confidant of Chin Peng and propaganda expert, and Ah Fat, a non-voting member of the Politburo. Rumours of a high-level 'mole' had to be pinned down. Matters were interrupted by one of the duty sentries who, after asking permission to speak and apologising for disturbing such senior comrades, announced that a courier from Seremban had brought such an important message that it had to be delivered orally. He was on such a tight schedule and in such danger of apprehension in his coming and going that time was of the essence. 'Can he come and make his report now?'

'Comrade Lau Beng, ask him who the messenger is,' demanded Chien Tiang.

The sentry was asked and said, 'Comrade Kwek Leng Joo, the barman of the Yam Yam.'

The Political Commissar explained what an important man Comrade Kwek Leng Joo was.

'Yes, Comrade Lau Beng. get the man brought in. This could be interesting.' That was Yeong Kwoh speaking, belatedly feeling that it was he who should have spoken in the first place.

Comrade Kwek Leng Joo was ushered into the meeting and Lau Beng, who knew him well, introduced him before asking permission to interrogate him.

Granted. 'Comrade, please tell us your news. It must be important for you to have made such a dangerous journey.'

'Comrades, as barman of a nightclub in Seremban, the Yam Yam, one of my tasks is gaining information from the *gwai lo* who talk to me as they drink their alcohol. One of the most persistent is a sympathetic English officer, name of Captain Alan

Hinlea, the Intelligence Officer of the *Goo K'a* battalion. He is a card-carrying Communist but is under the strictest orders not talk about it openly. He wants to join us and work with the Central Committee as an adviser on how best to counter colonial propaganda.'

A gasp like a soft wind escaped from every listener's lips.

'He also wants to marry one of the taxi girls and has mentioned taking her with him.'

Silence reined as the implications were considered. After a long, long silence Yeong Kwoh said 'Thank you, Comrade. This certainly is news we must take full advantage of. Other than the woman who will have to stay in Seremban for any marriage to happen after we have won our struggle, the extrication and movement of the officer will need the most careful planning, a fool-proof cover plan and the closest monitoring. We will go back and get permission one way or the other and let you know in due course. It will take time but, if permitted and successful, eminently worthwhile. The need-to-know principle is paramount.'

The messenger was briefed how to let the *gwai lo* know what was being planned and not to breathe a word to anyone at all. He departed and, with a considerable lightening of the original atmosphere, the meeting continued for another day. The three senior men left in high hopes.

When a courier next arrived at the Regional Committee camp, Lau Beng told him to wait while he wrote a letter. It was to Ngai Hiu Ching and all it said was that his suggestions had been noted and that 'we are preparing a thunder bolt that will do more damage than what you had in mind.' He hoped that his elliptical reference would be enough to put his friend's mind at rest.

Ngai Hiu Ching had heard the Radio Malaya broadcast about 'a senior person at Juasseh Estate whose name cannot be made public' and had wondered if it was Captain Rance being referred to. Later on, 'no', he learnt so he waited patiently for another occasion. He had already managed to contact, secretly of course, Lau Beng about the complaints he had received and his difficulty in suggesting how to resolve them. He was overjoyed at Lau Beng's letter.

Politburo permission to contact Captain Hinlea and organise his journey onwards reached the Regional HQ and preparations were made for Hinlea to be brought to the camp on Bukit Beremban. And brought he was, having managed to steal many of the secret details of what was known of the guerrillas held in Special Branch. The Gurkha, Padamsing Rai, thinking he was talking to Hinlea, had been overheard by Rance and Hinlea's reports were not Special Branch's but cleverly forged ones designed to bring alarm and despondency to the guerrillas. Padamsing, never having contacted Kamal, was gently eased out, never fully understanding where he had gone wrong and once back in Darjeeling became a Bengali politician. The reports Hinlea showed to Lau Beng had such a devastating effect on Lau Beng's morale he was unable to cope properly with his task.

Unbeknownst to the guerrillas, Captain Rance was alerted at Hinlea's absence and the *maskirovka* planned by the turncoat came unstuck. Rance and four Gurkhas were sent to track Hinlea's group, which consisted of the whole of the Regional HQ plus a military escort.

The tracking was of such a high standard that the guerrilla group never knew it was being trailed. It finished spectacularly: Lau Beng and some of his men were killed as was Hinlea, after a furious but unsuccessful attempt to kill Rance, otherwise he would have been captured. The news was never broadcast on Radio Malay so the Politburo had to guess that something on the way had compromised the operation. Also on the credit side was that Wang Ming, the Bear, and the few remaining MRLA soldiers were so won over by Rance's performance that they were persuaded to work for the Security Forces as a 'Q' team, often with Rance.

December 1952

Siu Tae, a girl with a sad, sweet, young-old face, felt that by hooking a *gwai lo* in marriage, future life, however difficult, would be compensated by the untold wealth that every foreigner had. She knew what her hoped-for future husband was intending to do and that it would be a long time before any news could filter back that he was well and happy working with the MCP Politburo. But before anything definite was told her she began to hear niggling rumours that her Alan was dead. She asked both her manager and the barman but neither gave her an answer that satisfied her. It might just have been careless talk from one of the 'Q' team that his so-called friend Captain Rance – never any proof, mind you – had killed him. He had told her all that class were just the same, none could be trusted. Certainly there was evidence that Captain Rance had not been in the camp after her man had left her. Good enough! Siu Tae, who was pregnant by Hinlea, vowed that her baby would be a son – it was – who would make amends. She sought out her uncle, Deng Bing Yi, who worked in a garage and blurted the whole story out to him. 'Don't worry about waiting for your son, it'll take too long. Let me see what I can do.'

He recalled a talk he had had with Ngai Hiu Ching when he had suggested trying to sabotage the *gwai lo*'s car when the *gwai lo* was inside, difficult though it would be to arrange it. Ngai Hiu Ching had acquiesced in principle but had suggested a more plausible occasion with detailed publicity would be more of a coup. It was now time for Deng Bing Yi to act. He was a skilled mechanic and during the war had sabotaged some Japanese cars by blowing them up and killing the occupants. *If the man my niece wants to eliminate has his own car, as some of those officers have, that's the best answer. I already service a couple of them. Time and place will be the problem, not what I can personally do.* He wondered how best to set about solving his problem.

He decided he had three main tasks, the first was to make a bomb that would blow up a car. That would not be difficult because he had, or could get, what was needed as he still had some hidden away from the war years. The second was to fix it in the car that this Captain Rance was about to drive away – or be driven, it didn't really matter – and the third was to get an accomplice to fix a date and place to an event that would ensure that the captain and his car would be there long enough for him to plant the bomb. The first two were comparatively easy as only he himself was involved: it was the third bit that was an unknown.

He looked at the calendar in his office and noted that on the 25th was Christmas Day which the British always celebrated. Was there any local who worked in the battalion who would be likely to throw a party for the officers, at his own place? If so, who? He racked his brain and came up with the idea of the fresh-ration contactor, Chow Hoong Biu, a friend of his. He knew that, in spite of his working for the British Army, his heart was not in it because the comrades in the jungle felt it was against their Cause. *I'll put it to him in such a way he can't refuse.*

Deng Bing Yi went to see Chow Hoong Biu one evening and, ever so gently, brought the conversation round to the comrades wanting information on operations. 'Tell you what, I've just had an idea,' he dissembled with an air of sagacity. 'Why not invite some of the officers to a Christmas party at your place, get them drunk and talkative. The comrades will put less pressure on you for that and on me for suggesting it to you,' he added dismissively. 'Also do you know of anyone who would like to know what Captain Rance looks like from close quarters? If so, as a friendship gesture, ask a couple or so to come along also.'

Chow Hoong Biu considered that for a while, remembering how he had been approached by Wang the Collector – *why not him as well?* – and said, 'yes, I like it. I do know someone who'd like to see him. When I next go to the battalion I'll see the Adjutant and ask him to come along and bring a friend.'

'Suggest he comes along with Captain Rance in the captain's car. I know he has one as I service it for him.'

And, that being agreed upon, Chow Hoong Biu rang Deng Bing Yi at his garage and told him so. He also sent a letter to Wang the Collector telling him about it. Wang was keen. He knew how to drive, slowly. He could borrow a car so need not worry about a bus.

It was now incumbent on Deng Bing Yi. He knew how to make a bomb that would cause the petrol tank to explode and the car to go up in flames and be completely gutted when it hit a bump in the road. He knew what ingredients he needed. Basically some plastic explosive and as the car was a pre-war model, half a pound would be enough and two electrical detonators.

He had managed to steal some explosive from the Japanese when they were trying to quarry stone for some defences against an expected invasion. He had looked after it and it would still be usable. As for the electrical detonators, he doubted that the ones he had stolen at the same time, all those years ago, could be relied on. He knew Lee Kheng and, taking his two electrical detonators, surreptitiously managed to change them for two new ones. *No worry now!*

He had his own soldering iron and a small stick of solder, a roll of black insulating tape, a yard of thin wire and a pair of cutters. He needed something sticky and opted for some plumber's putty. If he were to finish the bomb on the morning of the party it would not become too stiff.

Getting a nine-volt transistor battery, a small bulb one inch in diameter and two lengths of fine, single-strand, five-amp plastic-coated wire, each three yards long, one coloured red and the other blue, was no trouble. None was banned material, nor were some erasers to act as 'jammers'.

He had his own supply of condoms to keep the active ingredients dry and all he now needed was an air-tight tin. His wife had one of tea she had not thrown away.

Now to make his bomb: in the lid of the tin he made a hole

and cut enough of two pieces of wire to solder to both positive and negative terminals of the battery. Battery and wires went into the base of the tin and he inserted the detonator deeply into the plastic explosive. He filled the tin up so that it was full and the charge from the battery would fire the detonator and the plastic would then explode to ruin the car.

He then had fixed the trigger mechanism with a snapped hacksaw blade. He made a block of rubber with the erasers with the ends of the blade just wide enough to join when the car jolted so, with the wires in place the bomb, already live, was activated.

The possibility of Captain Rance not joining the party was something he had to accept but, no, on the night in question, he and the Adjutant, the latter driving, reached Chow Hoong Biu's house and, with other guests 'who didn't matter' as far as the bomb maker was concerned, gathered in force as the liquor flowed.

The bomb maker, from an advantage point, saw the Adjutant park his car under a lamp post. That was for Jason to get out. He did not see the car drive on as he was 'nursing' his stuff so did not see another car, very like the Adjutant's drive up and park where the first had, momentarily, been. The Collector, who had borrowed the car, unwisely left it unlocked and the ignition key in place so there was no problem for Deng Bing Yi to open the bonnet, nor to shut it later when he had placed the bomb.

He had brought the bomb from his garage in his own car. With bonnet open, and no passer-by would take any notice of someone looking at the engine, it took no time to strap the explosive charge opposite the steering wheel. *Two for the price of one* he thought cavalierly. In his excitement the only extraneous thought that passed through his mind was that the car was overdue its regular servicing. He lowered the trigger mechanism, connected to the main charge by two wires, down through the engine space to the ground beneath.

He then had to wriggle under the car, again nothing worthy of notice to any passer-by. Using his torch he found the front suspension and tightly wired the rear end of the trigger to a bracing-bar. The bomb would now explode the first time the car hit a hump or a pot-hole with the positive and negative wires joining. He got up, dusted himself down, closed the bonnet and drove himself off, highly delighted for his niece's sake.

The party at Chow Hoong Biu's was a lively affair. Drink flowed and the tidbits that circulated were delicious. One of the guests was the ebullient Teochew, Tay Wang Teik. Standing next to him with a drink in his hand was Wang the Collector and Jason came up behind the pair of them in time to hear Wang lean over to his right and ask who the tall *gwai lo* was. Unable to resist the opportunity and as Wang took a sip of his drink, a voice came from Wang's left, 'Lee Soong's bodyguard.' So startled was the hapless Wang that he did the nose trick, coughing and spluttering. By the time he looked to his left there was nobody.

Before the meal Chow Hoong Biu introduced Wang and Jason. There was nothing more banal than the 'how are you' type of talk, Jason using 'basic' Malay. 'Tau cakap Cina?' asked Wang. Jason shook his head, 'Ta' tau,' no, I don't know how to speak

Chinese.

The Collector soon had enough and, having seen Rance at close quarters was still not sure if he was the man who had delivered the message that night or the voice he had heard speaking Gurkhali on Radio Malaya, felt he had had enough for one night, excused himself, left the party and drove off, slowly, after all, it was dark and the car was not his. When well south of Seremban he was dazzled by a car coming the other way, swerved, drove the car into a ditch. The bomb exploded. The car's petrol tank immediately caught fire and the car, along with Wang the Collector, was unrecognisable.

Not long after the Collector had left, the Adjutant came up to Jason and said, 'I think it is time we left. Let's say our thank yous to Chow Hoong Biu and go home.'

Once outside the house Jason said, 'Where's the car? I thought you left it under this lamp post.'

'I did but I thought better of it so parked it over there,' indicating with his head, 'in the shade. Less likely any urchin muck it up.'

On reaching the car the Adjutant said, 'It looks all right. I doubt anything untoward would have happened had I left it where it was when you got out.' That remark was, neither of them were ever to know, the understatement of the evening.

When Siu Tae's uncle heard no news about the death of two British officers he was at a loss. He just could not understand how the bomb had not exploded. He had been so sure it would have. He did not know who to ask to find out where he had gone wrong. It was a few days before the remains of the burnt-out car were found and reported to the police. The disappearance of Wang the Collector was never commented upon and Deng Bing Yi never heard about it so, for him, the car's non-explosion remained an unsolved mystery. When it was time for the Adjutant's car to go to his garage for servicing he was utterly bewildered at finding nothing. When he again did meet up with the old schoolmaster and tell him how hard he had worked and what had happened, Ngai Hiu Ching felt it would do Deng Bing Yi's self-esteem no good if he suggested he had put the bomb in the wrong car, nor would he believe it, so tactfully he said nothing.

As for Siu Tae, she inwardly raved when she learnt that nothing had happened to 'that' officer: *it will have to be my unborn son …*

Sometime in 1954

A Company, 1/12 Gurkha Rifles, was one of many, many rifle companies engaged in a shooting war against the Communist Terrorists. For Malaya there were Malay infantry battalions, Police Jungle Squads, a Home Guard and some aborigine *orang asli* fighters as well as a squadron of armoured cars manned by any Malayan acceptable. From overseas there were eight Gurkha battalions, a Fiji battalion, a Rhodesian African Rifles representation and a Nigerian Regiment unit to say nothing of British battalions, made up of National Service and regular soldiers, and sometimes units with a specialist role. They were backed up by artillery and air reconnaissance, helicopter transport and supply planes, as well as an extensive staff, all of whom went back to their home country after three years, except for Malayans, Gurkhas and their British officers. Against them there was a diminishing band of guerrillas with no three-year limit, battle-hardened whose existence was tougher than any soldier's. Their tenacity was, in its way, inspirational, but history was not on their side yet even after six years of such an effort, no end of the conflict was in sight.

For both sides, sometimes good luck came its way, at other times bad luck but the unending slog of jungle work was common to all.

A stroke of good luck combined with clever tactical sense came to the commander of 2 Regiment, MRLA, Tan Fook Leong, on Friday, 13 August, when his ambush killed the CO of 1/12 Gurkha Rifles but his luck ran out a couple of months later when his camp was bombed and he was killed. His camp had been found by Special Branch putting a minute contrivance into his hand-held radio which, when switched on, could be picked up and the position located by a bomber flying to a flank. The Director of Operations in Kuala Lumpur had felt that such a ruse was unsporting and had suggested a really fluent Chinese speaker go to his camp masquerading as a surrendered terrorist to try and persuade Tan Fook Leong to surrender and lead a normal life. Commonly known among British troops as 'Ten Foot Long', the guerrilla had earned himself a good name and it seemed a shame not to give him the chance of living longer.

The person thought best to carry out this delicate task was

Captain Jason Rance, well known, if only by a relatively few people, for being able to speak Chinese like a native. However, before he took his company into the jungle on this gruesome task, he remembered he had Tan Fook Leong's home number, wife's and son's names in Penang. Although he felt he was, in fact, wasting his time in so doing, he felt it worth his while to ring the number so he phoned the house.

After several rings a male voice answered, giving the phone number, not his name.

'*Wei*, is that Tan Wing Bun, Tan Fook Leong's son?' Jason hoped that a Penang youth was a Cantonese speaker. He was.

'Yes, who are you?'

'Is your mother, Chen Yok Lan there?'

'What is that to you whether she is or she is not? Who are you?'

'Just someone telling you that shortly I am going into the jungle to talk to your father and unless you or your mother tells me to tell him you want him back home alive, he'll be dead within the week.'

Jason heard a loud intake of breath at this harsh and unexpected ultimatum. Silence. *This man cannot be a comrade. He'll be a government man, probably a turncoat. If I can recognise his voice and find out where he lives, maybe I can eliminate him if he is responsible for eliminating my father.*

'May I know if you have Politburo permission to address a comrade's family so abruptly?'

'I'm afraid there is neither any time nor any sense it contacting the Politburo on such a matter.'

'Who are you? Can't you tell me that?'

'I am just a simple foot soldier whose name would mean nothing to you or the Politburo. *Paan chue sek lo fuu.*'

Feigning to be a pig he vanquishes tigers! Who can that be? 'I am puzzled, say that again.'

'No, why should I. You obviously understood it. Here's another for you: "convenient water, push boat".'

By now Tan Wing Bun's mind was working overtime. He had another proverb ready, '"a soft-hearted person is liable to be victimised as a tame horse is to be ridden". No. Let my father suffer for his belief. For him to abandon all he has fought for since he was a youth is unthinkable.' As Tan Wing Bun put the phone down he told himself he'd never forget that voice *but whose is it?*

The announcement, on Radio Malaya and in the newspapers, English-language and vernacular of Tan Fook Leong's death caused cursing among the Communist Terrorists, especially in the Politburo now safely in south Thailand and relief, rather than joy among the Security Forces, although only a few knew how he was killed. One who did was Chan Man Yee, the woman Registry Clerk in Police HQ, a long-time Politburo mole. When Xi Zhan Yang, a special courier between Chan Man Yee and the Politburo next met up one evening after her work, he was told about how Tan Fook Leong's demise had happened. The commander of 2 Regiment was a personal friend of the MCP Chairman, Chin Peng. Both of them had marched in the Victory Parade in London in 1946 and both esteemed one another.

'His wife and son will have to know how that happened,'

Chan Man Yee said, then asked, 'Do you go back to MCP HQ by way of Penang where they live?'

Xi Zhan Yang considered that. 'I'd rather not, you know. Somehow I wouldn't feel safe.'Could you fight with the electric speech?' That phrase meant to 'telephone'.

'I don't have the number.'

'I can get it from the office when I go tomorrow. Stay safe in my flat. You can phone from here.'

That was agreed upon.

She brought him the number and he rang the house, properly identifying himself. He could scarcely believe the conversation with a Chinese speaker using four- or five-character phrases and he said he would try and find out who was responsible.

After he had rung off he thanked Chan Man Yee, not knowing that the phone had recently been bugged and that the Police HQ recording device had the whole conversation.[10] That did not stop a report being made to the Politburo. When Ah Fat heard about it he said nothing but felt Jason, it had to be he, who else, needed to be more than careful.

Tan Wing Bun was so incensed at what had happened to his father and that unexpected and worrying phone call that he decided only long-term revenge was the answer. He decided to offer himself as a member of Special Branch and work against the colonial, imperial oppressors from within. He told nobody of his intention.

---

10 See *Operation Red Tidings*.

PART II

1956

4

Betong, south Thailand, January, 1956

With the failure of the Baling Peace talks Chin Peng now felt that living in Peking, as they still thought of it, near the Chinese Communist Party was better both for him personally and also for the MCP, so he asked permission for this to happen. Even after that was granted it was not until December, 1960, that he departed. He had been worried about his successor so was overjoyed at the return of Comrade Ah Hai, who had gone to China in 1949 to be cured of tuberculosis, before he himself set forth. Once Ah Hai had settled in, Chin Peng told him he would be in charge in Betong as Deputy Secretary General with he himself remaining as Secretary General.

There was someone in the camp who had come from China before the Baling talks were started.[11] He was an emissary sent from Peking who had taken many months to reach Betong. He had two main tasks; one was to deliver a message so secret that it had to be remembered orally and of which he had forgotten some of the most important points. The other was, as a skilled radio operator, to mend the MCP HQ's radio that had not functioned

---

11 See *My Side of History*, Chin Peng, Chapter 22.

for six months. He was a middle-aged man, of medium height, with high cheek bones and a slightly protruding chin. His steady eyes that seldom blinked were calm and reflective. Even though he was exhausted on arrival he gave as much of his important message as he could remember before repairing the radio. In fact he never did remember the most important points so it was slightly ironic that his name, Meng Ru, was the same as the surname of Mencius, the Chinese Confucian philosopher, and Ru meaning scholar or learned man. A full Politburo meeting discussed his report, without knowing all of it, and on what was happening as far as the Communist Party of China's attitude to the MCP was. There were also little driblets of news – never gossip, scandal or rumour, oh no! – that could make the Betong people's job easier and as a background for Chin Peng's proposed sojourn. As a reward for his having faced so many dangers in his long journey he was allowed to stay in Betong for as long as he wanted to: he was given the soubriquet of 'Emissary'.

It had been during his move through western Laos that Meng Ru gradually noticed a change in people's demeanour. It had not struck him before but here, even though he was escorted by comrades, he saw that people did not have the same non-smiling, furtive glances when passing strangers as he had grown up with, so become used to. There seemed to be no worry as to the 'is he an enemy?', 'can I trust him?', 'will it count against me if I talk to him?' frame of mind. In Thailand it was more obvious and something deep inside him told him that that was the way to live, not the way he had known till then. It only later struck him: *by trying to keep the people in line through fear compared with how happy people seem when not bullied by 'party' functionaries has let me see that where I come from government sponsored life is one inhumane and least realised confidence trick. I must get out of it somehow.* And now, living in the MCP camp, he could the more clearly see and the more keenly loathe the same deadening, damping, yes, demeaning attitude again. It struck him forcibly. However there was one man, more than one if his small group was also counted, who had the hard-to-define manner of being his own self. The Emissary found out that this man's name was Ah Fat.

Initially the Emissary 'sniffed' at Ah Fat as dogs will sniff each other on first meeting but, in this case, only metaphorically and unobtrusively. He and Ah Fat became friendly. It was when the Emissary overheard Chin Peng telling Ah Fat that he had decided to send him back to Kuala Lumpur, that he made up his mind. *I can't lose anything by trying, can I?* he asked himself.

Chin Peng had a person 'mole', Chan Man Yee, who worked as the Central Registry clerk in Special Branch, Malayan Police HQ in Kuala Lumpur. Her superior was Too Chee Chew, a.k.a. C C Too, a brilliant propagandist who was the Head of Special Branch, so she was a 'gold mine' of information. Quite some time before the Baling Conference Chin Peng had sent Ah Fat down to KL to find out from her what high Malayan government officials were thinking about and planning on peace talks between the MCP and the Government, the better that the Politburo could plan its own arguments. Now the Secretary General wanted her views on Malayan Government policy, not knowing that Chan

Man Yee had decided to go back to China. Ah Fat had not told him otherwise and an excuse to go to KL and see his family and Mr Too was always welcome.

A day or two before Ah Fat, with his 'deputy', Wang Ming, a.k.a. *Hung Lo*, the Bear, were due to set off for Kuala Lumpur – it happened to be on Wednesday the 1st of March – the Emissary sidled up and said, 'Comrade Ah Fat, let's take a stroll together. I need to stretch my legs and I expect you do, also.'

'How did you guess?' Ah Fat answered with a smile.

After they were out of earshot, the Emissary said, 'Comrade, I overheard you being told to go to Kuala Lumpur. What is it like there? I was told about it by my grandfather who was born there but, due quite why I never discovered, he moved to Peking as we called Beijing in those days.'

'Oh, how interesting,' Ah Fat answered in a neutral tone of voice, only showing peripheral interest and purposely not using the almost obligatory use of Comrade.

'I expect in your job when you go to the capital city of Malaya you have lots of sensitive contacts, one way and another ...' and he let his voice trail off.

Ah Fat noticed that the initial 'Comrade' had not been uttered, thereby deliberately ignoring a required courtesy following his own non-use of the word. *Tradecraft still sharp!* he thought happily. After a judicious silence he said, 'Well, yes, in my job I am bound to, "one way and another",' letting the emphasis sink in.

Rapport had been established but it was necessary for both men to let it 'cook' for a while so for about five minutes they walked on without talking. Ah Fat waited for the Emissary to break the silence, wondering how not to let his own double life be thought to exist. The Emissary stopped, turned and faced Ah Fat, looking at him eyeball to eyeball. 'Is there anyone among those who you meet who knows how to get me back to my grandfather's Malayan standing and be ready to advise me how to set about it?'

So I was not wrong! Ah Fat gave himself a pat on the back as he felt it best how to answer neutrally but coded. 'Let me ask you a theoretical question, Emissary. Just suppose such an occurrence could be managed. Just suppose the answer was "yes for you alone". What would your answer be when you enquire if your wife and children can be brought with you or can you go back and fetch them?'

'I would say I had none, even if I had.'

So his mind has been made up already.

'Suppose, again theoretically, I say, yes, I will put your case forward when I am next in KL. What would be your reaction if any of those here who might hear about it wonder why you had particularly asked me and ask you?'

'I would deny it and say something to the effect that I was misunderstood when I had actually been saying how terrible such a happening would be.'

'You mean your northern dialect, your *kwok yi*, not being understood by us southerners who speak *hak ka wa* or *kwang tung wa*?' Hak Ka Wa, the language of the 'hak', guest people, because it was too far from Hong Kong to go back whence they had come straightaway, and Kwang Tung Wa, the language of Canton, also often known as *poon tei wa*, the 'local' language ,when referred to in Malaya. 'In Cantonese you'll be known as

167

Mang Yu not as Meng Ru. Will you be ready to recognise your name then or will your ignorance give you away?'

The Emissary grinned with eyes button bright. 'That is clever of you: yes. I can quickly get used to a southern pronunciation.'

Ah Fat smiled back conspiratorially. 'And, again theoretically of course, how much would you be willing to pay if payment were asked?'

'Only enough for moderate resettlement but, of course, I could answer questions.'

'Of course. It would be rude not to, wouldn't it?' said in a tone of voice that implied more than the words themselves might indicate.

They paced slowly on, turned and Ah Fat pointed to the trees and plants. 'If anyone were to be watching us I am teaching a northerner their names.'

That means he is on my side thought the Emissary.

Ah Fat had another question. 'Let us say, for planning purposes, that the answer is yes. There would be, how shall I call it? an incubation or quarantine period or to be more friendly a "getting-to-know-one-another" period. Any problems there?'

'Problems? I can't see any from my side. No.' The Emissary drifted off into a reverie and Ah Fat did not disturb him. 'None there but there is one condition I feel I must ask, without any disrespect to you.'

'And that would be what?' Ah Fat asked with a delicate tinge of doubt in his voice.

'Apart from you, I would want to travel with a British person, a fluent Chinese speaker.'

When Ah Fat did not make any comment, the Emissary continued 'it would make me feel I was accepted and that any Malay, Chinese or Indian we met would not bother me as he might otherwise. And apart from that, if the person concerned had some official standing he could explain about my lack of required documentation. The Chinese document I carry may not be accepted in Malaya.'

'It probably won't be so your suggestion is an eminently sensible precaution. I will see what I can do for you but here and now there is no guarantee I can succeed. Have you got any spare passport-size photos?'

'Yes, why?'

'Because were one to be asked for in Kuala Lumpur for a temporary document, I could give it to them.'

'I have a couple which I will give you. Now, supposing you do succeed, what happens then? I mean how and where do I meet up with the Englishman? That may not be easy.'

'I'll tell you something else that won't be easy and that is going on south rather than returning north without any suspicion arising among the Politburo members and other interested people. Likewise, just suppose you do get away without any trouble, what will happen if there is a follow-up and you get caught?'

The Emissary grinned sheepishly. 'I hadn't thought of that,' he confessed.

'Just suppose you had to make a journey through the jungle. Would you be ready for that?'

'Have to be if that is the only way.'

Footwear? 'What size are your feet?'

The Emissary told him. 'Say nothing to anybody. Give no hint in speech or body language. Your tradecraft must be flawless at all times.'

The Emissary nodded agreement and they walked back in silence, each immersed in his own thoughts, parting just before camp buildings came into sight.

Early February

Ah Fat and the Bear left for KL as planned on the 6th and in the normal way. Each had two passports, one Thai and one Malayan and they flew from Penang. Before take-off Ah Fat rang Mr Too's private number and, without introducing himself, merely said, 'if you are at home tonight I'll come and take dinner off you.'

'Yes, do that,' and the connection was cut.

Both travellers first went home, to the delight of wives and children who saw far too little of them but accepted it as the salary of both meant that the families had enough to eat, could dress properly, pay the rent and send the children to a good school. 'I have to leave you for a couple of hours,' Ah Fat told his wife while the Bear told his that he had come on holiday so would stay at home. His son, Wang Liang, a sturdy lad of fifteen years, asked after 'Uncle Jason': they had met a couple of months earlier and he had been enthralled by Jason's tricks. 'I haven't seen him since then,' said his father ,'but if I do, I'll tell him you asked.'

Ah Fat told C C Too how the Secretary General, intent on planning what to do next and his move to China, so there was no point in fixing any substitute mole, went on to talk about the Emissary, giving his name as Meng Ru. Too listened avidly, asking for more details than could be given without a much longer debrief. 'On the face of it I can't see any enormous difficulties but, with this new government and the British tuans not in the driving seat for much longer, it might be difficult.'

'But if he is presented as a Surrendered Enemy Personnel would that help?'

Too rubbed his chin as he thought. 'Just can't say. It has never happened before and Communists are barred, aren't they?'

Ah Fat nodded, then said, 'Even if you get a green light to bring him in as an intelligence prize the one other possible snag to getting him here is that he says he will only come if a fluent, Chinese-speaking British man brings him, him and me, to make three of us without considering any escort.'

'That should not be an insurmountable difficulty. Let us, for the sake of argument, say that permission is granted to bring him in. How would you get him out of the camp and what route would you take thereafter?'

'I have given a lot of thought to that, coloured by the request to have a European with him. In all there are three options for the way out. One, we arrange for motor transport on the road nearest. That would mean moving round Gunong Lang onto the road by Kampong Lalang, the same route Jason Rance took with the documents I gave him after I raided the Secretary General's safe, then on by car to KL. The second is to take him to Ha La almost on the border and then join the Betong-Prai road before driving south. The third is by not using the roads but crossing into Malaya by the pass to the west of Gunong Gadong on the border, a two-day walk along the river till a boat is reached and then on down along the headwaters of the Sungei Perak until either a heli point, a fixed-wing airstrip or the road at Grik is reached. That way would make any follow up from the MCP camp much harder so would be the safest. The pass is, in fact, not difficult to find and has a border stone marked with a hammer and sickle in its stem. We engraved it as we passed into Thailand when we had to evacuate Malaya. I was there at the time.

'The third option is, as far as any follow-up in concerned, the safest but it is difficult and remote country and could be dangerous as the thirty-odd guerrillas still on the Wanted List working under Ah Soo Chye, with Tek Miu and Lo See as his lieutenants, operate around there. We are not sure if they have a permanent camp in Thailand or Malaya, whether they operate in three small groups, two larger or one much larger one. I do know that they often stay with the *orang asli*. The leaders have wives in various settlements and it is much easier to be fed there rather than carrying their own rations around. But back to the rescue group: apart from rations, armed escort, communications, etc, what other factors need to be considered?'

'If I could get hold of any Temiar, the *orang asli* I've friendly relations with, I could count on them for advanced warning of anyone we don't want to meet. However, contacting them could take too much time to plan on them. In any case they're furtive as mouse deer and timid as birds and trying to plan anything with them is harder than knitting with eels.'

'It's a thorny one, isn't it?'

'Our next problem is finding the fluent Chinese-speaking European who can meet the bill. You can try the Chinese Affairs

Departments in the various states but even they are not field men, while any university professor will be too unfit even to consider. Not a big choice is there? It would be a pity to have to abort just because we can't find "the" man.'

'We need not find him if there is no agreement from up top, need we?'

'No. True enough,' Ah Fat countered, then asked 'Do you know the Director of Operations? Is he still the one we met when it was fixed that Jason Rance come and collect the paperwork I had for him?'

'Yes, I'll see if I can get an interview. But before we meet him, both of us if he'll agree, what do we do if we can't find a fluent Chinese speaker who can meet the bill working in the Chinese Affairs Department?'

'You know the answer already. Jason Rance!'

7 February

With the Malayanization of administrative posts, civil and military, consequent on the changing political situation, there had been a considerable exit of British staff but it was not for a few years yet that that post of Director of Operation went to a Malay General. However, the current Director's MA was new and when Mr Too rang and asked for an interview, he was quizzed. 'I think you need an official request put in to me by police protocol.'

'Of course. Yes you are quite right. I am sorry I forgot, quite stupid of me,' Mr Too waxed, somewhat overdoing it because, even though his English was of a particularly high standard he did not sound like an Englishman when he spoke. 'But I have the

General's personal word that I can talk to him if needs be.'

'In that case I'll pop in and ask him. Your name again please.'

'Too Chee Chew, a.k.a. C C Too.'

'Please say that all again, more slowly.'

'To make it easy, just say C C Too.'

'Got it! Thanks. The person I took over from didn't tell me this, sorry. Half a mo', please.'

The General came on the line. 'Mr Too. I know you never try and contact me unless it is something valuable that probably no one else has and most likely needs a decision one way or another in a hurry. Am I correct?'

Too chuckled his answer back. 'When have you not been, sir?'

The General chuckled in return. 'Now or face-to-face?'

'Not on the line, please. I have someone who you have met before and you listened to in earnest about a tall man, one who was Ten Foot Long. I am sure you can recall that.'

'Yes, I can indeed. Office or at my place?'

'Sir, the fewer people who see my friend in official places the happier we are.'

'In that case, you know where I live, don't you? Come around just after six, just as daylight is fading.'

There were five of them who sat in front of the desk in the General's office at Flagstaff House, each with a glass of something to their taste in their hand. On arrival they had been met by Colonel James Mason, the Director of Intelligence. He had met Too and Ah Fat before when planning the hand-over of secret

MCP documents to Captain Rance. So irregular had that been that the General and the Colonel had 'not wanted to know' when or how the operation was to be carried out. They shook hands and grinned at each other. Before they sat down the General said, 'Now that last lot's all over and done with, may I congratulate you on your success, Mr Ah Fat?'

Ah Fat bowed his head. 'I was only half, sir. The other half did just as well.'

'Yes, yes. Of course he did. That I know well.' They sat down. The General wiped his brow although there was air-conditioning in his study. He looked tired. 'So, what horrors have you come up with this time?'

Mr Too said, 'Sir, I'll ask Mr Ah Fat to open the bowling,' and, with a nod from the General, Ah Fat told him 'chapter and verse', slowly and coherently. The MA, new to it all, had sat goggle-eyed, his drink forgotten. The General, a tall man with imposing features that, at first blush, were intimidating, yet had a kindly smile soon dispelled that impression. He wore a 'walrus' moustache and had a deep voice. He listened intently, at times raising his eyebrows and looking with wide-opened eyes, at times just staring dully ahead. When the story had finished, the General said, 'Mr Ah Fat, I'm only so glad you and I are on the same side. This needs careful thinking about. On the face of it, this Emissary could be of great use. Of course, until he is fully debriefed we won't know if our mine is gold, silver or bronze but it just has to have some sort of metal in it of use to us. As to whether the government authorities will accept his grandfather's story, or even his grandson's version of it, is something none of us can say. The worst that can happen is a disappointed man being returned to China but once there won't live long, I expect. Too bad, as he is most certainly a brave man. Can you give me his name, please?'

'Yes, and I can give you his photo,' which he handed over.

'That is most useful,' the Colonel said. 'We might get some temporary pass for him.'

Ah Fat asked for a piece of paper and a ball-point and wrote 孟儒, Meng Ru but pronounced Mang Yu in Cantonese, and gave it to Colonel. I'd love to be able to speak, read and write Chinese but I'd never have any time for proper soldiering had I done so, he thought. 'Have you any other points?' he asked Ah Fat.

'Yes sir, my own personal position in the MCP organisation, as a non-voting Politburo member. If both the Emissary and I disappear together there will be an almighty large hue and cry' – I learnt that phrase in school but have never used it till today. Glad I remembered it. 'I can manage the Emissary's disappearance by getting him to say he wants to go back to China as he came, individually, rather than wait and go back with the Secretary General who is waiting for permission to go and live there. I could even volunteer to take him to the nearest road, towards Sadao to cross the border into Malaya at Danok rather than east to Ha La or to Songkhla but I expect they would want, even for protocol purposes, to have more than only me to take him there.'

He was interrupted at that piece of news of Chin Pen's intention of going to China as none had yet heard it. He was asked for more details, gave them, including that Ah Hai, now returned from China cured of his tuberculosis, would be the Deputy Secretary General remaining in Betong. Ah Fat continued.

'I am still held in high regard by Chin Peng who does not in any way suspect what I am doing here. I don't like the task I've set myself but I can't renege now. In other words, once I have returned to Betong I cannot leave of my own accord. That means I cannot escort the Emissary.'

'So how will you get round that problem without him changing his mind?' It was C C Too who asked.

'I have only one option and that is to get the Bear, sorry, my deputy Wang Ming, to take my place but only as far as the border. If there is an affirmative reply to his request I think the Emissary will accept him. I might just be able to start him off if I am allowed to take him to where my printing of that newspaper Red Tidings was done at Ha La. I have to go there in any case as it will no longer be published now that the peace talks have failed and I will have to get the equipment brought back. Even then I'll have a working party with me.'

'Not easy. Let's hope he accepts your deputy,' said the General, adding, 'Now, Mr Too, what about his Chinese-speaking Englishman? Any ideas?'

I'll answer this in a roundabout way. 'Sir, the Chinese Affairs Departments in the states and here in HQ must have Europeans who can manage the language but their jobs are sedentary. They may be fit enough for a set of tennis or a game of squash but other than that, no, they won't be fit enough to cover the ground that we have chosen.'

'Not even being met by car on the nearest road?' queried the General.

'They will have to meet the Emissary in Malaya at the border but even though he came from China on a passport, the countries he passed through were Communist but Malaya surely won't accept a Chinese passport with no visa.'

'Then that puts the road journey right out of play?' said the General. 'It looks like being the jungle or nothing. Yet quite how we fix his documents if he is allowed in is something we here can't answer. That means the jungle route is the one we have to take whether we or he likes it or not.'

'Yes, sir. It is,' said Ah Fat. 'Most probably the Emissary is not a jungle man, almost bound not to be but he is determined enough otherwise he'd never have reached Betong from China the way he did. But he will need escorting: there is only one man I know who is a canny jungle escort and a Chinese speaker of the standard needed.'

'You don't have to tell me who you have in mind, do you?' asked with an innocent smile.

'You know as well as I do, sir. There's only man who can do the job, Captain Jason Rance.'

'Yes, I agree with you on that but he is no longer a Captain,' said the General. 'I insisted on his promotion to Major after trying to persuade that Ten Foot Long to surrender and all the other outstanding jungle work he and his men have done,' *although, sadly, no bravery award was forthcoming.*

At that very moment the Major under consideration was again doing something that, as far as others knew, had not been done before quite like he was doing it. A well-known Communist Terrorist was reported by some 'friendly' rubber tappers to be due to meet them for rations during a period covering four days. The rubber estate was extensive and the cover crop was almost nil so there was no place to hide. Any of the Security Forces who laid an ambush in the area would be doomed to failure and, indeed, any guerrilla could be seen were he to contact the tappers so only a chance patrol might be lucky in a contact. However, there was a small stream running though part of the estate and, as the ground there was marshy it had no trees in it but unkempt undergrowth. It had been decided that Major Rance would take five men and lie up in the undergrowth and, if successful in capturing the guerrilla, Rance's language skills could speedily alert battalion HQ before any of the guerrilla's compatriots knew he had been captured.

The approach march was long and tortuous to avoid three sets of labour lines. In order not to give his position away by smelling where they had defecated, all six of them had taken a double dose of medicine to make them constipated. Extra water bottles were carried and hard tack only taken to avoid cooking. The group settled in before dawn on Day 1 and, while it was still light and before any tappers arrived, made sure there were no signs of their entry into the undergrowth. It was presumed that the tappers would put their stuff in the scrub and the guerrilla, more than one most likely, would come along the stream early in the morning and leave, with their booty at dusk. Mosquitoes were in profusion and face veils rather than repellent were used to avoid the smell. It rained hard on the first three evenings to the men's excruciating discomfort.

There was great relief among the ambush when they heard rustling at about nine o'clock on the fourth morning and they discerned a tapper furtively putting some stuff on the ground just inside the undergrowth. The tapper did not notice the Gurkhas who waited with the utmost expectancy all day. It was the sheerest bad luck that, although the guerrillas did come late on that last day, they had one ploy that no one had previously considered. A couple of dogs roamed ahead of them and, on finding the Gurkhas hiding in the undergrowth, set up such a aggressive barking that the guerrillas knew that it had to be someone hostile hiding there so long after tapping hours so they turn back unseen by the ambush.

'We nearly had them, didn't we,' said Jason. 'You did wonderfully well to stay so quiet in such unpleasant circumstances and I am proud of you. Time to go back. Pack up and on our way. Without any radio contact the vehicle should have come to pick us up by 1600 hours at the labour lines, a mile down the road.' He looked at his watch. 'It'll be there already.'

'Saheb, what she we do with the stuff the tapper has left lying around?' asked one of the men.

'I have a wicked idea. Finish any water in your water bottles and get rid of it naturally as you pass the stuff. That's the best way to relieve our frustration.'

The CO of 1/12 Gurkha Rifles, Lieutenant Colonel Eustace Vaughan, had served in 3/12 GR during the war. He was one of many Indian Army British officers transferred to the Royal Artillery after Partition before making his escape to command 1/12 GR, so he knew nobody. He was a small, barrel-chested, bouncy man, round-faced, bushy-browed and clean-shaven, with a deep voice. He handled Gurkhas well but his handling of British officers was apt to be clumsy. He had been CO since 31 July of the previous year.

The out-going CO had written the all-important annual confidential reports for the officers, brought forward because of the change in command. The then Captain Rance was graded 'C', average: with a 'C' grading no officer could expect to rise above the rank of major. Remarks on Rance's operational ability were cattily clouded because of the fiasco during one operation which was in no way his fault and a difficult interview with the Royal Air Force's top brass over bombing or not bombing guerrilla camps. 'Yes, he can be good but I advise you to watch him. He would not have been commissioned pre-war.'

It was less than a month ago that the Director of Intelligence had rung him about Captain Rance being 'needed'[12] - he did not know what for – so he was not best pleased to get yet another unexpected phone call from Kuala Lumpur, this time from the Director of Operations himself. 'Eustace, you are a patient man aren't you?' was the strange opening remark.

'Well, sir, one has to be in any army job if one does not want a gastric ulcer, doesn't one?'

'Surely so. I have the unusual task of having to steal an officer of yours once again and I am ringing in person for two reasons. The first is that I overcame your Brigadier's categorically telling you not to promote Captain Rance and made a personal request with the Military Secretary's branch in the MOD. Rather stepping

12 See *Operation Red Tidings*.

on your toes but needs be *et cetera*.'

'Understood, sir. I can't really cavil at that can I?'

'No good if you did, Eustace. Now listen. Hush-hush. I have just learnt, today as ever is, that there is an intelligence plum, a ripe and juicy one, that has fallen off its tree but has yet to be picked up by us. If we don't get hold of it soon we'll lose it and that would be a great pity. Whatever your thoughts of Major Rance happen to be, and I can guess both pros and cons, you may not yet realise his Chinese linguistic ability. I doubt there is another European his equal, certainly at sounding like a Chinese, in the country. I personally need him as he is the only man who fits the bill. He will require a small group of men, say four or five, one of whom is to be a radio operator. I cannot give you more details now but please do your best to lend him to me.'

He's got me by the short and curlies, hasn't he? 'Sir, there is no real difficulty. He is due home leave very soon and I have to appoint another officer to take over his company. While he is away I'll get his Company 2 ic to concentrate on getting the administration shipshape before the new man takes over. Any idea of how long Rance will be needed?'

'I'd like to think not more than a week or ten days at the outside. What I want is him up here pronto to be briefed, go back, prepare himself than to disappear over the horizon.'

'What shall I tell people this end, sir?'

'Oh, let's see. A general operational and intelligence briefing about his methods for the updated pamphlet of jungle warfare we are writing for the Federation Armed Forces when we finally hand over to them. He's done enough for a personal debriefing in depth.'

'I'll ensure he does what you want, sir. Have you anything more for me?' The question went unanswered as the General had already put his phone back on its cradle.

Colonel Vaughan had been influenced against Rance by his predecessor's report. He had also taken a dislike to him. The reason that no one could guess was that the Colonel's dead younger brother, whom he had idolised as being a better all-rounder than he himself had been, was not only the same age as Jason Rance but also somehow resembled him, was killed in the war whereas Rance had survived. *The wrong man died* was a recurring and secret mantra, acting as a recurring grudge in the senior's approach to the junior. In Gurkha regiments numbers of officers were too few for the junior in a personality clash to avoid discrimination without leaving the regiment. Rance had no intention of so doing.

10 February
So what do you think of all that, Major Rance?' Colonel Mason asked after giving him the whole story, Ah Fat having already told him his side of affairs, about the Bear standing in for him. It was a week after the two Chinese had left Betong. 'It really does look as if this whole business hangs on you personally. You can't say "no" can you?' There were in his office, which was wired off from the others. 'So far, so good?'

'Sir, being on a short list of one brooks so argument,' Jason said with a wry smile. 'So far so good, sir, as far as taking the job on and dealing with this Emissary man is concerned. On the reverse of the coin there is guerrilla activity to be considered as well. Without a very much larger force, I mean were we to meet all thirty of the notional guerrillas still on the Wanted List, I would need a minimum of two platoons. But for this task I don't want to be cluttered with all the administrative complications of having so many men to look after. In my mind's eye I was thinking of at least two escorts, gunmen if you like, and a radio operator.' He broke off and pursed his lips in thought. He turned to his boyhood friend.

'How long can the Bear and his few men be out of camp without raising suspicion of any unauthorised activity, shall I call it?' He spoke in English.

'Yes, I see what you mean and why you ask. I think the longest he can be away safely is the time it takes to meet up with you, hand the Emissary over and return.'

The implications of that were not lost on any of the listeners.

'So I'll be on my own in hostile territory. The map reading won't be hard, both ways just go along the course of the river. But meeting any hostiles puts another slant on matters. I can manage the language side of meeting them but that is not enough. I need to calm any initial suspicions if we do happen to meet head on. I think I can manage that but I may break military etiquette if I do.'

'You intrigue me. Explain please.'

'Sir, of course you will remember how we managed the follow-up of the killers of Colonel Ridings that was named *Operation Red Tidings*.'

'No need to ask. I most certainly do.'

'So you will also remember that four of Ten Foot Long's

people came over to my side, one of whom was the man detailed to look after his personal radio, the one eventually that led to his demise. I will take two of them, put them in CT uniform if I can, otherwise merely to wear a starred cap, and they will be my screen and liaison with any hostile.' He did not say that he and his Gurkha gunman and radio operator would also were similar headgear. *Something about some Geneva Convention will be flung in my face if I suggest it.*

'Are you sure they won't turn?' the Colonel asked, doubt evident in his tone of voice.

'Sure as I can be, sir. They will be fully dependent on me for a return to their families. They'll be lost in north Malaya.'

'I'll go along with that. Call them a "Q" Party.' He broke off, obviously in some distress. 'Sir, I must ask to go to a lavatory. I have just come back for four days of enforced constipation hiding in the middle of a rubber estate where such an operation would be given away by any smell of human ordure. I had to take a laxative on my return, all of my small group did, and only now is it working.'

He was shown where to go and came back, looking much more comfortable. 'And where you successful?' the Colonel asked.

'Sir, we would have been had the guerrillas not had a dog to go in front of them as a sentry. As soon as it smelt us it barked so gave us away. After such an effort by my men, yes, it was disappointing.'

He never mentions himself, does he?

'Now back to the "Q" Party: I'll fix it when I get back to Seremban.' Seeing a map on the wall Jason went over to look at

185

it. He found the Sungei Perak and traced it up to the Thai border, noting Gunong Gadong. 'No crossing the border for me and my men, that's correct, isn't it?'

Before the Colonel could answer Ah Fat broke in with 'there's a border stone marked with a hammer and sickle in its stem. We put it there as we passed through on our way to Thailand. It is a good reference point and easy to find. That could be a good RV as the Bear knows where it is.'

'Useful,' said Colonel Mason and continued, 'No crossing the border whatsoever. This venture is hairy enough already without anymore whiskers being added. Unwanted whiskers could well be meeting up with the opposing group.'

To the Colonel's surprise Jason grinned and said something in Chinese to Ah Fat who grinned back. 'Sorry sir, that was rude of me. What I started to say was that I can make jungle noises that Ah Fat can tell the Bear to listen out for.' He smiled delightfully as though enjoying a joke. 'He's bound to recognise one noise I make as it is unique.'

'I don't get you,' said the Colonel, a tad gruffly, not fully understanding what Jason was trying to say.

'Listen, sir,' and he cupped his hands and made some startlingly realistic cuckoo noises. 'Why is that unique?' the Colonel queried.

'Because there are no cuckoos in Malaya or rather, to be accurate, members of the cuckoo family that are in Malaya don't "cuck". When I used it to keep distance with my people the guerrillas heard it, knew it was not a Malayan bird and quickly left. In fact I was the only cuckoo there was,' and he gave a burst of laughter. 'I can also coo like a dove but that doesn't carry so far,' and he gave a lifelike call with his cupped hands,

Colonel Mason asked how such esoteric pieces of jungle lore had come his way and Jason explained, 'I learnt how to make the noise when a cadet at the Indian Military Academy to use as a recognition signal on patrol exercises in the Tons Valley. I "cuckoo-ed" to such good effect that a real bird answered and the patrol I wanted to call in to me went the other way towards the bird. By the time I had made several calls the poor fellows were going round in circles. Were they mad when they met up with me!'

'What other noises can you make?'

Jason answered by belling like a deer, first the male then the female, followed by the call of the 'dawn-and-dusk' bird, the *burong tetabu*, the great-eared nightjar. 'Ah Fat will tell his Bear to listen out for any one of those noises, each set to be three longs, two shorts followed by three longs.'

'Well, I'll be damned,' exploded the Colonel, shaking his head in amazement.

Jason continued, 'So to clear my mind, my old friend the Bear with a group of his men will bring the Emissary and meet me there then I and my men carry on down river?'

'Yes, just that, in outline. And before you go any further it now strikes me as it must have already struck you but you have yet to mention it, from just before till just after your suggested timings, there will be no other troops at all in the area. You must not have the worry of meeting any of our own people.'

'Thank you, sir. I was coming on to that,' said Jason, then asked, 'What is this pin here, quite a way up the Sungei Perak?'

Colonel Mason went to look at it. 'That is a Police Field Force fort, Fort Tapong.'[13]

'And are there police boats that can go farther up river?'

'Yes, they can be arranged. Sometimes their engines break down and their propellers break their shear pins but with a fitter aboard with plenty of shear pins that should not be a problem, especially if the engine has had an overhaul before.'

'The General is pretty keen on this, isn't he?' Jason asked.

'Yes, he is. He is still not sure whether the civil authorities will accept such a person but he feels that their reaction will be positive rather than negative if the man can be shown as being an intelligence bonanza and if he is brought in without a great fuss.'

He was interrupted by the phone ringing. He went over to answer it and Jason heard him say, 'excellent news, sir. So the civil boys are happy with what we're planning provided a government representative is with him from the moment he steps over the border. Yes, sir, I'll tell Major Rance who's here with me now.' He rang off.

'All systems green, Major Rance. You're on. Let us sit round the table, us three and work out a time and space programme, so beloved by military planners and what they make much of at Staff College.'

Within half an hour they had an outline plan. D Day, the day the Emissary was to start his journey, was fixed for 20 February. Today was Friday the 10th so that would give Ah Fat enough time

---

13 Your author was invited to spend Christmas day 1962 with the Police Field Force in Fort Tapong.

both to conclude his job in KL for the Secretary General and for the Emissary to start his journey on the 20th.

That should be plenty of time to brief the Emissary – they decided not to use his name for security reasons – and to get the Bear and his men rations without seeming to, not an easy task. During that period Major Rance would return, get his men ready – he said that he, his three escorts and a radio man were enough – and bring them to KL. He thought he would need five days for the journey – 'it's unknown territory for me and there are some inquisitive guerrillas to evade' – and he would like first of all to have an air recce in an Auster on Sunday the 19th, please for me and two others. I'm sure you'll help out if the air boys get sticky, sir' – and he and at least one other fly up the river, past Fort Tapong and, with his map, locate Gunong Gadong. He would like a heli for his team to fly to Fort Tapong the next day, the 20th, and one police boat to be there to take them up as far as the boat could go. That would be all in one day. They would take eight days' hard tack and scrounge meals in KL and Tapong.

For their return could there be a boat at the place they disembarked at, or two come to that if the police wanted an escort – and that would apply to the way up also – on the 28th and a chopper warned to stand by to pick them up from Fort Tapong for the 29th but only to be confirmed on re-reaching Fort Tapong, so it could be the 1st of March. 'On the way up I think the chopper should land as far away from inquisitive eyes as possible, don't you, sir?'

'Yes, I agree. I will arrange for transport to take you back to the battalion. In case it is too late I'll get the Gurkha Engineers at

Sungei Besi to look after you for the night. There will be someone to tell you about it, with transport, after you have deplaned.'

'Thank you, sir. That is all in the best case. May I turn to the worst case, being intercepted by the guerrillas and taking casualties? What I would like is to have a rear link close to you. There are some Gurkha Signals men who work nearby, surely. What I plan is a nightly sitrep with our grid reference. If you hear nothing it could be because our set has gone "dis" or that the set has been shot off the signaller's back. I'll take a Very pistol and green and red flares. When I hear an overfly I'll fire whichever colour is needed. If it is red can you arrange a stand-by group somehow to come to our aid?'

There was no need to go into details now but, 'yes, yes, yes,' came the replies.

The Director asked Ah Fat is he had anything to add. 'No, sir. I have yet to make up my mind quite how to play it my end but play it I will. If the Emissary does change his mind I'll have to get my Bear to disappear on some mission or other and get a message through to Mr Too. I can't think of any other way.'

'Any more before we finish off?' the Colonel asked.

'No, sir. I'll just say farewell to my childhood friend and leave you.'

'Before you go, let's have an operational code word for this. Any suggestions?'

'How about Operation Emissary,' suggested Ah Fat.

'Okay. That'll be it and Top Secret also.'

Before Ah Fat and C C Too left Jason and his boyhood gave each other a hug and wished each other well. The Colonel signed

Jason's pass and he left. Back in the car park he found his driver. 'Sorry to keep you so long, Ustad. Back now to the battalion.' He climbed in and was silent all the way back, deep in thought. *Unusual for him* the driver said to himself.

Ah Fat also left, did what he had to do for Chin Peng, not forgetting to buy a pair of civilian-type jungle boots for the Emissary, and got back to Betong where he reported in, once more to the Secretary General's satisfaction. That evening the Emissary strolled round, knocked on the door of Ah Fat's room, making sure he was unseen and, without being invited in, entered quietly. 'I have come to hear the result of your deliberations.'

'Sit down and pay great attention to what I have for you. Some of it will, I hope, please you; some, I fear, will not. But you have been allowed to go to Kuala Lumpur where you can expect gentle treatment.'

'That's wonderful news. We'll be together going there and when I am asked questions.'

'Not so fast. This is the bit I fear you will not please you ...' and all necessary details were given him, why Ah Fat was unable to go with him, why the Bear could only take him to the border, why the journey was to be the one through the jungle, how he was to be joined by two one-time guerrillas, two Gurkhas – the Emissary had never heard of such people – and 'the British Chinese speaker will be my boyhood friend, one I regard as a brother, who speaks Chinese like any Chinese person, who can write the script, whose name is Major Jason Rance and who I know as *Shandung P'aau*. He is a skilled jungle operator. You can trust him implicitly.' Ah Fat let that sink in and then asked, 'So do you still want to go or shall I cancel it and let you go back to China, back to your grim, artificial life?' Ah Fat rubbed his hands together as he sometimes did when under stress.

'So, if you don't go with me, who will look after me when I get to Kuala Lumpur?' which he pronounced *Ka Lum Po*.

'There is one named Too Chee Chew whom I know well. He is wise and awaits your arrival with eagerness. I guarantee you will be in safe hands.'

'Then I accept your conditions. Thank you for your efforts. I will now go back,' and he stood up.

'Before you go, try on these boots I have brought you to wear in the jungle. They should fit.'

'So that's why you asked about the size of my feet!' said with a smile. He tried them on and they fitted perfectly. 'A good omen.'

'Yes, take them off and leave them here.'

Before the Emissary left Ah Fat told him the date he was expected to leave. 'And before then I'll have worked out exactly how you will leave this place without any suspicion.'

Next morning Ah Fat and his Bear had a long session together. The Bear suggested that Ah Fat pretend to go and show the Emissary the place in Ha La where his newspaper *Red Tidings* was produced and let both of them drift off down south towards the border. 'I will have a man with me both ways and before then I will manage to go to Sadao and, under various pretexts, get enough to eat to last him to the border and us back again. You will have to buy stuff in such a way that there is no suspicion about people asking "why so much?" also don't forget he'll need quite a bit more for his journey on down south. See if we have a spare haversack to let him have rather than buying a new one.' A sudden thought came into his mind: *tradecraft* 'Buy a few tins of Thai sardines and a jar of Ovaltine to give to Meng Ru so if meets any Malayan guerrillas he can offer them one as "a present from Thailand" so allay any possible suspicion he has not come from where he says he has.'

Late on the evening of the 10th as soon as Jason reached Seremban he called in on Ismail Mubarak, the Head of Special Branch. The two of them had had excellent relations since the battalion had come to Malaya back in 1948. Jason told his driver to go back to the lines, have a meal, tell the Mess that Jason was back and ask the Duty Driver to come and collect him within half an hour. 'You've been hanging around all day, Ustad. Time you were free.'

The driver thanked him, thinking that not all the British sahebs were so thoughtful.

Moby, hearing someone at the door, went to investigate and greeted Jason warmly. 'Jason, what can I do for you? Not often I see you these days. Come in and have a beer.'

'Moby, no beer thanks but I'd love the largest and hottest and sweetest cup of tea you can provide.'

They went inside. 'Moby, I need your help for such a top secret and unexpected operation, so hush-hush I can't even tell myself!' and both of them laughed.

'Can you never be serious, Jason?'

'Sometimes. Now please listen. C C Too is on this, the Director of Operations and his staff and my old boyhood friend,

Ah Fat, whom you know.'

Jason broke off as his tea was brought in.

'Nobody else?'

'Yes, Moby, you. Joking apart this is what has happened …' and Jason gave him the background to the Emissary's visit to Betong and his wish to change sides. 'Planning has to be one hundred per cent safe from Ah Fat's personal side of affairs. The Emissary wanted him to go all the way to KL but that being impossible I am the lamb being offered to the slaughter as we plough our way down the Sungei Perak, hoping not to bump into the CT who are still in the area.' Jason was careful in not using the man's name.

Ismail Mubarak looked grave. 'Quite some task. You seem to be in the habit of being given them.'

Jason nodded as Moby asked him how many men he was planning to take with him.

'Five not counting me. Two of them will be my gunman-cum-batman and a Gurkha operator and other two will be – and this is where you come into it – Goh Ah Wah and Kwek Leng Ming.'

'But why them and not Gurkhas, Jason?'

'Moby, I do not want to take as big a force as a platoon. I am relying on speed but were we to meet any CT, my two ex-guerrillas, wearing caps with red stars and a shirt that looks like one of theirs, will provide me with enough time to sum up the military problem, shoot and scoot or just scoot, kind of effort.'

'Yes, I see your point. In other words, you can keep the initiative that way.'

'That's about it, yes, Moby. Now here comes my "but": what

I am about to ask you is forbidden by military convention. I and my two Gurkhas also need to wear similar hats and shirts, not the trousers particularly. If I were to suggest this or even tell my CO he would make a row, tell me I'd be for the military high jump if I wore such kit so that means I don't tell him. Nor do you. Please, not even your friend C C Too.'

Moby nodded his agreement. 'In that case I'll give those two men the kit, tell them it's spare and not mention who it is actually for. Okay?'

'Correct. Now, arming and rationing them. They can carry what arms they prefer or what you allow them to but for food, I am taking ten days hard tack, tea, biscuits and high-protein chocolate. It won't be popular with my three nor, probably with your two but, needs be where the devil wotsits, or something like that.'

Moby grinned. 'You're a hard man at times, Jason, aren't you?' and without waiting for an answer, went on to say that he had funds for that. 'If you agree, I'd really like to ask C C Too if he has funds to give my two something extra.'

'How long will it take to get hold of those two men? Can you call them here and now?'

'Give me ten minutes and they'll be here.' He called the duty policeman and gave the orders and ten minutes later both men came into the house. They seemed delighted to see Jason who, as normal, cracked a joke with them and got them laughing. He told them he had an important task to do and asked them if they were willing to go with him for ten days. Before they gave their answers he said that the food would be like it was when they went to deliver Tan Fook Leong's radio. 'Can you manage that again, please?'

'If we can buy some extra rations on our return, yes we will go with you.'

'I'll arrange that and thank you. I will fully brief you once we have started but before that I'll come and fix details,' and off they went, back to their lines.

'Give C C Too a bell now, will you and let me ask him.'

Moby rang and got an answer. 'Sir, it's Ismail Mubarak here talking to Major Rance. He'd like a word with you, please. A very quick one.' Moby handed the phone over to Jason who said he was sorry to bother him at this late hour. 'I have personally spoken to the two men I plan to take other than my Gurkhas and they are happy to go with me. However, when told they would only eat hard tack for ten days they both asked if they could have some money to make up what they had missed in the food line. Rashly I said I'd arrange it so I am putting my word in before Moby asks you officially.'

'Major Rance, you are one cool operator. Hand him over,' which Jason did and permission was granted.

Jason finished his tea. 'Moby that was great. I hear my vehicle outside and I'm ready to go back. I'll let you have firm details as soon as I can.'

Moby escorted him to the front door and they said their farewells. Jason got in the vehicle and told the driver to go back to the battalion. He thanked the driver, went to the Mess, bathed, changed, had a hurried meal and went to bed, thoughts churning in his head. He hardly slept a wink and woke up tired.

Monday 13 February

'I don't like my company commanders being pulled out from their normal jobs for "funnies",' fumed the CO, with Jason standing to attention in front of him, fixedly looking ahead. 'Well, what have you to say for yourself?' Jason had been called from his office to report to the CO at exactly 10 o'clock.

This is not how it's meant to be going! 'Sir, if you are suggesting that I pre-planned any of this without your knowledge and behind your back not only are you wrong but by showing so little faith in me tell the Director of Operations to cancel his operation and get me posted to 2/12 GR' – *and slap my wrist at the same time* – 'if I have misunderstood you, I apologise and cancel my last transmission.'

The CO sighed deeply and played with some pencils in front of him on his desk. He said nothing – *counting to ten so he won't burst out again?* – shook his head and started again. 'Major Rance, yes, now I come to think of it you could not have started this lark as you were in that rubber estate for four days and so were out of circulation, weren't you.' The CO had suddenly remembered that the Director of Operations had specifically said that the intelligence plum had been 'dropped from the tree' that day. 'I will still ask you what have you to say for yourself, in answer to being summoned by the Great Man in person so there was no need to have gone off into an unseemly huff at being asked.'

'Sir, I will tell you my task. I have been given it as there is a man from the Chinese communist party now in Thailand who wants to come over to our side and one of his conditions is that he needs a Chinese-speaking escort in case he meets Security Forces on the way down who won't recognise his documents. The chosen escape route from Baling down into Malaya is through the jungle to the Malay-Thai border where I have been asked to meet him and bring him down the line of the Sungei Perak as far as the top boat point where a Police Field Force boat will take us to Fort Tapong to be helied out to KL. Thence I come back here, sir. Estimated time of journey is five days up and five days back.'

The CO mulled that over. 'You say "us". Who are "us"?'

'Corporal Kulbahadur Limbu, Lance Corporal Minbahadur Gurung, as radio operator, Rifleman Chakrabahadur Rai, my batman and two of the men who went with me to try and get Ten Foot Long to surrender.'

'The General has only asked for you, for no one else. Let him work out who "us" are.' The CO looked searchingly at his junior, a smirk playing on his lips. 'And you really believe six can manage? That no back-up is needed? That you can manage any casualties? That your two Chinese won't turn against you?' He pursed his lips, shook his head and, with a small smiling malice shining in his eyes, said flatly, 'No, I won't risk my Gurkhas, even only three of them, on such a wild-goose chase. But I can't stop you, can I, as the General has personally asked for you? So, Rance, I do not agree with who you mean by "us".'

Jason braced his back as he did when angry, this time inwardly seething. *Don't answer back. Let him think he's won.* 'I cannot comment on that, sir. Have I your permission to leave?'

'Yes, and may the Lord have mercy on your soul if you have misjudged your prowess. When are you due to leave here?'

'I have planned for the 19th, sir.'

'In that time you will hand your company over to Major Kent and when you come back I'll send you on longer leave. Six months in England should be good for you' – *if you come back.* 'You are dismissed.'

Major Rance saluted and went to his A Company to tell people about the hand over and his departure.

5

February 1956

Every *orang asli* settlement, or *ladang*, was a masterpiece of making houses with nothing but bamboo and rattan and the Temiar ladang belonging to Headman Kerinching was no exception. He was the most powerful headman west of the central range of mountains that divide Malaya. Middle-aged, he was dark-skinned, with a flattened nose, a deep frown, creased lips and a receding hair line. His large eyes were two stones of shining hard coal.

The ladang was an hour's walk from the Sungei Klian, a small tributary of the Sungei Temenggor – itself a tributary of the Sungei Perak – about thirty 'air' miles south from the Malay-Thai border, roughly in the middle of the area the rump of the guerrillas tried to dominate. To reach it from the river one got out of the boat at the remains of a pre-war 'halting bungalow' used by the tin dredgers and now in disrepair. Twenty minutes later an old open-space tin mining area was crossed and some way beyond that, there was the ladang.

That particular evening, it happened to be the 1st of February 1956 and had that been mentioned it would have meant nothing at all to any of them, was a festive occasion as the three guerrillas most liked were present. They were Ah Soo Chye, the senior guerrilla and his two lieutenants, Tek Miu and Lo See, and a small armed escort. The Temiar liked them because they treated them well, not as many Malays did by looking down on and being inclined to bully them. Headman Kerinching had previously been given a shot gun by Ah Soo Chye. The three senior men sometimes stayed together and at other times operated separately against the Security Forces in the far north of Malaya. The reason they were there was because Zhong Han San, leader of Killer Squad in south Thailand, had been sent down on a rare visit to check that the MCP presence was as active as it could be expected to be. He was a sadist, a bully and had perverted tastes yet could be pleasant if he wanted to be. The hard-faced hitmen of his Killer Squad were unsuited to think kindly of the Temiar.

The three senior guerrillas, with their few followers, spent much time in ladangs with a 'wife' in most of them. Temiar women normally did not marry until they knew the father of the child they were carrying as the language reflected, *kuäsh,* a child when the mother did know the father and *papõöd* when she did not. Neither did the Temiar normally use names but relationships instead – such as *akoody*, elder uncle, *keloq,* elder sibling, *pöq* younger sibling – apart from the senior man Ah Soo Chye, who was known by the respectful name of *Tata,* literally 'old man' but also a designation of respect. Fictitious relations were sometimes used with strangers.

After their evening meal the people of the ladang had assembled, lit by a fire to one side. Everyone was happy and the whole atmosphere harmonious. Bare-buffed maidens sat on one side and sang. Their voices were not inharmonious and the pieces of bamboo they beat on a log as an orchestra produced an enjoyable, simple clunking cadence in time with their song and dancers' footsteps as a line of young men, wearing only a loin cloth, with a bunch of cut grass tucked in at the back and a crown of long grass on their heads – left, left, right, right, round and round. Some of the elder women followed the men.

One of the elder dancers wandered out of the line in a trance, mesmerised by the repetitive plunking noise, fell to the ground, writhing. The three Chinese leaders looked on, wondering whether to be amused, worried or to ignore what was happening. They saw an elderly man, followed by three others, younger, leave the audience and go to the writhing man. 'Who is that elderly person?' Zhong Han San asked Ah Soo Chye who, in turn had to ask because what had happened was so unusual he had never seen it before. He knew simple Temiar and the some of the Temiar spoke a little Malay.

'He is the *senoi bar halaaq*. He has gone to cure him.'

None of the three Chinese knew the words but presumed, correctly, he was the shaman. They saw the shaman grab hold of the writhing man's head and pull strongly, once, pause, twice, pause ... and wait ... and then the last pull. This time the man stopped writhing, got to his feet and moved off, unsteadily. The Chinese did not know that only three pulls were allowed and if the third had not been instantly successful death would have followed.

A group of men bearing blowpipes and slinging a wild boar from a pole with its feet tied with vines to prevent it falling off came into the firelight and put their prize on the ground. They were led by a small man with peppercorn hair, probably in his thirties. A man sitting next to the three Chinese asked if they knew the Temiar name for a blowpipe. He only knew the Malay, *sampitan*. 'No, we call it *blau*.' He shouted out for the leader to bring his over to teach the three Chinese the names of the outer casing, *log*, the inner tube, *tenaq blau* and the mouthpiece, *tabog*.

'We'll try and remember,' Lo See said.

Zhong Han San was interested in how much damage a blowpipe dart could cause otherwise he was disdainful of all else he and his group had seen.

Ah Fat and his loyal Bear returned to Betong as planned and the next day, the 12th of February, met the Secretary General, at least Ah Fat did. He gave a heartening report about Chan Man Yee not having left anything incriminating and also brought news of British troop reductions now that conditions were much quieter. 'I also heard that there will be an increase in the Royal Malay Regiment but I don't know how many battalions.'

Chin Peng shrugged that off. 'Won't affect us here at all,' he said in a scoffing tone of voice. Ah Fat asked to be excused, he was always ultra polite even though he had to force himself into being so, and went to his quarter, fully expecting the Emissary to visit him before long. Nor was he disappointed.

Ah Fat had a book on the birds of Malaya which he opened and put on his table, 'in case we are disturbed.' Meng Ru was almost beside himself for details and seeing Ah Fat was not looking doleful presumed he had good news, saying so.

'Yes, as far as the Malayan authorities are concerned, you

have permission to go and meet them. They will make some sort of card for you and you will be given it when you meet them. They do not want you to have it on your way down because of security for your sake if you were captured by the Communists, here or in Malaya. Without it you could say you lost your way but whether they would believe that is another matter. However, in case of such an eventuality, which we all hope won't happen, they agree that it is crucial you have an Englishman with you.' He didn't bother with other British nationalities, *keep it simple!* 'You didn't come armed so you can't go armed. Don't worry. Your escort will be armed. You will wear a khaki shirt and a cap with a red star in the front as cover. You will be guarded at all times so there is no need to worry.' Ah Fat was 'adlibbing' but he knew Jason's methods well enough to be sure of what he said.

'Now for some disappointing information: the planning authorities have decided that I had better not leave this camp for quite some time nor in any way be connected with your disappearance, for obvious personal security reasons. That goes for Wang Ming also. For the Chinese-speaking Englishman I have got my schoolboy friend, an army Major, to come and meet you at the border, on the Gunong Gadong pass ...'

'The what pass?'

'Sorry, of course you don't know the names. The place I mentioned that has the hammer and sickle badge carved on a boundary stone. Just take it that the Major cannot under any circumstances whatsoever step foot on Thai territory. He will lead you down towards a big river, along a track to where the river is deep enough for boats with outboard engines to reach. They will take you downriver to where a helicopter will pick you up and fly you to Kuala Lumpur. So far, so good?'

Meng Ru cogitated for a while. 'Is the Englishman as good in the jungle as you say he is in speaking Chinese? Are you sure that is the only way I can get there?'

'First, there is none better than the Major, both for the language and for the jungle. You are not a jungle man so leave everything, everything there is, to him. As far as the route is concerned, I am one hundred per cent sure it is the only safe way and, moreover, if you say "no, that is not for me", I will somehow have to abort the operation so stop the English Major from making an unnecessary journey.'

Meng Ru cogitated further. 'How much of a risk is there going this way?'

I could strangle him if he says no. Ah Fat answered bluntly. 'There are always risks but this way fewer than any other and more comfortable way. And I could ask you, how many risks were there in your coming all this way from China? You managed then, didn't you? Six months, wasn't it, on the way? Come on, this is only for maximum of ten days.'

Meng Ru had the grace to look abashed. 'I accept. I will go as you say.'

They shook hands on it. 'Now we must plan how best you can disappear without raising any suspicions.'

Major Rance left the CO's office in, unusually for him, a vile temper, completely baffled by the refusal to let even three men go with him, gritting his teeth and looking like a man possessed.

What has come over the fellow? he wondered. *Had a row with his old woman? He can't think that I'd be such an idiot to do anything of this nature behind his back!* On his way to his company office he answered salutes punctiliously but those saluting him knew something was wrong, wrong, wrong. His company clerk saw the black look on his OC's face. *Not like him to look like that, is it?* he said to himself as he turned back to the file he had open in front of him.

Rance, taking a grip of himself, sat down to look at his in-tray and a few minutes later the office runner came in with a mug of hot tea and put it on Jason's table. 'Major saheb. I have put an extra lot of sugar in this for you because from the look on your face when you came back from seeing the Commanding saheb I saw you needed it.'

Jason was enormously touched. '*Keta*, you were quite right but with this inside me I'll be fine once more.' He lifted the mug and took a sip. 'Yes, you have had it made just as I like it.' He looked at his watch. 'Please give the 2 ic saheb my salaams.'

The office runner saluted and within a short while the Gurkha Captain came in. 'Saheb, you sent for me.'

'Gurkha Captain saheb, I did. Please be seated and listen to what I have to tell you. The first thing is that during the next week I am to hand over A Company to Major Kent saheb. After that I have to go on a secret operation, just for ten days, and on my return the Commanding saheb has just told me I must take my six months' home leave.'

'Saheb, we will all be sorry to see you go but if you are due home leave you have to take it.'

Jason made a little bow as an answer and continued, 'and my second point is about the operation' and out came the outline story. 'Why I have been chosen is that the man who wants to defect will only do so if a Chinese-speaking Englishman escorts him and the General saheb wants to use me and my Chinese language ability for that reason. Saheb, you and I have been in the battalion together now since 1948 and we know each other well enough for intimate trust and respect – both ways. You are the only person I want to tell about what I am going to do. Please listen well. Perhaps you will ask me questions when I have finished.'

The Gurkha Captain looked at his company commander with puzzled, brooding eyes but said nothing as Major Rance got up and went to the map on the wall and pointed out the extent of the operation, where Betong was, the route he intended to bring the Cheena down the Sungei Perak for a boat pick-up prior to the heli flight for them to Kuala Lumpur. 'It is top secret and only seven other people know about it, five in KL, here the Commanding saheb who seems angry with me because of it.' Jason shrugged his shoulders. 'The other person I have had to let know is the one we know as Moby. He has to know because I need to take two of the men who went with me to try and get that daku to surrender. They are Goh Ah Wah and Kwek Leng Ming. From here I needed Corporal Kulbahadur Limbu, Lance Corporal Minbahadur Gurung as my radio operator and my batman, Chakrabahadur Rai ...'

Most unusually the Gurkha Captain interrupted. 'Saheb, excuse me but this is madness. Only six people all that way. I know your planning principles you always work to, firm base, alternative and a reserve. Here your plan has none of those yet that is how you have decided to operate?' A sudden thought struck him. 'Or is that what you have been told to do?'

'... Saheb,' Jason continued remorselessly as though his 2 ic had not spoken. 'The Commanding saheb has forbidden me to take any Gurkha at all. I must now ask Special Branch to let me have all four of the surrendered Cheena with me so that if we do meet any daku they, armed and wearing a daku cap with a star in front, can keep them occupied while I and the man I am escorting can quietly move out of the way. I am going to disobey the strict orders about not wearing enemy uniform by wearing a daku hat, the one with the peak and the red star.'

The Gurkha Captain broke in, taking the conversational initiative. 'Saheb, can I go and tell the Commanding saheb this is wrong? How can you cope with just four surrendered Cheena daku? You'll be on your own and out-numbered.' He shook his head in frustration and in disgust. *Can I say we all know that the CO does not like our saheb? Better not. He knows that himself.*

'Saheb, I thank you for your concern. No, please say nothing to anybody. I am only telling you in case I do not come back alive and you can get my home address from the office and get the clerk to write to my mother. My father is dead.'

The elderly Gurkha was stunned into disbelief. *I did not know the gora sahebs could behave like this.*

Jason smiled. 'Saheb. I have a secret weapon: bluff! This is what I plan. If we are met by daku on our way up to the Thai border to collect this man I will tell them I'm deserting to their side with all the office secrets and if I meet them on the way down

I'll tell them I'm a Russian spy disguised as an Englishman going to penetrate the government because I was unhappy in Moscow. My new name will be Bluff Bahadur Rance,' and he laughed so hard his company 2 ic had to join in, shaking his head with a sort of awe.

'Now, let's have a meeting to discuss the hand over to the new OC. I think he is due to report in on Wednesday the 15th so we don't have much time for planning and getting everything ready.'

Jason decided to take rations that did not need cooking and to buy some self-heating soup. He would take some solid fuel cookers to light a fire at night to keep animals off. *Normally guerrillas don't move at night but if they do they use a fire brand or torch so we'll be safe but, if it rains, uncomfortable. I'll take an extra lot of oil to keep the insects off us. Weapon? I'll decide later.*

That same afternoon he phoned the Head of Special Branch. 'Moby, during the war people in England were constantly told "Walls have ears" and so do phones. I simply must come and see you when you are free. When will that be?'

'How about taking pot luck with me this evening?' Moby was intensely proud at knowing that phrase.

'Suits me fine. I'll take the duty truck down and hope you can get me back from your resources.'

'No bother. See you around 6.30.'

Jason and Moby sat at the dinner table and a sustaining meal of rice and curried chicken with vegetables from the garden were served by the Head of Special Branch's serving maid, Leong Bik

Fong, the middle-aged wife of one of Moby's Special Branch detectives, Lee Kheng, a Communist 'sleeper'. Jason told Moby that he had decided to tackle his operational problem differently from how he had originally told him.

'Oh, so that's why you have asked to come to see me?' Moby asked, 'how can I help you?'

Leong Bik Fong came to collect the dishes and bring in some fruit. Jason wondered how she had been so quick to come in when Moby had called her. She left and Moby repeated his question. Jason took a piece of paper out of his pocket and wrote 'Keep talking' on it. He leant over, showed it to Moby and got up, quietly tiptoeing towards the door which he opened abruptly – and in fell Leong Bik Fong who had had her ear to the keyhole. 'That was quick of you,' said Moby as he went over to the woman, now getting onto her feet and looking more than embarrassed. He severely upbraided her and told her to get back to her quarters. 'I'll consider what to do with you later,' he told her as she shamefacedly left the room. 'Her husband is one of my detectives. Could it be that the pair are not really working for me?' Moby looked troubled then said, 'That's for me later on. Now tell me how I can help you.'

'Moby, I have decided not to take any Gurkhas and instead take all four of the men I brought in that time.'

'Jason, may I know why you have changed your mind?'

Jason hesitated. 'Let's keep that for later. I am thinking that with the four men on our way up if we are met by any guerrillas they can say they are escorting me, a turncoat government agent, on my way to joining the MCP in Betong. On the other hand, if we meet any on the way down, I'll pretend to be a Russian emulating an Englishman to keep the struggle alive now the Baling peace talks have collapsed. The presence of Gurkhas would be out of place, especially one carrying a radio.'

'Jason, you are one cool, cool operator. What does your CO think about that?'

Jason didn't temporise. 'It was his idea, What I want to know is if the four surrendered men are to act sincerely in good faith, is it possible to promise them not only a reward, as we have already managed for two of them, but permission to return to civilian life with no blot on their copybooks? No longer be Surrendered Enemy Personnel, SEPs. Let them be armed with a pistol each and ten rounds of .38 ammo – oh, and yes, get them all to carry a torch and a *parang* to cut with.'

'I'd love to say "yes" but it is not up to me. I'll have to find out from the omnipotent C C Too who will also have to delve even higher.' He gave Jason a hard look. *Something's not right. He's being loyal but then he would be, wouldn't he?* 'When are you leaving?'

'In five days' time, on the 19th, a Sunday, early as I have asked for an air recce early in the afternoon. That means I must know the very latest on the Friday."

Moby shook his head, got up and went to the phone. Jason heard an answering voice and recognised it as Mr Too's. 'Sir, sorry to bother you after hours but needs be *et cetera*. Veiled speech as time is short. I have the Southern Mountain Cannon with me. He has had to re-organise his planning, he'll tell you in detail when he meets you in KL, but he is not taking any of his own people ...'

Jason heard a splutter. '... You remember that man who was over ten feet tall? Yes, of course you do. The Cannon wants to take all four, not two, of those who were his. To pave the way for success and a happy group he is asking for these four to be regarded as carefree citizens with no extra obligations. Can you see any difficulties?'

'Do these four know of this proposal?'

'No, sir. I was only told it minutes before I rang you.'

'Can I speak to him?'

'I'll hand him over,' said Moby, giving Jason the phone.

No preliminaries: 'and if they say no, then what?'

'Then nothing. No Operation Emissary.'

'Leave it with me and give them a provisional yes' and the line went dead.

'Moby, I now need your help more than before. Can you somehow get five guerrilla hats, shirts and trousers? The CT kit is to wear on the trail and their issue kit is what we must wear to start with and, if we are successful, at the end. I will borrow five pairs of puttees and equipment from the QM. If I have to explain it I'll say it is "captured enemy kit".'

Moby grinned like a knowing goat. 'Jason, it's lucky there aren't more people like you asking me to do this otherwise I might find myself in difficulties. But for you, yes. I'll fix all you want.'

'Bless you! I'll bring a sack for the kit when I come to collect my gang.'

Planning for the Emissary's departure was a two-phase affair, what to say and what to do. Meng Ru and Ah Fat worked out what he

212

had to say when he announced that it was now time to go back to China: he felt he had outstayed his welcome and, although he would – but of course! – liked to have gone with the Secretary General when he went to Peking, he thought that would be too much of an imposition as well as not knowing his departure date yet. The time lag was too long. 'I came by myself with a relay of guides and I told them that when I returned I would contact them so they could escort me as on the way here. It's all in place.'

The Politburo said they would be sad to see him leave but quite understood his concern. 'We will give you a send-off because you have done us so well.'

'That is a kind thought which I appreciate. What I'd like to do is see this place Ha La and find out how Comrade Ah Fat and his people produced such an outstanding newspaper. I have seen copies of it and I think it is an object lesson for the comrades in China to do the same thing on their borders, both provincial and country.'

Yes, that was a good point. Why waste all that effort without passing it on? After all, it was almost on the way, wasn't it? 'When do you see yourself moving off?'

'Not before the 20th and today is the 13th so I have plenty of time to fix myself for the journey. Of course I don't need much as I will be escorted from one place to another but, as on the way down, sometimes we were stuck without anything to eat or anywhere to sleep for a night so I need to be prepared, just in case.'

'Yes, that is a sensible and wise precaution.'

Ah Fat had already made sure that Meng Ru had enough

basic kit to last the journey through the jungle. He had given him a spare haversack he had as his own was no longer waterproof and a cape was brought from the local market, as well as a torch. Basic rations had to be produced surreptitiously because on his journey back to China he would be looked after by his escort.

20 February

Meng Ru and Ah Fat spent the night in the same room and long before dawn the Bear and his four-man squad silently came in to take charge. The Bear had taken the precaution of going to see the Guard Commander the evening before and telling him how many men were going to leave camp at dawn and who they were. He had not forgotten an incident of earlier on in the year when a man, a courier in fact, who had come over to government side, had been left off the list so arbitrarily shot. That must not happen again.

He had checked everything and packed all his stuff before going to sleep and now, with a candle lit, all the Emissary had to do was dress and put his pack on. Ah Fat, along with the Bear and four men, went to the main gate, spoke to the Guard Commander and bid Meng Ru an effusive farewell. 'Comrade, have a safe journey back to China. We, in the Politburo, sincerely thank you for all you have done.' Traditional farewells were expressed, 'May the fortune star shine on you from above' with 'Wishing you a tailwind journey throughout' as it was a long, long way back to China.

The Emissary raised his arm in the communist salute and, as he turned to leave, took Ah Fat's hand and squeezed it in thanks.

Saying no more the group left the camp turning the way the route led to Ha La, three of the squad in front, the Bear, the Emissary and the other three men. They were quickly out of sight. 'You do know who that man is, don't you?' Ah Fat asked the Guard Commander. *Keep him unworried.* Yes, the Guard Commander did and was glad that man's aim had been accomplished so he could now go back to his family happily.

'We need people like him, don't we Comrade?' he asked.

'Indeed we do,' Ah Fat answered with an inward and outward smile.

By now Jason had collected what he needed from the Quartermaster and, before he left the battalion lines that same morning, he drew a pistol as he felt that was the most likely weapon the notional man he was pretending to be would take, and ammunition from the arms' kote. There was now no need to take a Very pistol with four reds and four greens. He had already had a long and earnest conversation with his four men, Goh Ah Wah, Kwek Leng Ming, Sim Ting Hok and Yap Kheng, all four originally from the 2nd Regiment of the MRLA commanded by Tan Fook Leong. The first two named men were of a high quality: the last two named were originally 'gardeners' on plots in the jungle to increase the MRLA's food supplies and were not quite of the same calibre. Jason had wounded Sim Ting Hok in August 1954 but had managed to 'save' all four's lives from a mock, illegal shooting. That should have sealed all four's loyalty. All four were delighted to be free once more so Jason had no worries that 'the green hell' would recall them. And, in any case, in the area they were going

215

they were unknowns. They had been so struck by his unusual character that among themselves they had given him the nickname of *Fut Sum Pao*, the Buddha-hearted Leopard. This was because of Rance's sometimes fierce and terrifying appearance that belied his Buddha-like kind heartedness. *They don't look unlike my A Company men, do they? Same age as the riflemen, same eyes, same high cheek bones, a bit fairer in the face. Do? Of course they'll do. Damn well have to, won't they!* He knew they did not belong to a Secret Society: he had seen them stripped and there were no tattoo marks. Moby had told him that they belonged to the same *tong*, brotherhood.

He decided not to go to A Company where the new OC might not have welcomed him so went to the Police Station to collect his four Cheenas where he met Moby and before setting off for Kuala Lumpur, all of forty-two miles off, checked each man's kit. *Good, all present and correct.*

They drove to the Defence Platoon who had been warned of their arrival. Rance had told the driver he'd go back to Seremban on the morrow. After settling his men in, he telephoned the Director of Intelligence, announced his arrival and asked what was the time the recce.

'Be at the Air Flight lines at 1400 hours, you and two others. When you come back, come to my office and see me. I'll warn the relevant people. I hear you have changed your group's composition and want to know why after all we talked about.' He did not sound the best pleased.

Jason acknowledged the flight timings and said he would report back on his return. *So far, so good – but how far is so far?*

The pilot of the Auster had over-flown Jason and spoken to him by radio on several operations. 'Great to see you in person,' he said, introducing himself. 'You seem to get around a lot. The last time was away over to the east.' 'Goes with the job,' answered Jason, smiling broadly as they shook hands.

He told Goh Ah Wah and Kwek Leng Ming to get in the seats behind the pilot, showed them how to fasten their belts and shut the door. Both were thrilled and a bit frightened by this new venture. The pilot took out his map and spread it open. 'Now, I gather you want to fly up the Sungei Perak. Exactly where do you want to join it? Surely not from the coast inland?'

'No, no. Please take her up straight to Fort Tapong and then fly alongside the river up to the border, but of course not flying over it. If you fly to one side on the way up and the other on the way down my two men can see it clearly.'

'Yeah, that makes sense. Your men don't look like or sound like Gurkhas,' he said enquiringly.

'No, they don't because they're not.' Jason opened the door and, putting his head inside, and said, 'from here we are going to fly to Fort Tapong. That is where we fly to tomorrow and from where we will go upstream by boat. I can't say how far the boat will take us but we will have to walk to the border once the boat can get no farther. We are going to fly along the river to the border and I want you to look out of the window going and coming and remember what you see. When we are on the ground it will help us recognise any danger points.'

The pilot listened in, amazed at Jason's fluency. The two men nodded their understanding and a few minutes later they took off. From Fort Tapong onwards the river narrowed. Watching from the plane they could see some dangerous rapids, bends and twists in the river and the jungle coming to the water's edge, even disappearing under the canopy for most of the last quarter of an hour's flight before turning back. Jason always looked down on the jungle seeing it an impenetrable sea of cabbages, but knowing full well it wasn't. What struck him was that he could see no traces of any bombing, The only 'holes' in the jungle were away to the east and looked like Temiar ladangs. For the two Chinese it was almost too much to digest but it gave them a sense of proportion and importance that would otherwise have been lacking.

As the plane flew up and down the river Temiar and guerrillas looked up to see if they could spot it. It was not often planes flew above them but this one was flying straight: what could it mean? Ah Soo Chye, about to leave Kerinching's ladang, thought it could be following the Sungei Perak. *Does this foretell Security Force movement? If so we might try and ambush what comes along.* It would take a day or so to get to a good spot he knew about.

'I have been told that you have decided not to go with any Gurkhas, nor to take a radio set with you,' said an ill-humoured Director of Intelligence. 'Instead you have four SEPs and no radio. Isn't that military madness in the extreme? Won't it mean that the operation is bound to be a failure?'

Jason knew that he had to handle this one carefully. Colonel Mason noticed Major Rance's hesitation before answering. 'Sir, on mature reflection it struck me that I would be safer with an all Chinese group and therefore to have a Gurkha with a radio set would be out of place.' He said no more.

'That's all very well if you were going on a guided tour in a peaceful area or on a picnic but, man, this is guerrilla country,' retorted the Colonel, still not liking Jason's idea one little bit. 'And what about you?' Before Jason could answer, 'Does your CO approve? Does he even know about your ridiculous idea?'

'Yes, sir. He does.'

'And his reaction?'

Jason stayed silent.

Exasperated, Colonel Mason said, 'Major Rance, answer my question, what was your CO's reaction to your idea?'

'There was no reaction at all, sir.'

'How can that be so? There must have been a reaction. How can there not have been one?'

'Because it was his idea, sir, not mine.'

'His idea? Do you know why?'

Again Jason did not answer.

Colonel Mason, normally a placid man, exploded, 'For heaven's sake, answer me.'

'Sir, he told me he would not allow any of his Gurkhas to go on such an operation so I had no choice but to re-plan.'

The Director of Infantry realised that Jason had been in a quandary and his silence was merely loyalty to an order he was in no way responsible for so he immediately calmed down. He stayed silent as he thought out the enormous strain that would attend Jason. Calmly he asked how Jason visualised contact with any guerrilla.

'Sir, if I tell you, you will indubitably forbid me. Wouldn't it be better to let you know after my return how I managed to bring back the Emissary?'

It was now Colonel Mason's turn to be in a quandary. It was a situation that he had never previously encountered. He temporised. 'Aren't you being over-theatrical in giving me such an answer?'

'Sir, you will, I expect, have read Sun Tzu,' Jason began to his superior's amazement. 'You will recall that he wrote "Supreme excellence in generalship consists of breaking the enemy's will without fighting." I am basing my plans on that theme. If you can keep this to yourself and not stop me from going, I will grasp the nettle and let you know how I will manage.'

'All right, go on then. In my job I know how to keep secrets.'

'Sir, once we are on the ground, we will wear guerrilla kit, shirts, trousers and caps. If we meet anyone hostile on the way up we will not be Security Forces. I will be a turncoat from the government trying to join the MCP in Betong so ask for free passage so I can be taken as a comrade. I'll have my face covered so won't be recognised. I have no fear linguistically so it will also be "in plain sound".'

The Colonel listened, eyes button bright. 'And on the way down?'

'Say I am a Russian pretending to be an Englishman coming to infiltrate the government as a double agent. I travelled from Moscow to Peking and on down to Betong, where I have just left.'

The Colonel's eyes probed him like a scalpel as he considered the implications. 'And that is the only way you think you can manage?'

'Not "think", sir, but "know". Under those circumstances, nothing else came to my mind, sir. There is a Nepali proverb, "the goat to be sacrificed has had the gods enter it by sprinkling it with water; all that remains is for something to go wrong",' and his face was lit by a fleeting smile.

The Colonel digested this piece of esoteric Nepali folklore before saying 'I must ask this. Who else knows of what you have decided?'

'Only three, apart from you. One is Ismail Mubarak, Head of Special Branch, Seremban, who had to be told to get the CT kit ready, and one is Mr C C Too. Let me explain. I felt that to ask these four SEP to undertake such an operation with no recompense was asking too much. I needed authority to give them a bonus and permission to let them off the SEP list and be free men once again.'

'Yes, I go along with that. You said three others. Who's the third?'

'My Company 2 ic, sir, my Gurkha Captain.'

'Why him particularly?'

Again Jason hesitated before answering, 'to write to my mother explaining everything in case I don't come back.'

Some way along from the camp at Betong along the path to Ha La was a track that led south towards the border. The Bear's squad reached it towards mid-afternoon. By then the Emissary was tired. Although he had regained his strength after his arduous journey, he was no longer a fit man and by now he was lagging. The Bear knew that the only reason he himself was still alive after so many

221

years of jungle living and so many near misses was because he took nothing for granted. He didn't believe that anyone from the camp would follow up but one could never be sure. He had travelled along that track so many times he knew it like the proverbial back of his hand and knew that about half a mile ahead was a north flowing stream. Once there he would take his group up it for a few hundred yards then jink back to the track until he found a place they could spend the night. That way, were there anyone following them, they would be safe.

The Emissary didn't like getting his new footwear wet – the others went bare-footed – but kept quiet about it. Back on the track the Bear found a place where they could spend the night. He had divided some basic rations, rice chiefly, among his men, and, with their *parang*s, they constructed rudimentary shelters by cutting branches, which they covered in leaves and topped with sheets of waterproof material to keep out the rain.

After their meal logs were collected, a fire was lit to keep animals away and, taking a risk of not bothering about sentries – after all, they were not at war in Thailand, were they? – they drifted off to sleep.

21 February

Colonel Mason was quietly shocked at what he had learnt about Jason's change in plan and felt it was in everyone's best interests to say nothing about how matters had developed. He was in two minds to ring the CO of 1/12 GR but decided against that until, when? Until Major Rance had gone on leave? He had had his

Deputy, a major, arrange the heli and transport for the five men. He had also arranged for Police Field Force boats – originally he had said only one but better to have a spare with such a tight programme so two had been ordered – to arrive at Fort Tapong the previous night but he himself thought it would be a gesture of solidarity if he himself went to see the group off.

The Royal Air Force 'Whirlwind' helicopter pilot was the same person who had lifted Jason, some Gurkhas and the same SEPs out of the jungle previously. He waved to them as the crewman ushered them inside and told them to belt up. The engine was switched on and the rotors started turning. No one bothered about the sack Jason carried. When all was ready it lifted off, Colonel Mason waving as it did, Jason's Nepali proverb running through his mind.

Ah Soo Chye heard the heli in the distance. *Must be something to do with the plane I heard yesterday. There'll be someone somewhere along the river. On, on.*

22 to 25 February

The Bear's group with the Emissary found the going hard. It was not just the terrain that was getting rougher, steeper and colder but the nearer the line of mountains that formed the border the more it rained. Meng Ru didn't grumble, he wasn't that sort of man, but he slowed everyone down so it was lucky that the meeting on the border was not scheduled until the 25th. Wild animals were the only threat and the noise the group made – much too loud for the Bear's professional standard – was, if anything, a bonus as it scared the forest creatures.

The helicopter ride took more than half an hour as Fort Tapong is a good way up the Sungei Perak. The Police Field Force had been alerted to marshal the heli and once it had landed, Jason and his men, having been bare-headed in case their hats blew off and damaged the rotors as they exited, quickly deplaned. Once they were clear the marshaller gave the sign for take-off and away it flew.

The OC was a Malay Inspector and his number 2 was a fine-looking Sikh. 'Welcome, sir, welcome to Fort Tapong. It is not often we have people landing by heli.'

'Thank you for marshalling us in so successfully,' Jason answered, his smile open and friendly. 'Let me introduce my men' and, in Malay, told the policemen their names. They shook hands.

'Would you like a meal before you move off in the boats? Both came last night. They want to move off as soon as you are ready but a quick meal will not harm matters.' He looked at his watch. 'It is only half past nine. I'll tell the crews to be ready to caste off at ten o'clock.'

Jason asked his men, still in Malay, if they'd like a meal – 'we don't when we'll see hot food again' – and the offer was eagerly accepted. 'For me a cup of coffee would go down very well,' he added. 'I'd like a word with you while my men are eating.'

'Come along in,' said the Inspector. They went to the upper floor where the open windows caught a breeze. Coffee was brought and Jason asked how much of his operation they knew.

'All we have been told that there is a top-secret operation

with the planning name of "Emissary", nothing else.'

'Let me explain,' Jason said, sipping his coffee. 'I have been tasked to go to the border and bring down a Chinese man of huge political importance and that is why my squad is one of SEPs. We are going to walk up to the border to meet him and bring him back ...'

'Yes, your boats will be here on the evening of the 26th to meet you at the boat point on the 27th.'

Jason nodded agreement at the dates. 'Not having operated in the part of the country yet, although I had an aerial recce yesterday, my first two questions are how much river traffic is there and what is the CT situation? By that I mean how much is that activity out of the ordinary and/or how much would it alert the CT?'

'Since the Baling peace talks life has been much quieter. In this area there has been a Special Branch operation, "Bamboo", for some time, winning over the *orang asli*, or trying to win them over from the CTs. It is possible that any CTs who heard yesterday's and today's air activity would be suspicious.'

Jason thought about that. 'You will have noticed I have no radio. That is on purpose. Also we are not carrying anything heavier than pistols. The last thing I want is a firefight. What I am asking is, is it at all possible for a squad of yours to move with us to the boat point, walk up and down in the vicinity, leaving tracks that show them to have gone back down river? The boats can wait half an hour at the disembarking point for the crew to stretch their legs. Also, a patrol moving around this area locally might make the CTs think the heli reinforcements were for here and not upriver.'

The Inspector looked at his Deputy and asked, 'What do you think of that? I think we can manage that, can't we?'

'Yes,' the Sikh answered. 'The stand-by section is always rationed and ready to move. Let's send them.'

Jason thanked them saying it was a great bonus and it made him feel much safer than before.

Orders were given and the two boats, one with Jason and his four and the other with the police, moved off at a quarter past ten.

To start with, the journey was of interest with flocks of hornbills, and monitor lizards on the sandy banks, otherwise it was much of the same: thick jungle either side with, initially, an occasional Malay village. The river narrowed and was slowed by his boat breaking its shear pins on underwater snags several times. As the hours passed it grew uncomfortably hot with no awning, and cramped. The river wound around the contours, with a strong current in the main channel. There was one place where the river fell a couple of feet – *this is what I saw from the plane* – and Jason asked if they could get out and walk the short distance to where the river was calmer. 'It will make the boat lighter and let us stretch our legs.'

It was early evening by the time they reached the point where the boats could go no farther. Out they got, glad the uncomfortable journey was at an end. The boat drivers were adamant that it was too late to start going back. They and the police squad were prepared to spend the night where they were. Jason said to Goh Ah Wah that there was time to go on farther. 'We can't change into guerrilla clothes with these people watching, can we?'

'*Sinsaang*, no. That is wise. In any case those people make too much noise for us.'

'Goh, let them. Any guerrilla will concentrate on them and not on us.'

Two of them recced forward a couple of hundred yards, saw nothing and came back by which time Jason had found a small cave. At the back of the cave they hid the sack with their Security Force clothing in, wedging it into a corner. 'We won't cover it with leaves as they will be out of place,' said Goh Ah Wah. Half an hour later there was just enough light to make a rude camp, collect wood to make a fire, take out their hard tack, eat it and before they went to sleep Jason got them to listen to his plan, which he had yet to tell them. 'You know we are going as far as the border. That was why we had that recce yesterday. We need to move quickly and act as though we were not Security Forces but as real guerrillas. That means all four of you will walk in front and I come along at the back. If you meet any guerrilla your cover story is that you are escorting a European from the government who is a turncoat going to join the MCP in Betong. I will hide till then and, when you call me as proof, I will join you with a camouflage veil over my face. There should be no difficulty as we will be on the same side and not hostile to one another. Incidentally, the chief guerrilla's name is Ah Soo Chye and his lieutenants are Lo See and Tek Miu.'

The four Chinese were greatly amused at Jason's plan and laughed softly. It appealed to their sense of humour. '*Sinsaang*, that is fine for the way to the border. What happens if we meet these people on the way down with the Emissary?'

'Oh, I have a different story. I am a Russian pretending to be an Englishman. I travelled from Moscow to Peking and my job is to try and join the government and spy for China. The Emissary, the man we are escorting back, is my Chinese guarantee that I have been accepted as genuine. When we get to Malaya I will find him a job to work with me.'

That unheard of ruse was meat and drink to the four men: they already had a high opinion of the Buddha-hearted Leopard and now it was higher still. Jason felt what he thought of as 'friendly vibrations' emanating from his four and felt more confident that he had yet to feel. They stoked the fire then settled down and went to sleep. Next morning, dressed as guerrillas with Jason's camouflage veil round his neck for instantly covering his face, they set off for the border.

The track that ran along the river was easy to follow and they made good time. They found signs of men moving both ways and only once met anyone, a group of *orang asli* with their blowpipes. No words were exchanged, neither party taking any notice of the other. Jason felt it was almost too easy but none of them ever let up their guard. Game abounded in the area: bear, elephant, rhinoceros, tiger, deer and pig, recognised by their spoor. They also found a large patch of trampled and bloody undergrowth and a pig and a python that had fought to the death. They heard high-pitched animal noises and had the rewarding sight of three otters fishing in a stream as they were making their way for the pass to the west of Gunong Gadong on the border.

They reached the pass over Gunong Gadong on the 24th.

By then they were alert as wild animals and, although none mentioned it, tired, dirty and hungry. They looked around and found the stone border marker with a scratched hammer and sickle in the stem. Against everything that had been said about not crossing over the border, Goh Ah Wah and Kwek Leng Ming went about five hundred yards over on a patrol, looking for signs of the others.

The Bear was worried lest he was late reaching the pass. Meng Ru was so whacked that at one point up a particularly steep slope his pack had to be carried and he pulled up. At midday on the 25th the Bear was delighted to hear a cuckoo noise in the distance, thrice drawn out, pause, twice quickly, pause, thrice drawn out.

'We've arrived,' he told the Emissary and made a noise like a gibbon, thrice drawn out, pause, twice quickly, pause, thrice drawn out. Jason's men looked at each other smiling broadly. 'As planned,' muttered Jason before putting his hands to his face and repeating his signal. The gibbon answered, much nearer and Jason's men heard people coming. Jason called out 'bird, monkey and now men, all welcome.'

The Bear's group came into sight and automatically everyone, except a dazed-looking elderly man, waved at each other. Jason and the Bear hugged each other, and Jason shook hands with the rest of the group in that he knew them all before the Bear introduced him to Mang Ru, who had flopped down on the ground, panting heavily. Jason saw he was wearing ordinary civilian dress and a floppy hat. 'Greetings and welcome. You have covered the uphill part of your journey. It is all downhill from now on. We will look after you as you are now ours. Your new companions are …' and he pointed out his four men, naming them as he did. They started talking to him to make him feel at ease.

The Bear looked at Jason, nodded and moved off. Jason followed him. When out of earshot the Bear said 'you will have a job to get him to move as quickly as you want.'

Jason nodded. 'Yes, I can see he's in a poor state.'

'I have told him that I am only responsible for him until I hand him over to you. Of course he knows you will supervise him until you reach Kuala Lumpur but has no idea of details as neither *P'ing Yee* nor I know them, nor has he asked me about them. He seems a placid man who doesn't fret unduly. He'll do whatever you decide.' The Bear looked at his watch. '*Shandong P'aau*, it is time I started on my way back. I am glad we have met. Before I go, take these two tins of Thai sardines and a jar of Ovaltine for a present for any guerrilla you might meet. He'll know you really are from Thailand, won't he?'

'That's tradecraft in a really big way! If we meet any they'll love the Ovaltine. Thank you. And a present for your son' Jason put his two hands in front of his face and made them talk to each other. 'Don't forget to tell Wang Liang I remember him,' said one hand. 'No, I won't,' said the other. He had done this in front of the Bear's son, Wang Liang, to his unforgettable delight only a month or so back. The Bear broke out laughing. 'I'll tell him but I won't be able to demonstrate.'

Jason's four men had seen that little play. They knew he was a ventriloquist and were enraptured. Mang Ru had seen it and smiled gleefully as it was something new and unexpected.

Farewells said, the Bear's group moved off and got back to Betong where they reported that the Emissary was now safely on his way home. It was not a lie: only which 'home', old or new, was not specified.

'*Sinsaang* Meng Ru, I am the man my boyhood friend Ah Fat told you about. These four men are also my friends. They are all jungle trained as indeed am I. Our task is to take you safely to Kuala Lumpur.' Meng Ru was impressed. 'I see you have hope in your face: you may also have it in your heart. My plan for the next two days, three if you find our pace too quick, is to move on quietly along the line we came up. Until now we have not met any Malayan guerrillas. Whether we will or not is an unknown. If we do, we will claim also to be guerrillas. That is why we are wearing these clothes.'

Meng Ru nodded then said, in objection to Jason's plan, 'but how can you pass as a Chinese guerrilla? Nobody would ever think you were Chinese.' He looked perplexed. 'Surely that will prevent our getting to where we have to reach?'

Jason's answer was a five-character Chinese phrase, 'feigning to be a pig, he vanquishes tigers'. 'No, I do not pretend to be a Chinese person. I will pretend I am a Russian who speaks English like an Englishman. I have been to Peking and you have come down from there with me to help me surreptitiously join the Malayan government, both working to overturn the present system.'

The Emissary loved it. 'But suppose we meet some government troops. That will be dangerous, won't it?' and gloom spread over his features.

'There are none. I have arranged for the area to be left to us. Anyone we meet will either be to *t'o yan* or guerrillas. Ready to move?' Yes, they were. 'On our way' and slowly downhill they went.

That first day they moved slowly, confident they had no worries about where to go having only come up the track recently. At the first night stop Jason talked to them all. 'We may meet some guerrillas. What we will do tomorrow is practise what you leading four will say if a guerrilla walks around the corner, sees us, takes us for one of his crowd and calls out.'

Yes, that was sensible. 'What I'll do is clap my hands loudly and that will be the sign for a guerrilla spotting us and asking who we are. You all know our cover plan but until you have done it a couple of times the answer may sound unnatural. Think up a suitable reply and call it out when you hear me clap.'

It had been on the hesitant side the first time but by the fourth time a suitable answer came naturally. 'Something like "We are on our way south. Is the track safe for us? Come and tell us about it." Only when you think it time to call me and the Emissary will we appear, you having told them that the other two are waiting to be called for.'

24 February
That heli we think flew to Fort Tapong a couple of days or so back. Just the one. It has only just struck me. That hasn't happened before, has it?' Ah Soo Chye was talking to his two lieutenants.

232

No, the others could not remember it having happened but it could have done without their hearing it. Certainly they had heard helicopters flying over Kerinching's ladang area but not so far west. 'It could be a survey group, it could be soldiers but not many so there is no real threat to us. In any case we'll move as we normally do, a *t'o yan* screen in front and their dogs in front of them. That way is how we are still alive after so many years working against superior forces, both in numbers and weapons. Let's go and check. We'll start at the place we know the police boats stop. It will take a couple of days to get there, what with collecting the *t'o yan* who have no idea of time. Even with four fingers they only know how to count up to three.'

The others thought it a good idea.

'We can't cross the river any lower than that boat point unless we come across a *t'o yan* raft which I don't think is likely but they will know if there is one. We'll only take one bodyguard each. Quicker that way.'

Loo See objected. 'Suppose the people are those special ones who sometimes drop by parachute. They have good weapons and are quick on the draw. Better to take more than a bodyguard.'

'I'll take one. You can take as many as you like. Just make sure there's enough tapioca for us for a few days before we set off.'

27 February

Ah Soo Chye's group waded across the river at the boat point having spent the night on the far bank and, once ashore, caste around. All of them, Temiar and guerrillas, could read ground

233

signs like a book. The signs of where boats, two of them it seemed, had been tied up were noticed. Once on land they soon picked up where the Police Jungle Squad had traipsed around, tracks moving a couple of hundred yards up the path before returning. Not a lot here, not worth worrying about, was the general opinion. 'There's lots of game a bit higher up,' said one of the Temiar. 'You have your weapons and we our *blau* to shoot with if you don't want to make a noise. Why not get some meat instead of dried tapioca? The best place to start looking is a couple of hours walk north.'

27 February

Jason's group moved slowly, his four Chinese in front followed by Jason and behind him Meng Ru. The Emissary had fully appreciated the role he had to play and had rehearsed what to say if asked as he walked, his feet hurting, behind that curious, optimistic foreigner in front of him. Having come so far it would be devastatingly disappointing to fail now so he simply had to play the part thought out for him. He had not had a decent meal for so long he felt a nagging pain in his gut. He hadn't washed properly for so long he itched. He hadn't been as tired as this for so long for … and his mind drifted and he lurched to one side of the track and tripped on a root that jutted out, nearly falling. Jason turned and said, 'Let's all stop for a rest. There's plenty of time and it is still early afternoon.'

They sat down and rested.

The guerrillas in north Malaya never went any distance from their base without a Temiar 'screen' ahead of them to warn them about any Security Forces in the area and the Temiar had their dogs as their 'screen'. It was such a foolproof system that Ah Soo Chye and his lieutenants had not been seen by any soldier or policeman for more than five years. That day it just so happened that the Temiars' dogs had slipped away having smelt a wild boar so it was the leading *t'o yan* who instinctively 'felt a presence' ahead of him. Slowly, oh how slowly, he peered round a bend in the track and saw four guerrillas sitting down resting. *No sentries? Or are they hidden?* He slipped back and told Ah Soo Chye that there were some guerrillas sitting on the track, resting, just round the corner. 'I did not see any sentries.'

Ah Soo Chye knew there were none of his men up in these parts but, of course, couriers from Ha La or Betong whom he did not recognise often used this track. He went forward, saw the four men about twenty yards ahead and called out to them politely, in the traditional Chinese method, 'have you had your rice today?'

'Yes, and have you?' and before any response could come continued 'We are on our way south. Is the track safe for us? Come and tell us about it.'

Ah Soo Chye called his men forward and joined them. 'I was not expecting to meet anyone here,' he said, hiding the fact that that was why he was where he was. 'We have come from the other side of the river and,' pointing to the men with blowpipes, 'these men said we could find some animals for meat in this area. Have you seen any on your way down?'

'No, but we have heard them and seen traces.'

'You have no sentries out?'

'Not in front but behind, yes.'

'Let us introduce ourselves. We are ...' and Ah Soo Chye turned to his two lieutenants, giving their names. We are the main link between the *t'o yan* and the MCP HQ in Betong. Who are you?'

'We four were very close to the late Tan Fook Loong, Commander 2 Regiment. The equipment we are wearing and our pistol were all captured from the enemy we managed to kill. Now we are under Comrade Yeong Kwoh.'

'Now there's a warrior for you,' said Ah Soo Chye. 'Yes, indeed, we have heard so,' echoed the others.

'How it is you are so far north in our area without our being told?' asked with just a tinge of anxiety in his voice.

Goh Ah Wah looked around, furtively, lowered his voice conspiratorially and said, 'it had been hoped to tell you but our task is of vital secrecy so I can't tell you how our commander saw himself doing this.'

This fascinated Ah Soo Chye so much that, against all his training, he asked if he could be told. Goh Ah Wah deliberated, said, 'please wait just a moment. I'll go and ask.' He got up and, to the others' astonishment, disappeared round a bend in the track. *Where could he have gone and why?* was in each mind.

Goh Ah Wah told Jason what was happening. 'Yes, tell them and if they want to see us two, come and fetch us,' so he went back and sat down again. 'Listen well. There is an English-speaking Russian who is based in Moscow. He was sent to Peking where he met a man associated with the Politburo of the Chinese Communist Party.' Goh paused and saw nothing but radiant astonishment in faces around him. 'The Party ordered a man, Meng Ru, to escort him all the way to Betong. It took them six months. Once there they rested. The Russian's aim is to pretend he is an Englishman. He speaks fluent English. He hopes to keep Meng Ru hidden until he can place him where he knows a government worker has died but the government won't have heard of it. That bit may be tricky. The two sentries behind us are those two' and he let that amazing story hang in the air while the others contemplated it. For a while silence reigned.

'We would be honoured to meet there two extraordinary men. May we?'

'You know how much either's life will be worth if any of this gets out. I cannot stress how secret it is. However, if you will promise to say nothing I'll go and ask them if they're willing to talk to you.'

'We promise, we promise,' the three leaders said, almost in unison.

'In that case I'll go and see if I can persuade them to come and talk to you.'

Jason, face tightly bound with his camouflage veil and only his eyes showing although his fair hair not covered by his cap could be seen, and Meng Ru came round the bend in the track with Goh and greeted the three leaders. 'I won't tell you my name and if I were to give you one it would not be mine, nor will I tell you my friend's' was his opening gambit. 'Also, if you want to put a sentry whence we have come, do so.' They sat down in a small circle, gunmen guarding them.

'I am Ah Soo Chye and these are Comrades Tek Miu and Lo

See.'

Jason's play acting came into its own. 'So I am privileged to meet the famous trio!' he exclaimed happily. 'While I was in Peking I actually spoke to the Great Helmsman and he knew your names ...'

He was interrupted by gasps of unexpected delight – and Jason's four thought *the Buddha-hearted Leopard can be as wise as he can be wild.*

'... and he said two things. "When the trio belch, the *gwai lo* defecate with fear" ...' – more gasps of delight – '"and their work with the *t'o yan* I regard as the bridgehead of the next invasion that will lead into the nation's capital." That is why I am honoured and pleased with this unexpected meeting.' *And if that doesn't keep them on my side nothing else will.* 'Comrade Ah Soo Chye, before you tell me about yourself please take these as a good-will present,' putting hand into his pocket he pressed two tins of Thai sardines and the jar of Ovaltine into the surprised guerrilla's hand.

The guerrilla trio was dumbfounded by such generosity and showed it. Jason blessed Ah Fat and the Bear for their forethought. Then the guerrillas opened up and the main thrust of the trio's remarks was that often they seemed to feel forgotten by those in Betong – 'not at all. You are fervently appreciated' – and that only by keeping the *t'o yan* happy, fostering their dislike for the Malays and trying to ensure that the government does not send soldiers to their *ladangs* did they think they would succeed in their task.

During the conversation Meng Ru was fully aware that Jason

was learning all about what they were doing and added his bit. 'It is not easy for me to speak *kwang tung wa* you are using as I am only fluent in *kwok yi*, which is not properly understood by you southerners. But if you speak slowly I can understand most of what you say.'

'How will you manage to get to Kuala Lumpur, that's where you're going, isn't it? It's a long way from here.'

Jason saw Goh slightly ill at ease so said, 'My escort has arranged couriers, safe houses, other dress, food and shelter from a bit farther downstream onwards. We think it will take quite a few months before we are settled in.'

'Do you need escorting downstream?' Loo See asked. 'We are ready to help you if you do.'

This time Goh Ah Wah rallied. 'No that's not necessary but thank you for the offer. We arranged it all on our way up and any alteration will spoil matters.'

'Fully understood,' said Ah Soo Chye.

Jason looked at his watch. 'Comrade Goh, our friend has had his rest so we must push on,' saying which he stood up and helped Meng Ru to his feet.

'Stay the night with us. Have some wild boar the *t'o yan* have gone off to shoot with their blowpipes. When they come back we will show you how to shoot with them.'

Jason laughed. 'Comrade, you make my mouth water but please don't tempt me. We will be on our way. Up lads and put on your packs.' He shook hands with the three guerrilla leaders. 'You said this was not your area. When will you be returning?' The last thing he needed was a confrontation at the boat point.

'You say there are no enemy anywhere along the track?'

'That is correct. It is as safe as anything.'

Ah Soo Chye looked at the others. 'Time we had a break, isn't it? We could all do with a few days good meat.' At that moment one of the Temiar came back with a small boar. 'This is Senagit from Kerinching's ladang' called out Lo See, not realising that none of Jason's group knew what he was talking about. 'Let him show you how to shoot before you leave.'

Senagit showed them, Jason pretending he had never seen such before. 'Are they used against men?' he asked.

At that question, which was answered by a shake of the head, Ah Soo Chye turned to Lo See and said, 'by the way, from what we've heard there's nothing to worry about.' What he said next made Jason prick up his ears. 'That helicopter we heard must have only been someone important on a visit. Nothing to worry about; no special forces.'

'In that case we'll bid you farewell and wish you good luck and a full belly,' Jason said. 'You will know it is boar meat, not dog meat' and, in a joyous mood, went to where Senagit was holding the pig. Remembering he was not supposed to know Malay he gently took the dead pig out of the Temiar's hands and, to Senagit's horror, the dead pig started grunting. When Jason made to give it back Senagit jumped away.

Jason went back to his group and off they went, almost with a swagger although every one of them breathed a deep, deep sigh of relief.

27-28 February

Before Jason's group reached the boat point they went to the cave where they had hidden their other uniforms and changed before later that evening reaching the boat point where they were delighted to meet the police squad and two boats. The squad had brought an extra amount of rice with them, knowing how the five men had been on short commons. Jason told them about Ah Soo Chye, Tek Miu, Lo See and their men being a day's walk up the track. 'I doubt they'll bother us but it is better to be alert.'

Nothing untoward happened during the night and at dawn they caste off. With the current the boats made good time, luckily needing no shear pins to be changed, and reached Fort Tapong before sunset and were made welcome. Jason introduced Meng Ru, not by name, merely saying that he was their target they had been sent to escort from across the border. As they were having a refreshing shower, Jason in the officers' shower and the four men where the rank and file of the force did, a radio message was sent saying all was well and that could six men be heli-ed out on the morrow? One of the group, no name was given, was obviously suffering from malnutrition and acute tiredness so could a medical officer be handy?

After a bumper supper they all, dog tired, retired to bed early.

Next morning the Malay Inspector got his answer. 'Expect a heli at 1100 hours.'

At Kuala Lumpur they were met by Colonel Mason, C C Too, Ismail Mubarak and a doctor. Meng Ru was taken away almost immediately but was allowed to say his farewells, which were touchingly warm and obviously sincere. *That Rance man's magic worked* thought Colonel Mason, *I need a long session with him.*

'Jason, all well?' Moby asked.

'Everything went like clockwork. They are a fine bunch of blokes. Are you taking them back now?'

'Yes. I've got a vehicle all ready.'

'Do me a favour will you? Take this sack along with you,' and he gave a wink, unseen by anyone else. 'I'll say good bye to them before you take them away.' He went over to them and thanked them. 'Now you'll be free. I hope we can meet some time as we are friends.'

They bobbed their heads, smiling, turned and Moby led them away, thinking that the Buddha-hearted Leopard had indeed done them well.

'Jason. I have told the battalion I'll take you home for the night and we'll talk. I'll arrange an Auster for you sometime tomorrow. You must have an enormous amount to tell me.'

'Sir, I have. I've nothing else to wear but these clothes. I'll pong a bit.'

'I'll lend you something to wear. And, in fact, considering you have been to the edge of Thailand and back, it's amazing how your clothes don't seem to pong after so many days without your getting a proper wash!' and the ghost of a smile twitched the Colonel's lips.

The main point of Jason's talk with Colonel Mason was the importance of maintaining good relations with the Temiar and other similar groups of people, of which there were quite a few.

'Sir, I don't speak Temiar and from what I gather few on the government side do either. That ought to be rectified.'

'I agree with you but it's a thorny one and more than tact and charm will be needed to put it into action.'

The Colonel drove Jason to the airstrip and, before he emplaned, thanked him effusively. 'I can't tell you how much I admire what you have done but,' and here his face clouded, 'sadly no recognition can ever be awarded as the citation would result in a court-martial not a bravery award.'

Jason felt like saying 'there's no need to tell my CO' but forbade to, merely saying, 'thank you sir for your hospitality and letting me run my show my own way: some might say that two indulgences were an extravagance.'

Without Jason knowing about it, C C Too had taken a comprehensive statement from the Emissary, taking all of two weeks, before deciding how he could use his input and how to present it to his masters. It took a lot to horrify him – he was constantly shocked but seldom horrified – but his reaction to Meng Ru's description of being met on the Thai border by a tall Englishman wearing guerrilla uniform with four Chinese guerrillas similarly dressed, did momentarily horrify him. *This must be kept under wraps and not appear in my report* Mr Too decided but lest something did leak out, he felt he had to tell the Director of Operations about it. So a meeting was arranged at Flagstaff House and the General was, frankly, appalled. 'How and why could Major Rance have had the audacity, the stupidity, the, the ...' he stammered 'to have acted in such a forbidden and foolhardy way? He ought to be court-marshalled. He still could be.'

'Sir, I can't tell you why. I am also unhappy about what happened. In KL he was looked after by Colonel Mason. All I do know is that earlier on Major Rance rang me to ask if I could make a special case for four SEPs, the ones that had gone with him to try and persuade Tan Fook Loong, the successful commander of 2 Regiment, MRLA, to surrender, and he needed them for Operation Emissary he called it. I saw no difficulty as such: they had proved their worth already.'

Relations between the outgoing British and the new Malayan Government were going through a difficult period and the General feared unpleasant repercussions were such a story to get abroad. 'I must get to the bottom of this as soon as I can,' he said and reaching for his phone dialled Colonel Mason's home.

'Colonel Mason speaking.'

'James, it's the General this end. Are you irreversibly tied up here and now? If not could you come over to see me, please, now, at my place? There's something I simply must get straight. It won't take long, just a few minutes then you can go back to what you were doing.'

In twenty minutes a car was heard outside and in the Director of Intelligence came. He was offered a drink and told to sit down. 'James, I'll come straight to the point. Why did that idiot Major Rance behave so irresponsibly in going and fetching that man from the Thai border dressed as a guerrilla? He should be court-martialled for behaving like that.'

The Colonel put his drink down on a side table and said 'Sir, rather me than him,' with a sheepish and lop-sided smile. 'Let me tell you exactly what happened …' and out the story came. 'So it was a case of stopping the entire escape with heaven-knows-what difficulties the other end or rolling with the punch so I let him go ahead. He seemed as confident as he normally did.'

'Were he and his men wearing CT rig in KL?'

'No, sir.'

'In Fort Tapong or in the boat going upriver? Have you heard anything from the Police Field Force?'

'No sir. Nothing of that nature at all. I think we would have heard by now if that had been the case.'

C C Too broke in. 'General, the Emissary said that on that last night before meeting the boat people the Englishman, who never gave any name, went into a small cave, produced a sack, took out a different lot of clothes and all five of them changed.'

'So no one except that man knows what they wore.'

'Well, except for the four SEPs and Inspector Ismail Mubarak and that's our way out if needs be. We'll merely say it is nonsense and ask, rhetorically of course, if the asker is trying to be funny.'

'So no courts-martial are needed,' the General added.

Mr Too looked at his watch and fidgeted. 'Sir, if you've nothing more for me I've nothing more for you. Have I your permission to leave?

'Of course, Mr Too. Thank you so much for coming round to talk to me. I'd have been yorked as we cricketers say if you hadn't.'

After Too had gone, the General said to the Colonel, 'Can you really credit a CO not allowing any of his men to go out with their own company commander on an operation as potentially hazardous as this?'

'General, it certainly takes one's breath away.' He scratched his chin reflectively as he remembered something else. 'There is something else that has just come to my mind. I asked Rance who he had told. There is one other to add to the list of those who know, his company 2 ic, the Gurkha Captain.'

'That was unnecessary of him, surely.'

'Not to him it wasn't. He only told him because he wanted him to write to his mother if he did not come back. The CO's diktat must have upset him.'

'Yes, and who can blame him,' said the General, standing up to stretch his legs. The Colonel followed suit. 'So, between us there really is only one answer, isn't there, however we dress it up?'

The Colonel nodded in agreement. 'And we'll keep our lips as sealed as that man Rance did his.'

During his six months' leave in England Jason had a letter from a brother officer telling him that 'Colonel Vaughan has been suddenly posted to the embassy in Germany where his German-language ability was needed.'

Rance was never told that his former CO knew not a word of German.

1961
It was not until five years later that Major Rance, working with the Temiar on Operation 'Bamboo' in the area of the Sungei

Temenggor and Kerinching's ladang was met once again by Senagit, as he was carrying a dead boar. Without thinking Jason, now a good speaker of Temiar, took it from him and grunted: Senagit, initially taken by surprise, later remembered the man who had done just the same when he brought back that young pig near the Sungei Perak headwaters.

When Senagit next met his friend Ah Soo Chye he told him, 'just like that time before.' This time he was not dressed like you wear clothes but as a soldier with a weapon. Ah Soo Chye, disbelieving Senagit at first, carefully questioned him and came to the conclusion that, indeed, the two men were one and the same. He was flabbergasted, outraged and bewildered. *One day revenge will be mine* ... but it remained an unfulfilled pipe dream as by the time Jason Rance did return to the area he had retired, permanently, to the Betong area of Thailand.

PART III

1963-1968

6

April 1963

After a decade of fighting guerrillas in the Malayan jungle, 1/12 Gurkha Rifles were posted to Hong Kong for a two-year spell where, apart from obligatory duties – Force Guards, Border Protection, Community Relations activities and Aid to the Civil Power when the police requested it – modern warfare could be practised from section up to brigade level. Classification on the range on the Bren light-machine gun and rifle was also an imperative as were, at long last, games and athletic competitions. It was certainly the first time since 1942 that any of the Gurkha soldiers had permanent accommodation to live in.

Two years later the Battalion left Hong Kong and returned to Malaya, this time going to Suvla Lines in Ipoh. It was then that Major Jason Rance was detailed to undertake a special task: to arrange for the return, by way of Malaya, of two Gurkha ex-prisoners-of-war who were stranded in Thailand. It meant working with Ah Fat, the Bear and the *orang asli* and Jason became dependent on Senagit. Successful though he only just was in getting the two wartime soldiers away from Thailand, in the guerrilla follow-up the Bear and Ah Fat were captured: the Bear was hideously killed and later Ah Fat died of wounds suffered

251

under torture. Following on from that Jason was sent to Borneo to command a recently raised armed Auxiliary Police Force, the Border Scouts, 'eyes and ears with a sting'; he nearly lost his life once a month for the year he did the job and was both broadcast as dead by the Indonesian Radio in Pontianak and by the *Sarawak Gazette*. He was then put in charge of the Gurkha Independent Parachute Company, based in Kluang, with more adventures in Borneo and Brunei before handing over prior to being posted to the Jungle Warfare School, near Kota Tinggi, not far from Johor Bahru – now Malaya no longer but Peninsular Malaysia. That was in July 1968.

There were two people who, during this time seldom if ever forgot Major Jason Rance, by whatever name they called him, polite or impolite. One was Tan Wing Bun, son of Tan Fook Loong, who only recognised his voice, at least to start with; the other was Wang Liang, son of Wang Ming, the Bear.[14] In January 1955 Tan Fook Loong, the commander of 2 Regiment, MRLA, was killed by bombs. The plane carrying them had a gizmo that linked it with a similar one in his portable radio. Jason Rance had been involved in getting some surrendered guerrillas to buy a new radio before Special Branch 'doctored' it. Before the bombing decision, which was considered 'unsporting' by the Director of Operations, was reached, it was decided to go and talk to him in person in the jungle, Rance masquerading as a surrendered guerrilla. But even before that Jason, who had secretly found out the guerrilla's

---

14 See *Operation Red Tidings*.

home phone number earlier on, had rung his son, Tan Wing Bun, in Penang. The son could never forget the day the phone rang. He answered it and a voice asked: '*Wei*, is that Tan Wing Bun, Tan Fook Loong's son?'

'Yes, who are you?' he answered, not recognizing the voice.

'Is your mother, Chen Yok Lan there?'

'What is it to you? Who are you?'

'Just someone telling you that I'll be talking to your father and unless you tell me to tell him you and your mother want him back home alive, he'll be dead within the week.'

To dedicated Communists such as were that family, surrender was anathema. As Tan Wing Bun put the phone down he told himself he'd never forget that voice *but whose is it?*

The news of his father's death was a shock to Tan Wing Bun, as was another phone call by the same voice. 'Wei, is that Tan Wing Bun, Tan Fook Loong's son?'

'Yes, who are you?'

'The same person who rang you before. I went to talk to your father in the jungle. I told him who I was, that I had rung you, that you did not want to talk to me. If you had gone with me your father could be alive today but, no, thanks to you he is dead. During the war, Japanese bullets didn't kill him and in this guerrilla war government bullets couldn't either. But his own pride killed him. Feigning to be a pig he vanquishes tigers.'

'Tell me who are you are,' the son shouted but the caller had put his phone back on the cradle. Once again the son felt he could always recognise the voice if he heard it again.

Almost all CPM members used aliases and some of their

families did also. In this case Tan Wing Bun was an alias: his real name was Tan Wing Hoong and that was the one he now used on his documents. After leaving school he tried to 'get his own back' and become a Special Branch officer but his alias was discovered so he was turned down. He became a contractor for supplying the goods that hawkers took round the streets. He opened his business in Penang and it spread as far as Grik. One day he was in Grik in his car outside the Police Station. He was interested to see a British army Land Rover outside, with a Gurkha driver. Instead of getting out of his car he sat and waited and watched. Quite why he did so he never really fathomed but something piqued his curiosity. Then one of those intriguing coincidences happened, nothing spectacular merely that a British officer came out of the Police Station. History can turn on a very small point.

One of the people he supplied, a Chinese itinerant seller of noodles, caught sight of the British officer and eyed him speculatively. He, as had some others like him, had been supplied with a photo of Jason Rance and told that on the odd chance the face in the photo was seen immediately to report it to his local party secretary for onward transmission to MCP HQ in Betong. The photo had been taken by the hotel manager at Sadao when Rance and one of the still stranded Gurkhas had stayed there during Rance's attachment to the South-East Asia Treaty Organisation in Bangkok in 1959. Rance had written an anti-Communist message on the organisation's headed notepaper and had secretly reached the MCP camp. There he had left the message on a bush and enticed the sentry to take it to the office in the camp. While he was away the hotel manager had taken the passport, given to him to put in his safe against loss from his room, out of the safe and had taken the photo – 'they' would ask for it, 'they' always did for any foreign visitor. And ask they had. It was subsequently circulated widely in the hope that the writer could be caught and vengeance taken.[15]

The vendor of noodles said to himself that one looks like the man in that photo. I'll have to do something about him.

Inspector Wang Liang, peering out of his office window, saw him. He had noticed him on more than one occasion and became suspicious of him. Not again? Leaving the office by a side door, he unobtrusively crossed the road and went behind the large tree in front of which the noodle-seller had parked his barrow. He saw a car had drawn up beside it. He noticed its registration number, P 9678 – remembering registration numbers was now second nature.

Happily unconscious of any unfolding drama Rance, in his faultless Chinese, called out to someone inside the Police Station, 'I'll go and have a meal in the camp before I go back to Ipoh. See you next week when I go upstream to meet the Temiar.' It never occurred to him why but he added, 'feigning to be a pig he vanquishes tigers', a phrase that tickled his senses of humour.

Tan Wing Hoong's heart stopped several beats when he heard that ... it can't be but it must be. It's that voice and that stupid phrase I've never heard anyone else use screeched through his mind, but yet he just knew it had to be the speaker on the phone. I must act now ... He called the noodle-seller over and told him

---

15 See *Operation Blind Spot*.

what he had to do ... and do it quickly ... and make a good job of it. The Bear's son heard and, equally surreptitiously, went back to his office.

After their meal in the camp Jason and his four men left for Ipoh. Jason, sitting in the front, still had his side window shut when, minutes later, as the vehicle slowed down to go round a sharp bend above a stream, a large rock was hurled at the side window of the front-seat traveller. A web of cracks spread though the glass with a few shards splintering into Jason's face, the rock falling back onto the road. The driver slammed on his brakes and he swerved, his vehicle nearly overturning. The four Gurkhas, as one, were out of it in a flash and gave chase to the rock thrower, a Chinese noodle seller whose barrow was by the side of the road.

He had reached the edge of the stream when the leading Gurkha, eyes reddened in anger, drew his khukri as he caught up with him and wielded it with all his strength. Out of the corner of his eye the Chinese saw what was about to happen and lunged forward. The Gurkha's khukri managed neatly to slice off the edge of the stone thrower's left buttock as he fell headlong down the bank into the water.

Jason caught up with the red-eyed Gurkha. 'Much damage?'

'No saheb. Hardly anything. Look, there's more cloth than skin and blood on my khukri.'

The chief doctor in the small hospital in Grik was intensely interested in the type of injury that an almost inarticulate Chinese man, brought in face-down by some unknown person in a car, had suffered. It was a particularly sharp knife wound in the buttock which was messy with cloth that had been hacked into it. The man did not specify what had happened, however hard the doctor and nurses tried to make him speak. A phone call to the Police Station brought a plain-clothes officer in to investigate. It was Wang Liang who of course could identify him. He also noticed a car in the car park and saw the registration number was P 9678. He took a statement from the doctor and said he would put the police onto the case. 'Can't have that happening, can we?' he said as he left.

Tan Wing Hoong, who had kept out of sight but had monitored the Land Rover's departure, cursed fluently at the near miss and vowed for another opportunity, another day. He paid an advance for the injured man and later on that day as he passed the Police Station he saw a young Chinese, dressed in civilian clothes, enter. On an impulse he stopped the car and called out to him. 'Can you help me, please?'

The other man turned. Neither knew each other. 'If I can, yes.' Instinctively he noticed the car's registration number. P 9678.

'I wanted to talk to a British officer I saw earlier on. I thought I knew him but was not sure,' he lied plausibly. 'Do you know who I mean?'

'Yes, his name is Major Rance, a fluent Chinese speaker. May I know your name please?'

Unthinking, he gave his alias, Tan Wing Bun, not his real name so happy was he in having solved the mystery of 'that' voice. 'I think I have seen him before,' he dissembled. 'He was the one who told me he'd be working up here. Am I right?' he asked, smiling guilelessly.

'Did he tell you that?'

'Oh yes, that is what he told me. Thank you,' and he drove off, not knowing that the man he had spoken to was Special Branch Inspector Wang Liang. The Bear's son had already come across the name and knew the owner was a dedicated Communist. He reported it and the answer came back, 'Be alert for any re-appearance.' *I'll most certainly mention that to the Siu Gaau Sinsaang* – the 'Major sahib' – *when he next comes here.* He made an entry in the report book but did not follow it up with any vigour.

As Tan Wing Hoong drove away a frown creased his brow as he tried to work out how best to get his own back now he knew who his enemy was. *He was responsible for killing my father in the jungle. Where best to kill him? In the jungle, yes, but where?* It was common knowledge that 2 Federal Infantry Brigade was conducting operations in Temiar country. *That* gwai lo *can only have been in Grik for future work with the* t'o yan, he mused. Then it struck him: he had heard 'next week'. *I'll get him in the jungle and where better than with the Temiar?* he asked himself, smirking. *All these military people give their operations names so I'll have mine.* An idea flashed into his mind. *I'll get him killed by poisoned darts from blowpipes – a lingering death – so the name of my operation will be Blowpipe. If not immediately, later: I don't mind how long it takes. My Operation Blowpipe will be victorious.*

The Bear's son had met Jason when he and his father were about to go and get some secret documents Ah Fat had 'stolen' from Chin

Peng's safe during the Baling Peace Talks at the end of December 1955. The two were being prepared for their task by C C Too in the house of his girlfriend when the Bear's wife brought her 15-year-old son round, unexpectedly, to meet Jason. Wang Ming said that he had often spoken about how Jason had initially won them over and it would be a great kindness if *Shandung P'aau* could show his son his tricks. Jason, realising a happy companion on a dangerous mission was always better than an unhappy one, adroitly played up. He held Wang Liang spellbound and so had a friend for life before Wang Ming sent them back home with a smile, the boy chuckling all the way.

Ah Fat had seen the Bear's hideous torture and after his own recovery, sadly only temporary, he went and told the Bear's widow and son what had happened. Both were utterly disgusted and the son felt that his one job in life was to revenge his father's death. His problem was 'how to?' He asked 'Uncle' Ah Fat who was against the son's trying to work his way up the ranks of the guerrillas and be a 'mole' or by trying to organise a group to make a raid into Thailand – 'that's only for cowboy-type films' – but a better and less targeted idea was to join the Malayan Police and see if he could get a posting into the Special Branch. For this 'Uncle' Ah Fat suggested 'Uncle' Too had the answer so went to see him. Because of the sterling work the Bear had done for his country over many difficult and dangerous years a generous reward for his family would not be out of place. Indeed there was an answer but, unfortunately, not one that could be bypassed. It was explained to the lad in detail: potential recruits needed certain basic laid down physical standards and academic qualifications, the latter the Cambridge School Certificate, with a Pass in the English language. The Recruit Selection Board, which always included a senior Special Branch officer, would determine from the interviews who among the successful candidates were potentially suitable for such work. When the Probationary Trainee Inspectors passed out from the Police Depot, they were posted to different branches of the Force, and those already earmarked for Special Branch work were posted to that branch.

Uncle Too asked Wang Liang what his school results were and, on being told, pursed his lips. 'You are just about good enough for an ordinary policeman but for Special Branch work you also need to be able to write Chinese and speak one more, better two more, dialects.' He saw the lad's face fall but knew that a really keen recruit was not easy to find. 'Look, I'll tell you what. If you really, really intend to do what you have vowed, I am prepared to fund you' – he had his own sources – 'you will have to work hard but if ever I see you not up to standard, I'll stop the funding.'

'Uncle. I'll do my level best, I promise you. I won't slacken.'

'Once I am sure you can manage, I'll recommend that you join the police force as a Probationary Trainee Inspector if you pass. Let's say you do and we both hope so. You have to undergo six months police training at the KL Police Depot. There you will learn foot drill, arms drill, weapons training, law (focusing on the Criminal Procedure Code, the Penal Code and the Evidence Ordinance) and Malay. Are you prepared for all that?'

'Yes, Uncle,' was the answer, given confidently.

'Let us say you are successful and become a Probationary

Trainee Inspector. You will pass out from the Police Depot and, if already earmarked for Special Branch work given your ardour and your family background, as I am sure you will be, there you will be posted.'

The boy nodded his head.

Uncle Too continued: 'You will be given on-the-job training and, not necessarily immediately but certainly at some time in the future, you will be sent on courses at the Special Branch Training School in KL.'

The lad stood up and sincerely thanked Uncle. 'Now go home, tell you mother all about it and I'll let you know in a few days which school to go and study at.'

By August 1968 the Bear's son was a Special Branch Inspector in the Grik office, where he had the added job of learning about those he knew as *t'o yan,* Temiar aborigines, although this last word was no longer politically correct in all circles.

Jason knew that before he could extract the two Gurkha ex-prisoners-of-war from Thailand he had to penetrate then use the Temiar for knowledge of the border area and around Ha La on the Thai side. He knew that without a good knowledge of Temiar he would not succeed. He thus had acquired a good working knowledge of Temiar. Now, years later, Mr Too had asked him to try and find out about Ah Soo Chye, Tek Miu and Lo See as sources about them had dried up. Initially, even with the support of the one Temiar who by then was not afraid of him so could help him, Senagit, it took quite a time for the leaders of the Temiar community, including Headman Kerinching, to trust him enough to talk to him. One of Jason's original ploys was to tell them that if he was successful he would try and get the Gurkha soldiers then on the ladangs, not liked by any of the *orang asli*, removed. So before any headway could be made in getting some Temiar to go with him and a small team of Gurkhas to the border to meet and escort the ex-prisoners of war to safety and rescue, movement to their border crossing synchronised, a meeting was held. Jason was hopeful that any progress he could make would be a bonus. In the end he was not as optimistic.

One of Jason's three Gurkhas was making a recording of the talk without the Temiar realising it. It was later edited and a copy sent to Special Branch in KL. The report on that meeting Jason submitted was seen as a hallmark of how the Temiar mind worked: Mr Too and the Director of Intelligence circulated it to all concerned: 'I had earlier been told by one of the Temiar that tapioca in a nearby plot was being stolen. I wanted to find out if it could be Ah Soo Chye who was digging the stuff up or was it a rumoured man – but from whose ladang? After I had persuaded the senior men of the ladang I wanted to have a talk with them and hear their views, they came to where I had a temporary base. They sat in a semicircle on the ground in front of me and my three Gurkhas. Once they had settled down I felt it time to ask them to let me know, one way or another, where Ah Soo Chye was, dead or alive? If alive, what was he feeding on?

'I did not bother to mention his two lieutenants as I thought it would be too much for them but if they did I could talk about them. By then I was known as "Tata", literally Old Man, but used to a person as a mark of "one of high standing". By then I knew that any straightforward question to start with was unproductive so I had to begin carefully. We started talking at 4 o'clock and went on for two and a half hours. The talk went round and round and round, frustrating in its elusiveness. My head swam by the end of it and I did not know what to think. After welcoming them, I started off as a normal Temiar conversation and the report's conclusion was that it was still uncertain whether Ah Soo Chye was dead or alive and, if the latter, where he would be:

'With what news?'

'With no news.'

'I hear, I hear strong, I hear wind, tapioca it steals.'

'How you hear?'

'I hear wind. True or not?'

'Hear women talk. Talk tapioca it steals.'

'I hear,' I continued after that part of the conversation had been repeated many times and had taken five minutes, 'I hear mad Temiar he from that side of the river, he steals tapioca, true or not?'

'Tata, I say, and if I say good luck, good, and if I say bad luck, bad, if you are angry, what am I to do? But I say, yes.'

'Yes, what?'

Came the devastating answer, 'Yes, no.'

So I started again: 'Is there a mad man?'

'Yes.'

'Tell me about him.'

'He lives in the jungle. Sometimes he comes. He has long hair and we are afraid. He has no knife. He has no fire. He cannot eat.'

'Where is he now?' I asked.

'Dead.'

'When did he die?'

'One day in the past.'

'So he does not steal tapioca?'

'No.'

'Who does?'

'The mad man.'

'But you say he is dead.'

'No, he is not dead.'

This point, try hard though I might, was never satisfactorily resolved, despite twenty minutes solid cross examination. So I switched tack.

'If the dead man does not eat, does not steal tapioca, then inland man steals?'

'No.'

'But tapioca it steals, mad dead man not, inland man not, who?'

'It steals.'

'The bad man China, that Ah Soo steal?'

'He is in the high hills. What am I to do?'

'What does he eat?'

'Food.'

'If no food?'

'No food.'

'If no food he dies?'

'He dies.'

'How long they no food he dies?'

'Long.'

'Dead now?'

'Yes.'

'Dead now?'

'No.'

I gradually brought them around to thinking the guerrillas might be living off the land, lying up, stealing tapioca and here having to use the word 'river' (even to the extent even when there was no actual river but where it would have been had there been one!) as an integral part of any location as otherwise the Temiar could not visualise where I was talking about:

'Ah Soo is near?' I asked.

'No.'

'Ah Soo is far?'

'No.'

'Where is Ah Soo?'

'If near, near, if far, far, if this side of the river, this side, if that side, that side, if upstream, upstream, if downstream, downstream. If you are angry what am I to do? I hope strongly.'

'What do you hope?'

'Yes.'

'Yes, what?'

'Yes, no.'

'Ah Soo is upstream?' I asked.

'Ah Soo is upstream.'

'Ah Soo is downstream?'

'Ah Soo is downstream.'

'How is he upstream and downstream?'

'Yes.'

'Yes, what?'

'Yes, no.'

'Where is Ah Soo?' I started again.

'In the high hills.'

'Is Ah Soo in the high hills?'

'No.'

'What is no?'

'Yes.'

'Yes, what?'

'Yes, in the high hills.'

'If he is hungry?'

'He gets food.'

'What does he eat?'

'What he can get.'

'What does he get?'

'Tapioca.'

'From here?'

'Yes.'

'Yes, new of it?'

'Yes.'

'Who, new of it, it steals?'

'The mad man.'

'But the mad man is dead?'

'No.'

'Not dead?'

'Yes.'

'Yes, what?'

'Dead.'

Mr Too said it would have left him crazy; and the Gurkhas listening in, but not understanding, praised their OC for his patience. The mere fact that Jason never showed any impatience whatsoever and kept a smile on his face was enough initially to convince the Temiar of his eventual ability to get troops removed from ladangs, always an imperative, and this is what eventually happened. It was found out and confirmed later that the guerrilla trio had not been in the area for some considerable time, having returned to the Betong area a year or so after the Secretary General had left Thailand for China.

May 1968

By then the Emergency that involved British and Commonwealth troops, later but not then known as the First Emergency, was well over. Malaysia was a fact and Confrontation with Indonesia was already history. The British Government decided that, come the end of 1971, their 'East of Suez' policy was that the only UK forces in southeast Asia would be in Hong Kong and Brunei, where the host countries could pay for them in whole or in part. The one unit of the British Army to work full time till the end was the Jungle Warfare School. By 1968 all those army officers 'with stars in their eyes' were no longer interested in serving in a theatre where points for promotion were not as valuable as they would be in Western Europe. That meant that officers with sufficient jungle expertise and seniority to command the British army's Jungle Warfare School were an endangered species.

The Military Secretary, a most senior officer, was wondering who could fill the recent vacancy for the job during the last couple of years of its existence. He called for a list of possible starters – it was a very short one – and his eye fell on the name of Major Rance, 1/12 GR. He asked for his file and read it. *He is not as well staff trained as a lieutenant colonel should be but he has earned 'staff qualified' for a job he did in Bangkok, he has much jungle experience and a prodigious linguistic ability.* 'Let him be promoted to do the job,' the Military Secretary advised the Promotion Board, which agreed. Thus it was that Jason Rance, despite the forebodings of the bevy of brigadiers and covey of colonels who had thought otherwise, found himself a lieutenant colonel, the last ever incumbent of the Jungle Warfare School, in July 1968.

Jason's time as OC of the Gurkha Independent Parachute Company, the job that gave him the most satisfaction in his long career, like all good things, came to an end in the May of 1968. Two days before he was given a farewell that was emotive in the extreme, he had as yet no idea what, if any, his next job would be or if he'd be sent on redundancy. On his last day in office a personal letter was given him by his Chief Clerk, 'to be opened by you yourself, Saheb,' he said.

To his utter delight, amazement and relief it was his posting order for promotion and command of the Jungle Warfare School. He saw he was wanted to take over on 1 July. That meant he had a month with nothing to do. He decided to motor down to Singapore to meet old friends. He went to Tanglin Barracks to doss down in a friend's room. It was on his second day there a uniformed Malay policeman came looking for him, in the evening, just before going to the mess for his meal. 'Tuan, I have a message for you. Here it is.'

Jason thanked him for it and asked him to wait until he opened it to see if it needed a reply. Inside the envelope was another envelope, marked secret. It came from Special Branch in Kuala Lumpur and was signed by the evergreen Mr C C Too. He wrote that no one had visited the Temiar since he, Jason, had left them those five years before 'when you produced your famous report'. There was no news of any sort, of guerrillas, or Temiar thoughts of the government. 'I want you to go there and find out. If you are willing. As an individual. If the Malaysian government and military authorities or the British Army were to know about this you will, I know, be severely punished, even to the extent of not being allowed to stay in the country. And yet you are the only person I know whom the Temiar trust and can speak fluent Temiar. Will you please go, secretly? Take one man, a Gurkha. A pistol each will be lent to you by the police at Grik. I know you have a car. Use that. Report to Grik Police Station and the Bear's son will arrange for a boat to take you up the Sungei Perak, then the Sungei Temenggor to the Sungei Klian to Kerinching's ladang. I am calling this *Operation Blowpipe*. Phone this number and say yes or no the day after you get this at ten a.m. Tell no one, not even your escort, where you're going till you get there. The Bear's son will meet you at Grik Police Station and stay with you.'

Jason thanked the constable and said no, there was no answer to take back.

His room boy, Tan Yee Faat, came in and asked him if he wanted his bed tea at the same time tomorrow and Jason, with the letter still in his hand, answered in Chinese only using his first name so calling him Ah Tan, no, half an hour earlier if possible. The room boy said yes, he'd do it, expecting a substantial tip for it.

Jason put the letter on his table and went to the mess. Ah Tan went to look at the letter. As one of the Tan family, he was related to Tan Wing Bun and had heard about a Chinese-speaking English officer. *I'll let him know as soon as I leave here. I know his Penang phone number and the news can be forwarded. In order to keep this secret I'll tell him to know it as* Operation Blowpipe.

Next morning at daybreak Jason drove hack to the Parachute Company in Kluang and spoke to the new OC. He told him he was bored with Singapore and had decided to spend the rest of his leave going places that had been too dangerous in the Emergency. I'd like company and, just in case I do meet any baddy or need help in a breakdown, please let me have my batman, Chakrabahadur Rai, to go with me. We've worked together well in the past and who knows we may need each other again.'

'Of course, old boy. Sorry, can't say that now to a colonel, can I? Yes, sir, of course you can.'

Jason laughed. 'I'm still a major till the 1st of July.'

The Bear's son had been posted to two other places and had hurriedly been sent back to Grik by C C Too a week before he had alerted Jason so he not seen the noodle-seller since the day he had been slashed, way back in 1963. The police report had 'lapsed'. He was, therefore, surprised and suspicious to see him yet again outside the Police Station. He was even more suspicious when he saw the man who sometimes called himself Tan Wing Bun and sometimes Tan Wing Hoong draw up in a car, lean out of the window and speak to the noodle-seller before driving off. *Could it,* he asked himself, *just be a coincidence or is it linked to* Operation Blowpipe? *If the latter there must have been a leak – but, if so, how?*

He called two of his men and from his office window pointed out the noodle-seller. He gave them the background of yesteryear but forbade to mention Jason's impending visit. 'When the man leaves here follow him. Find out where he lives and, without rousing any suspicion, bring him back here after dark.

'If he asks why?'

'Tell him his papers need to be looked at and not to lose face with people who know him it is better to check them after dark.'

They brought him in at ten o'clock and led him to Wang Liang's office. He was told to show his permit to trade. This he did. 'It is in order,' he said, looking at the three men who glared at him ferociously.

'Take off your pants and show me your bottom,' commanded Wang Liang.

'No. I'm not one of those. Why should I?'

A nod from Wang Liang and the other two gagged him, tied his hands and stripped off his pants. The man wriggled, twisted and turned in desperation, spluttering the while. Once his rump was bare, Wong Liang said, 'I see you have a scar. If you promise not to make a noise I'll take the gag out of your mouth and you'll tell me how you got it. If you do not keep your promise,' and he picked up a nasty-looking *parang*, 'I'll make another scar on the other buttock.'

The man's eyes bulged. 'No, no,' he tried to shriek but merely spluttered in his spittle.

Wang Liang put the *parang* away. 'Will you talk?'

The man nodded his head, relief in his eyes. 'Ungag him but keep his hands tied,' Wang Liang commanded.

He was ungagged and tried to wipe his mouth.

'How did you get that scar?' the Inspector asked him. 'Answer truthfully.'

'I, er, I slipped when I was about to decapitate a sheep for us to eat and the knife cut me,' he stammered.

'Liar,' and his face was slapped, not hard but hard enough to bring tears to his eyes. 'If you don't tell me the truth be ready for the other buttock to be cut even though there are no sheep here.'

The man was no coward but, in the end, he admitted he had thrown a rock at a military vehicle hoping to cause an accident.'

'Why? What made you do that?'

It took a long time to unwind two reasons, one was about a photograph that had been given him to try and find the man in the picture and to report it to his next senior and one was 'I was told by the man who employs me to do it.'

'And who is he?'

Nothing would get the man to say. He was obviously terrified. 'You know we could put you in jail for throwing that rock if you don't tell us.'

The man was desperate. 'He'll kill me if he knows I've told you,' he gasped.

'What, since so long ago?'

'No, now.'

'I'll give you one minute to tell me. If you tell me the truth you can choose to be tried by a magistrate and go to jail for a few months so you can hide from him or not to be charged for your offence and with a thousand ringgit go elsewhere.'

What a choice! Either way was a way out. 'I'll tell you if you hide me in jail.'

'As soon as you've told me I'll arrange for a magistrate, not here but in Kuala Lumpur.'

Relief spread over the man's features and out came the story: something about wanting to kill a *gwai lo* using a *chui cheen toong hang dung.* He knew 'blow-arrow-tube' but the 'operation' bit had stumped him so he had just nodded as though he had understood it. The man he knew as Ah Tan would follow the Englishman into the jungle and, once he was engaged with the Temiar, get him shot by a blowpipe.'

'He told you all that?'

'Yes, he and I were drinking brandy and he was talkative.'

'When?' asked sharply

'Oh, very recently. He also told me always to stay in sight of the Police Station so I would see the man he was waiting for and let him know when he had come. He'll see me tomorrow morning.'

Wang Liang shook his head in amazement at the stupidity of over confident and careless people and told his men to take him outside while he made a phone call. He phoned C C Too's private number, as he had been told to and related the story to him. He heard a deep, deep sigh as his boss tried to fathom where a leak could have happened.

'Well done, Son of a Bear. Send the man down to me tomorrow, escorted, in the station's lock-up vehicle but first look up the details of the case, if there are any, that is.'

'And what shall I tell the *Siu Gaau Sinsaang*?'

There was no answer for a while as Mr Too considered his options. 'Say nothing at first. Go with him in the police boat and once you are at Kerinching's ladang, get all his men and warn them to keep watch and ward.'

'And how, sir, do you think that Tan Wing Bun by whichever name he'll be going by will get news to the Temiar?'

'I don't know, sadly, but I'm sure he's worked it all out.'

And he thought he had! The morning after telling the noodle-seller about his plans he drove towards the Police Station, bewildered at not seeing anyone there. *Should be there by now* he thought *but it is on the early side so I'll come back later.* On his return he was glad to see the barrow but the person with it was not the same, merely a lad. Tan Wing Hoong stopped his car just short of the barrow, leant out of the window and asked who the person was and where was the normal vendor?

'He was taken away by police last night. They came to fetch him after dark.'

Tan Wing Hoong was shocked. 'Why? And who are you?'

'Why? How should I know why. Who am I? His fifth cousin and helper. I'll look after the barrow now until he comes back.' A thought struck him. 'If he comes back,' he added.

Tan Wing Hoong was not sure what to do. He could hardly go

to the police and ask them because, as far as they were concerned, it was nothing to do with him. He had not mentioned the fact to the man he had spoken to outside the Police Station – *what was his name?* – but if he were to go and ask, claiming that the missing vendor was, in fact, one of his men, he might be implicated in his arrest so be under suspicion himself. No, he would have to arrange matters and act on his own. *My name Wing Hoong means 'forever heroic' so it will all come right in the end.* Before he left he asked the lad if he had seen any military vehicle. No, he had not so that meant the man who was his target had not yet come. *At least that is one plus factor*, he thought as he drove off.

Jason and Chakré left Kluang at midday and reached KL late in the evening, having stopped on the way for leg-stretches and a snack. In KL they stayed the night with the Bear's widow. Although they hardly knew each other, she was glad to see him as she associated him with much of her husband's life. She missed him badly and Jason kept her amused with his reminiscences. She was especially glad to think he would be working with her son. She had a phone and, knowing C C Too's number, Jason rang him to say he was on his way. C C Too thanked him, wished him good luck and passed the message on to Wang Liang in Grik.

They left early the next morning and on the way Jason briefed Chakré on their task. 'Chakré, I must tell you why I have asked for you to come with me. I have been contacted by the senior Chinese in Special Branch to go into Temiar country for him and I need you as an escort. On the face of it, it is not a difficult task, merely to try and find out how the Temiar are managing without any troops on their ladangs and are there any guerrillas. No contact has been made with these people by Government, police or army for five years. The senior Chinese thinks I am the one man they trust and who can speak to them in their own language. You've seen me with them, haven't you?'

Chakré grinned. Yes he had.

'Now, there is so much jealousy between the Federation Army and the police neither must know about this journey of ours. Once we get to Grik we'll be armed. But if the British sarkar were to find out what we are doing it could be serious, even a court-martial with lots of inter-government embarrassment. So we can only hope and pray nothing unusual happens and, if it does, you Chakré must have eyes in the back of your head to prevent any repercussion.'

'Saheb, of course you can rely on me. But how strange the people in this country don't have their own men for such a job.'

By evening had arrived in Grik where there was a company of 6 GR, commanded by an old friend. There was plenty of room for them both as one of the platoons was out on a local patrol. Jason rang the Police Station for Wang Liang, got the number of his lodging and told him he had arrived with one gunman.

'Good. I'll come and pick you up at seven o'clock. We'll all wear plain clothes but I'll have a couple of .38 pistols, ten rounds of ammo and some cleaning kit for you both. I'll also bring some basic rations. You will give the Temiar much pleasure by letting them feed you on their tapioca but that won't be enough for a growing lad,' and he giggled at his own feeble joke.

'That's good,' Jason rejoined, 'as we've nothing with us. How long do you think this jaunt will take us?'

'Let me see. A day up to Kerinching's ladang, a day to get news around that it's you who've arrived, that's two and a day down. At least another day for talking so let's say four days.'

'That's no problem. I'm on leave for the rest of the month.'

'You do realise, don't you, that no one has visited them since you persuaded the government not to station any troops on ladangs so, although they don't want gossip about the wider world, they'll feel they are not neglected so will want to talk.'

'My Temiar may be a tad rusty by now as I've had no practice.'

'Don't worry, it'll all come back quickly enough. Quite why we are behaving this way is a bit of a mystery. You may not know this, the police and army are hardly on speaking terms so this is the only way Mr Too can find out if there is anything he should know about.'

'Okay Ah Wang, see you tomorrow,' and Jason rang off while the Bear's son rang 'uncle' to confirm the Major sahib's arrival.

The police vehicle left the police lines before the new vendor reached his post and went to the camp to pick up Jason and Chakré, who were waiting at the camp entrance for it.. There was only one road to the boat point but Wang Liang did not drive back by way of the Police Station but by another road to collect the Malay boatmen. They reached the boat point, at exactly the same place on the Sungei Perak where work with the Temiar had started for Jason so many years before. He found it almost unreal and felt it acutely as, this time, he was returning, not starting out.

Now he knew what to expect, what it was all about. The boat was ready, having had its tank filled the previous day and spare cans were brought from the stores. In they got and moved off into the river, where the main current was strong.

He was once more thrilled by the skill of the boatman as he steered his way up the rapids, happy to count over a hundred hornbills and to see the large monitor lizards sunning themselves on the sandy slopes. As he was travelling as a civilian he had brought an umbrella to keep the sun off but, as the day slowly passed, the inactivity and the hardness of the bench were the same as before: hard to take. Both he and Chakré were glad of the shade as the sun rose. Jason's was big enough for Wang Liang to sit under. They reached the dilapidated Halting Bungalow an hour before sunset and got out, delighted to stretch their legs. Wang Liang told the boatman he wanted them back in three days' time.

'In that case we'll go and stay in the nearest Malay village, which we have done before. It is much nearer than going all the way to Grik and back,' said the driver.

Jason thanked them for bringing them safely and waved them goodbye before moving off on the path he remembered so well, now more overgrown. Some distance along he met a young Temiar lad whom he asked where Tata Kerinching's ladang was. He was told he had moved his house and directed them towards it. They got there just as the sun was setting. They found Kerinching, with five others Jason knew and he remembered the names of four of them, his Temiar language skills instantly returning. All showed the greatest joy at his unexpected appearance. 'I knew you would came back one day,' said an ageing Kerinching. 'You are the only one who ever cared for us. You make your mouth look like a chicken's arse, but you have a kind heart.' He smiled the old smile and the others nodded their agreement. By then Jason had introduced the other two.

Being unexpected, nothing was ready to eat so Kerinching told a younger wife to prepare some tapioca. She fetched a bamboo cylinder full of water to wash it. She put the cylinder of water between her knees, having first lifted her sarong up. She then tilted it up to her mouth, took a swig, replaced it between her knees and picked up the piece of tapioca, holding it a little away from her. She then squirted the water out of her mouth, jet-like, on to the tapioca, deftly cleaning it before her supply ran dry. It was then put into the ashes to roast, with a slight dowsing of the flame until it dried off.

Jason was told that Senagit had died a couple of years before, probably of tuberculosis, he thought, what with the dry cough he had. The others who gathered around were now much more confident than he had seen them before, with no military or guerrillas to come and bother them. They carried themselves more proudly with a superior almost disdainful look in their eyes. They were soon laughing as they talked of old times. When the tapioca was ready it was given to them. After their meal Kerinching said it was too late for a dance but maybe the next night ... or the night after that ... or the one after that also. But now it was bedtime. Space was made for them in part of Kerinching's house and they slept well, except for Chakré who had a bad dream. In fact, three bad dreams he remembered when he woke, one was when he spilt some milk, one was when his ploughing oxen broke loose and one was when he saw his village house and went inside. All were bad omens with this last one really bad and he knew bad luck would be his before the end of the day. Almost unthinkingly he loaded his pistol, covering it, in its holster, under his shirt. It never occurred to him to make any mention of it: dreams were not to be spoken aloud about. He had been worried ever since Jason's briefing.

Next day there was more talk as more people learnt that the man with a kind heart and a face like a chicken's backside had returned. Mid-morning the three of them went for a walk when there was a rain shower with the sun still shining. To all Gurkhas this meant either seeing a jackal's wedding or a death. On their return Jason went to talk to Kerinching by himself. He brought the conversation round to the guerrillas and was told that, since his last visit no one, no one at all, had visited them or bothered them. 'It is like it was when I was much younger, so many years ago,' smiled the old man. 'We are all pleased.' He looked at Jason, smiled again and said there would be a dance. 'And after that you will make the children laugh.' He was referring to when Jason, on a previous visit, had held them spellbound, first frightened then laughing with his dummy. All of them fully believed it had a spirit of its own.

Back in Grik Ah Tan was getting worried at his quarry's non-arrival. He asked the noodle-vendor if any European had been seen and was told, no, the only European he knew about was the English Major commanding the Gurkhas in the camp just outside the town. *I'll leave it till tomorrow. Maybe the whole thing has been cancelled* but he somehow doubted it.

Again, the next day there was no news so on the spur of the moment he drove to the boat point where, to his horror and anger, he learnt that a boat had gone upriver the day before with a tall Englishman, a Chinese he knew was a Police officer and, they thought, a Gurkha. Spitting his rage, he managed to get hold of a boat at treble the normal rate and, that ready, he told the driver to take him over the river to Kantan's ladang. There he cajoled the headman to lend him his three best blowpipe shooters with some poisoned arrows. He paid a lot of money – not all that much to him but a lot to Kantan – to move straightaway.

By then it was far too late to go more than halfway. In fact the driver stopped off at the last Malay village where Jason's boat crew were and the following day the two boats moved off together, Ah Tan almost berserk that his boat would not move at first light. They eventually reached the boat point not long before dark and Ah Tan, on asking the way, was shown the path. Off he set with his three men. He got lost and only when he saw the light of the fire did he know where he was. The four men quietly went towards the ladang.

Despite Chakré's bad omens, it had been a happy day. After Jason and Kerinching's talk the old man had ordered a dance and, of course, Jason was hauled out. He remembered the steps, left, left, right, right, left, left and enjoyed the clunking cadence made by pieces of bamboo the maidens' beat on a log. After a while he pulled his two friends into the circle to join him. This time no one fell into a trance and it was dusk when it was over. They then went and sat outside Kerinching's house and Jason, with the children clustered around him, got them into hoots of laugher. This the blowpipe group heard as it approached the ladang.

Ah Tan peered into the crowd he saw in the light of the fire and spotted Jason, wearing a floppy hat. Jason had, in fact, just lifted it slightly to let the mouse that had squeaked inside it – frightening the younger watchers – and had yet to replace it. The Chinese avenger, saying 'hat, hat' in Malay, pointed it out to his shooters, making a gesture of roundness with one hand. They had inserted their darts, now they lined up their pipes on Jason and blew. Three darts shot into the centre of his hat, knocked it out of his hands and it fell on the ground. He looked at it with amazement and, before he could even pull them out to see if the tips were black with *ipoh* poisoning, his batman, Chakré, having felt on edge all evening, saw what had happened in a glance and instantly turned, drawing his pistol as he did. Peering forward he saw the three Temiar fixing more darts and a taller Chinese behind them. He aimed and fired three shots, to the consternation of the ladang dwellers, and hitting the taller man in the forehead, a most lucky shot. One of the other two bullets knocked a blowpipe out of the blower's aim and the other, startled by the noise of the shots, jerked and the dart flew wild, hitting a dog that ran away howling loudly.

Jason and Wang Liang ran forward, their pistols at the ready but the men from Kantan's ladang, completely surprised and frightened by the unexpected firing, fled. Only a dying Chinese man was left.

'My, but that was a close one,' Jason said breathlessly.

The wounded man stirred and, trying to focus his eyes on Jason, stuttered out a few faltering words. Jason and Wang Liang bent forward and heard, haltingly and in a low voice, 'it was you who killed my father ... my father in ... in ... the jungle. I ...' his voice weakened, spittle formed on his lips and blood dripped from the wound in his head. It was a wonder he was still alive. He made another effort, his voice fading, 'so ... so to avenge him ... I planned to kill you in the jungle.' His last words sounded like '*chui cheen toong hang dung*' but the two listeners were not quite sure.

On seeing that the man was dead Wang Liang asked 'What do we do now?' He called for a bamboo fire brand and, when one had been lit and brought, looked at the dead man. He gave a low whistle. 'Yes, this is the man who was enquiring after you, so many years ago. I'd forgotten him.' He searched his pockets and found nothing. In his haste the dead man had left his wallet and identity card at Kantan's ladang. 'I checked on him after he gave his name. He was the son of a highly placed and successful guerrilla commander. You won't have heard of him, probably, his name was Tan Fook Loong.'

If ever Jason did a 'double take' it was then, 'We can't leave the corpse here all night,' he said. 'The Temiar will be frightened out of their wits and go and sleep in the jungle. But what do we do with it?' Chakré, what are your views on this?'

'Saheb, he deserved to die. We can't take his corpse back as too many questions will be asked and I will be blamed and probably so will you.' He paused, considering his options. 'Saheb,

283

we three with one volunteer Temiar will take the body to the river, not where the boat will be, but in a different place. There we will drown it. As far as anyone else is concerned, he was never here. As far as his boatman will be concerned, he ran away in the night. As far as the Temiar are concerned, they won't have to move their houses, as I remember hearing they do, because of a death. He died just outside.'

The Bear's son asked what he was saying so Jason told him. 'I like it but it is against the law. But, and there always are buts aren't there, no one else will know he is dead if we do what your gunman says. The Temiar will never mention it and no one will be any the wiser. Let me first check with Kerinching.' The old man, who had not run away, was happy with the idea.

It was a grisly business that they undertook, none of them liking it one little bit. With enough bamboo fire brands properly to see what they were doing, they wended their way towards the river led by two Temiar lads. Jason wondered out loud whether it were better to leave the body for wild animals rather than drown it and find it floating. The Temiar agreed, as long as it was taken to the other side of the river and the river crossed below their drinking water point and above the boat point. They waded the river which was not quite knee deep and found what the Temiar thought was a suitable place. Wang Liang, who was not squeamish, took the clothes off the dead man and left the corpse nude, his watch still on his wrist.

'Back in the ladang we will get the clothes burnt or, if Kerinching doesn't think they are tainted, let him wear them,' suggested Jason.

'No,' said Wang Liang. 'If, just suppose, if any search party were to find them, they could implicate him in his disappearance. The clothes must be burnt. That is why I insisted on leaving his watch on his wrist.'

Next morning, farewells made, the three men went to the boat point. There they saw the other boat and the three Temiar lurking nearby. 'Talk to them, Jason,' said the Bear's son. 'Tell them if they came in the boat to go back in it,' before asking the two boat men if they knew where they had come from.

'We picked them up from Kantan's ladang.'

Jason called out, in Temiar, 'if you want to go back to Kantan's ladang, your ladang, get in the boat and go back. If you don't want to, find your own way back.'

They looked at him, saying nothing. They knew who he was because, some years back, he and his Gurkhas had spent a few days on the ladang, talking with Kantan. *When? One day in the past* was the nearest any of the three could remember.

Jason, Wang Liang and Chakrabahadur got into their boat. Wang Liang called out to the other boat's two crew, 'if these three want to go back, take them. The other passenger has decided to stay around here a little longer so don't worry about him. Give these three a quarter on an hour to make up their minds, then, with or without them, go back to Grik.' And, as an added afterthought, 'have you been paid?' he asked.

From the grins on their faces he knew the answer without them replying.

As they boated downriver they cleaned their pistols. 'If you can't manage to get your properly cleaned,' said Wang Liang, 'I'll get the station armourer to buff it up for you.'

Silence reigned for a while than Jason said, 'Chakré, you were marvellous. You saved my life and so averted a diplomatic crisis that would have done none of us any good. Thank you, thank you,' and he leant over and clasped the Gurkha's hand.

'Saheb, it comes with the job,' was the smiling reply.

'I'd love to put you in for some sort of award but sadly that's impossible.'

'I know, Saheb, in its way it was payback for all the time you have spent looking after us.'

They smiled at each other and let the subject drop.

Before Jason and Chakré continued on their leave from Grik Wang Liang asked for a report to be sent to Mr Too. 'You only need say what Kerinching told you. That the recommendations you made after your previous time with them have been carried out so well that they are all happy. There is neither sniff nor smell of any guerrilla activity nor has there been since you left them, whenever it was. For my report I will merely say that from what I saw what you told me of your talks in Temiar with Kerinching bear this out.'

The report made Mr Too happy. *That Rance man did a good job and they were glad to see him. My idea of* Operation Blowpipe *was the most calm and one-sided affair that has been my luck to instigate. I need not have been so concerned about international reaction, need I?*